Advance Praise for *Wedding Bel [Blues]*

"*Wedding Bel Blues* sparkles . . . A rollicking read and an auspicious beginning to a new series."

> —Carolyn Hart, *New York Times* bestselling author of the Death on Demand mysteries and the Bailey Ruth Ghost mysteries

"McConnon blends humor and intrigue like no other."

> —Laura Bradford, author of *A Churn for the Worse*

"It's a lucky day for mystery fans when disgraced Manhattan chef Belfast McGrath returns home and dons an apron at Shamrock Manor, run by her eccentric Irish family. Bel's got plenty on her plate with murder and mayhem on the menu, as she stumbles upon one deep, dark secret after another."

> —Susan McBride, *USA Today* bestselling author of *Say Yes to the Death*

"Top Chef meets Sherlock Holmes to cook up a delightful menu of mystery, humor, and romance. In *Wedding Bel Blues,* you'll find a whodunnit to die for, characters you'll love, and dialogue that will make you laugh out loud. Maggie McConnon knows the secret of concocting the perfect soufflé of fun. Bon Appetit!"

> *Murder*

"Don't [ ] [de]licious myster[ ] [is] drawn with w[ ] Bel McGrath [ ]

> —Nancy Martin, *New York Times* bestselling author of the Blackbird Sisters mysteries

WEDDING *Bel* BLUES

Maggie McConnon

St. Martin's Paperbacks

WEDDING BEL BLUES

Copyright © 2016 by Maggie McConnon.
Excerpt from *Bel of the Brawl* copyright © 2016 by Maggie McConnon.

For information address St. Martin's Press, 175 Fifth Avenue, New York, NY 10010.

ISBN: 978-1-250-00189-4

Printed in the United States of America

St. Martin's Paperbacks edition / June 2016

St. Martin's Paperbacks are published by St. Martin's Press, 175 Fifth Avenue, New York, NY 10010.

10 9 8 7 6 5 4 3 2 1

*To my big, loud, fantastic, talented Irish family.
Thanks for providing ample fodder
for the stories I hope to tell.*

ACKNOWLEDGMENTS

Someone once asked me, "What's the scariest book you've ever read?" to which I replied, "The first draft of any one of my novels." So thank you to Kelley Ragland, an editor who always makes my books better, a talent that cannot be underestimated. Thank you, too, to Deborah Schneider, my agent, who spends more time talking me off the creative ledge than any one person should have to.

I am lucky in my friends and colleagues.

CHAPTER *One*

It never bothered me when Caleigh McHugh, my first cousin on my mother's side, insulted me when we were teenagers. We had been competing with each other since we were kids, and today, her wedding day, was no exception.

Because I was pretty sure that my IQ was higher than hers and since I come from a family that has always valued brains over beauty—well, most of the time—her insults didn't really hurt. "You look plushy in that dress, Bel," Caleigh said, giving me the once-over, making sure she looked better than I did.

"I'm not sure that's even a word," I said to her, smoothing down the front of the raw-silk monstrosity she called a maid-of-honor dress. "But I'm pretty sure I know what it means."

"It means 'zaftig.' 'Curvy,'" she said, trying desperately to recover.

I was fine with that. But you're the only one who seems to care. For me, if being the same size as Caleigh McHugh, standing before me in her size 0 wedding gown, meant giving up my beloved Blue Moons and my favorite bakery's chocolate-chip scones as well as my own coq au vin, count me out.

We were standing in the bridal suite of the historic mansion that my parents own overlooking the Hudson, where Caleigh was to marry the robotic but filthy rich Mark Chesterton in under an hour. The guy seemed nice enough, but would I have picked him for Caleigh? Not in a million years. My cousin usually went for the bad boy, the guy your mother warned you about, your older brothers keeping an eye on in case he got too close. Older brothers, as I had come to learn—as I had four of my own—were the original restraining order.

My mother, queen of the Manor, as I liked to call her, had shooed the bridal party out of the room, along with her own sister, Aunt Helen, the mother of the bride. As maid of honor, I had the pleasure of being at Caleigh's beck and call, a role that was my birthright, apparently. I had learned long ago that letting Caleigh be the star of the show was sometimes my sole reason for being.

One last person remained in the room, Caleigh's mother's boyfriend, Frank, a man of few words but someone who seemed overcome by the events of the day, events that hadn't even begun yet. "Beautiful," he pronounced, tears filling his eyes as he clomped out of the room, his dress shoes clearly new and, from the looks of it, terribly uncomfortable.

"Caleigh, look away from the photographer, but smile," I said. The photographer gave me a side eye; I had obviously stepped on his toes here. I had forgotten how difficult it was for Caleigh to do two things at once. But here, in the bedroom, and not in the safe confines of the kitchen where I had once spent the better part of my days bossing people around, I still fell into my old role as chief cook and bottle washer/battle-axe. "I don't think you should look at the camera every time," I said, even though I knew that telling Caleigh not to look at the camera was akin to saying "don't think about pink elephants." See? Happens every time.

"You've been back what? Two months, Bel? And you're

already bossing everyone around," Caleigh said. "We know what we're doing here."

"You do?" I asked. "Then I hope you enjoy a wedding album of photos that make you look like you've just seen a ghost," I said. I looked at the photographer. "With all due respect, Jacqui," I said to the tall, thin, African-American man with the camera.

"It's pronounced 'Jock-quee,'" Caleigh whispered urgently.

Duly noted. "My cousin's got a great smile," I said. "Do you think we could get a couple of shots where she doesn't look like she's going to a funeral?" I asked.

"And you are?" he asked, looking up at me from the crouch he had folded into, all the better to get a shot of Caleigh's one physical flaw, the weak chin that melted straight into her short neck.

I held out my hand. "Belfast McGrath. 'Bel,' for short. Cousin of the bride." He accepted my hand in a limp approximation of a shake. "Maid of honor." He had already photographed us and knew the pecking order of the bridal party so the snub was for my benefit and mine alone.

When it was clear that my suggestion for some new poses had fallen on deaf ears, I gave up and took my place by another window, looking out at the setup below, the giant tent that would accommodate the cocktail part of the reception, the artfully decorated area where Caleigh would marry Mark, he of the trust fund, summer home in Nantucket, apartment in New York, house in Bronxville, and ability to give Caleigh the life she always wanted. She had strong-armed the chef, a guy named Goran Cilic, a Croatian ex-pat who was talented but had no finesse in the kitchen and whose grumpy manner made him the bane of every other member of the staff, into making a few items for the cocktail hour that were outside his comfort zone, including mini lobster tacos, something with quail eggs, and yet another thing that required gold leaf as a garnish. I wish she had asked me; I could have whipped up two-hundred-and-fifty canapés that would have brought tears to her eyes but she hadn't asked. Goran didn't want my help either, but he needed it, so I had shown him how to make a special chicken liver mousse recipe that Caleigh had seen on *Barefoot Contessa*. It took all I had not to tell him how to cut a filet properly at Caleigh's tasting because, as my parents had told me numerous times, Goran had been known to throw more than one tantrum.

I scanned the crowd below. My four brothers were in attendance as were all of their wives, my brothers assembling with their instruments next to the platform where Caleigh would marry Mark. The boys couldn't cook, but they could play Irish music like it was nobody's business, a trait that had been lost on me. Arney, the oldest, played the piano accordion and Cargan the fiddle, a skill that had taken him all over the United States and the United Kingdom; he was that good. Derry was our resident drummer, and Feeney did double duty as the lead singer and guitarist. Each and every one of my brothers was a diva in his own right and many a wedding had ended with Dad breaking up a fight over their "creative differences."

Their fights were epic. Creative differences bring about a lot of emotion apparently. I said a silent prayer that in addition to Goran's good behavior in the kitchen we would also have a pleasant day in which my four siblings played the music, smiled for the crowd, and packed up their instruments without anyone being the wiser that Feeney had pulled a butter knife on Arney the night before at the rehearsal dinner in retaliation for Arney's dismissal of Feeney's suggestion that they begin their first set with "Everybody Plays the Fool."

And people wonder why I was reluctant to come home after fifteen years away.

I spied my mother and father down below, both looking serious, but probably just unhappy that Caleigh wasn't having a Catholic nuptial Mass. Mark was a Protestant— something that my parents only said in a pointed whisper— denomination unknown, so whatever service was being held for the joining of the couple, it wouldn't "count," "counting" for attending Mass on Sunday being the sole reason for having a wedding after three o'clock on a Saturday.

In my devout Catholic parents' book anyway.

A handsome guy approached my father and shook his hand, my dad looking surprised to see him. No hug was exchanged, an odd thing, because my dad hugs the UPS guy when he brings my mother's almost-daily Zappos deliveries to the house. Next to them was Caleigh's uncle Eugene. "I didn't know you'd invited Uncle Eugene," I said. "He's allowed to travel now?" I said.

Caleigh let out a pointed sigh. "Of course he's allowed to travel. He was never convicted," she said.

News to me. Uncle Eugene was her late father's first cousin, so technically not my uncle or blood relation but we called him "uncle" regardless. He had fled the bucolic confines of Foster's Landing what seemed like a hundred years ago. I was little when he left, I remember that, maybe six or seven. I also remember that his abrupt departure had something to do with guns. Lots of guns. And the Irish Republican Army, which was a big deal in the eighties and whose existence was acknowledged in my house but never spoken about. So, how did I remember Uncle Eugene? He was hard to forget. He was as small as a man could be without being considered a little person but had hands that looked like they belonged to a much bigger man. He had a shock of white hair. Freckles to beat the band.

And one leg.

I never did find out the reason for Uncle Eugene's missing leg but had seen his prosthetic, something that had haunted my dreams when I was young. I remember my father taking us to Eugene's place over in the Hadley section of the Landing and whispering feverishly to the five of us—four boys and me all crammed into a Volkswagen Vanagon—"don't look at his leg!" As a result of that directive, Arney, on the one hand, the oldest and hence the most obedient and polite of our entire squad, spent most visits at Eugene's with his eyes closed shut, not trusting himself to look away from the visual pull of a prosthetic foot in a sneaker, a whisper of a plastic ankle just above a short sock. Feeney, on the other hand, always asked to play with the prosthetic, a request that Uncle Eugene was thrilled to honor.

From what I knew, Eugene had been in Ireland all this time, so seeing him at the wedding was a surprise. "I don't know why you're surprised, Bel," Caleigh said, adjusting her veil while looking in the mirror. "He's staying in the Manor."

"He is?"

"Yes, he arrived last night."

That's why I hadn't seen him. After coming home, a broken engagement smarting like a lemon in the world's deepest paper cut, I had stayed holed up in the apartment in the building adjacent to the Manor after the rehearsal dinner. Being at a wedding so soon after my own was supposed to take place was completely demoralizing.

Caleigh read my mind. "This must be hard for you," she said, showing uncharacteristic sensitivity. "I mean me, this gorgeous dress . . ."

"The wedding?" I asked. "This?"

"Yes, this," she said. "You've always been good at compartmentalizing things, Bel. It's your gift, I think."

That was her nice way of saying that I could ignore the obvious, pretend that things that were happening really weren't. That I could go to a wedding so soon after mine had been canceled and act, just for a few hours, like nothing had ever happened. We McGraths were good that way. Maybe it was a gift.

I turned to look out the window. "Who's the guy down there?" I asked Caleigh, still fussing with her veil. "Tall, dark hair, good-looking?"

"You've just described every single one of our cousins," Caleigh said. "Not a clue."

"Nice suit? Fancy shoes? Shiny?"

"Him or the shoes?" Caleigh asked.

"Um, the shoes," I said.

"Bel, I don't know. Now could you come over here and help me?" she asked, her hands wound up in yards of tulle so diaphanous that it almost wasn't there.

I took one last look at the guests below. The guy was cute. I'd have to find him later, ask Dad for an introduction. With my luck, the guy was my second cousin once removed.

"Please, Bella, some footage with the bride, please?" Jacqui asked, pointing to the phone in my hand.

"It's Bel. And you want video footage of you and Caleigh?" I asked.

"Yes, please. For my Web site."

Oh, now you need me, I thought. Jacqui and Caleigh preened for the camera, making small talk that basically centered around how gorgeous she was, how talented he was. He did some acrobatic photograph taking, jumping up and catching Caleigh as she did some supermodel turns, the requisite duck lips that graced every single photo of everyone on social media. If they kept it up I would be too nauseated to eat Goran's famous pigs in a blanket that I saw circulating on trays below, and that did not make me happy.

Caleigh had declared professional videographers "tacky" and was only having still photographs. I was surprised by that. Maybe Francis Ford Coppola was busy today and that's why there was no one filming every minute of what to me was a wedding nightmare.

Aunt Helen knocked and stuck her head through a crack in the door. "Caleigh, we're ready downstairs."

I adjusted the fake diamond necklace around my neck; Mom had lent it to me that morning, keeping the matching fake diamond earrings for herself. It had a habit of slipping, as cheap jewelry is wont to do, showing the clasp at the nape of my neck.

Uncle Jack had died two years earlier and since Caleigh was an only child, it was Aunt Helen's duty to "give her away," as the family said. Dad had volunteered but had been summarily dismissed, as he often was by Caleigh and Aunt Helen. I would gladly have given Caleigh away when we were children, but I was stuck with her, me an only daughter and she an only child. We were paired up from birth, our birthdays only a few months apart, and we grew up alongside each other, me getting brainer and chubbier by the day, she going from a not-so-ugly duckling into a beautiful swan who needed help with math. I kept my phone camera trained on her as she swept out of the room in her twenty-five-thousand-dollar dress and into the hallway, standing at the top of the stairs for a moment. She turned around and looked at me, forgetting I was filming.

"I'm doing the right thing, right, Bel?" she asked, her face under the mask of makeup she wore looking just like it had had when she was twelve and I was her best friend in the Landing. Or anywhere, for that matter, her e-mail pen pal in France, the presumed fourteen-year-old Jean-

Louis, turning out to be a forty-seven-year-old guy named Darryl who lived in Poughkeepsie.

I put the phone down. I would have to edit that question out later so that Mark Chesterton never knew that Caleigh McHugh had doubts about him. Good thing I was a nice person. "You are, Caleigh," I said. I didn't want to marry Mark, but that didn't mean that Caleigh shouldn't. "He's a great guy. You'll be really happy together." Okay, Bel, cool it, I thought; any more with the platitudes and she'd be on to me. "Second thoughts?" I asked, seeing her pale beneath the little spray of freckles across her nose, the bronzer on her cheeks. "It was a mistake. A onetime thing," I said, referencing a secret she had begged me to keep, the black-and-blue fingerprints on my upper arm a testament to the force with which she had pleaded. We made our way down the stairs, through the foyer and to the door that led to the long aisle.

"No. No second thoughts," she whispered, glaring at me as if I were the one who had professed doubts about marrying the guy standing at the end of the carpet runner that bisected the two sets of chairs for the guests: his on the right, hers on the left. I spied the cute guy who had been talking to my father, and he gave me a quick wink as a greeting. He was definitely not from these parts, as we say here in Foster's Landing; the cut of his suit and his shiny black shoes gave him away as someone from the other side. The "old country." Ireland's 32. I smiled back and then turned my attention back to Caleigh, making sure my nervous cousin looked like the princess she always wanted to be on her wedding day, fixing her veil, spreading her train out behind her.

I gave her a hug and told her I loved her. Because I did, when all was said and done. We were family, and although we had had a bit of a rocky relationship over the years, I would do anything for Caleigh, even lie and tell her that what she had done two nights before was no big deal. Water under the bridge.

Caleigh smiled at me through her tears and I knew I had calmed her down. No one would know that she really looked like she wanted to vomit right before she stepped out the door of Shamrock Manor and that deep down, as she had confessed to me the night before over a bottle of really cheap white wine—okay, maybe two—she knew that she maybe had cheated on Mark, more than a little bit, just the night before.

CHAPTER *Two*

I was watching the most raucous Siege of Ennis I had ever seen at any social gathering, let alone a wedding, with 100 percent of the bride's side and 0 percent of the groom's participating. The groom's family watched in perplexed horror.

If you've never seen a Siege, it's pretty amazing. Two lines of dancers face each other and advance and retire and advance and retire before each grabbing a person from the opposing line and spinning them around so hard that it's not unusual to see an older lady or gentleman get winged into a bus tray, sending champagne glasses flying. The dance originated in county Clare in the west of Ireland and represents the battle that took place when Ennis was under siege. As always, the siege had something to do with Catholics, Protestants, and a dispute over land, which, if you know anything about Irish history, is the root of every problem in the culture.

That and flat beer.

Anyway, it was an epic Siege. It went on for twenty minutes, and when it was clear that the remaining dancers had worn themselves out and I could get across the dance floor without being whisked into a bus tray I headed straight for the bar, where I got a pint, found an empty table, kicked off my shoes, a gorgeous pair of fake Jimmy

Choos that I bought used on eBay, and took a breather. Jacqui, I noticed, had taken the newly married couple out to the lawn and was doing some still shots in his patented *Night of the Living Dead* style, not a smile exchanged between man and wife.

Caleigh never told me whom she had slept with the night before and I didn't ask. It seemed curious to me that she wasn't dying to tell me, secret keeping not being one of Caleigh's character traits. She liked to spill the beans and spill them often, which led her to tell my mother things about me over the years that I didn't want my mother to know, ever. I had learned a long time ago that if you wanted the entire world to know something you told Caleigh. The fact that she had kept her paramour's identity a secret was telling, in and of itself. I scanned the crowd, wondering if that person was here.

It was a little hotter in the room than I would have liked and, coupled with the mass of sweating Irish bodies, it was downright unbearable. I grabbed one of the busboys.

"Hey, Padraic. Go turn the air-conditioning down to sixty."

The kid paled beneath his freckles. Mal McGrath was notoriously stingy when it came to creature comforts. "But Bel . . ."

"Just do it. I'll take the heat," I said. "So to speak."

I found a napkin and fanned my cleavage vigorously just in time for the cute guy in the sharp suit to come over and have a seat next to me.

"How ware ya?" he asked, and I've been around enough people with thick Irish brogues to know that he was in-quiring after my state of mind, not asking if he could don me like a raincoat.

"Grand, thanks," I said, speaking his language.

"Declan Morrison," he said, holding out his hand.

"Bel McGrath," I said, thinking that I was correct: he

was from Ireland and we were definitely related. He looked like my cousin Jimmy on my dad's side, but then again, everyone looked like Jimmy. And me, a bit. Declan also resembled my brothers, who when together looked like they had just come from a casting call for *Riverdance*. "Caleigh's first cousin on our moms' side of the family."

"Caleigh's third cousin, once removed," he said. "Do you know the groom?" he asked.

"I do," I said, keeping mum.

He leaned in close and I got a whiff of the suave-guy odor. Musk. A little hint of sandalwood. Something else that made me swoon just a tiny bit. "Thoughts?" he asked.

I thought about it for a moment. "Nice. Smart."

"And?"

"Well, there's the family money and the incredible good looks, too," I said. "It's all good," I added, more to myself than to the guy across from me.

He leaned back in his chair. "Fair enough." He asked for a sip of my beer, a little intimate for a first meeting, I thought, but I had been engaged recently to a really cheeky guy, so I was used to it. As I sat here looking at this guy, I found myself not missing my former fiancé all that much. That was a good sign, the ever-present pain in my gut diminishing a little bit. "So, what do you do, Bel McGrath?" he asked.

"Chef," I said, spreading my arms wide. "Currently on sabbatical."

His eyebrows went up. Saying you're a chef always impresses people. "Really?"

"Yep," I said. I resisted the urge to tell him that I had won the Rising Star Chef of the Year from the James Beard Foundation ten years prior, because if I told him that then I'd have to tell him the real reason I was back in Foster's Landing and why I was thinking about becoming a line cook at Five Guys.

"A chef?" It seemed my beer was now his and I watched as he made quick work of it. I don't know why he was so surprised at what I did, but I have found over the years that people often mistake curvy redheaded females for jobs other than head chef. Bartender. Waitress. Busgirl. Nanny. "Been doing it a long time?" he asked.

"Cooking, yes."

"And no job right now?" he asked.

"No. I came back to the Landing about two weeks ago, so I'm still looking."

"Came back from where?"

We must be related. He was as nosy as any other Mc-Grath or McHugh, curiosity running through his veins. "I was in New York City. Working at a restaurant." I didn't say which one. Even if he was from Ireland, he might have heard about the one-star Michelin restaurant where a former president of the United States had nearly choked to death on a fish bone that had inexplicably remained in his red snapper. And how the actor who owned the restaurant—a famous curmudgeon in his own right—had fired the chef on the spot.

And how that chef, a small redhead with a fiery temper that she had seemed to have since misplaced in favor of a dulled sense of not belonging, had—after apologizing profusely to the former president, who just minutes before had propositioned her in her kitchen—stormed out, telling the curmudgeonly actor that the Oscar he had won for playing a North Dakota farmer with the secret CIA past should have gone to another A-list actor for his role as Rambo's grown, angry son in *Axis of Terror,* a roundly panned film despite the A-list actor's performance, an acting tour de force.

And there was also a flipped table and a broken bottle, but I can't actually say that I remember that part.

I do remember, however, the face of the restaurant critic

for the *New York Times,* who between bites of my famous shepherd's pie—the one made with foie gras—was greedily taking in every detail of the passion play unfolding before him.

Not my finest hour.

The curmudgeon had always wanted a *Times* review. Now he had one. And a front-page story about the restaurant, the ending paragraph insinuating that the chef who had previously wowed diners with her artistry would never work in this town again.

I didn't wait to find out. I was out of my apartment, and the New York restaurant scene, within days.

Declan's eyebrows went up, almost as if he had read my mind and heard me tell the story out loud. "Sounds exciting. I've never met a chef."

It was exciting. And thrilling. And life affirming.

And over.

"Yep," I said, staring into the bottom of my empty glass. "But I'm back here now and . . ."

". . . and so happy to be among family again?" he asked, knowing that that wasn't the answer I was going to give.

"Right. Back in their loving arms."

"Do they do anything here but weddings?" he asked.

"Not really. Just my luck," I said.

"Why?" he asked.

"Not sure. I guess they like weddings," I said. Sure, we had the odd bar mitzvah and one or two christenings, but weddings were Mom and Dad's stock-in-trade.

"Not that," he said. "Why just your luck that they only do weddings?"

"You really want to know?" I asked.

He smiled. "Sure, I do."

"Broken engagement," I said. I held his gaze, waiting for his reaction. People always had one, I had found.

Declan studied my face in turn. "Well, that stinks."

"It's not so bad," I said when, in reality, it was too painful to acknowledge. The thought of the wedding dress I
had left hanging in my apartment's closet, available now
to the super, the landlord, or the next tenant, was something I had tried to banish from my mind. I focused, instead, on my lost career, the thought of never being in a
New York City restaurant kitchen again. That was easier
to think about, though difficult in its own way. It was a
broken heart, but of a different sort.

"What have you been doing since you got home?" Declan asked, changing the subject in the nick of time.

"The first month, I hid," I said. "And the second month,
I got up and decided that my life was better than that." I
had also come to the conclusion that it was possible that no
one in Foster's Landing really gave a hoot about a formerly
engaged, disgraced chef. They had their own concerns.
I probably wasn't even worthy of their gossip.

"Are you happy now?" he asked. "Is not being in hiding
working out for you?"

Guy was a regular Dr. Phil. Caleigh's third cousin once
removed and wedding therapist. I could get behind that
kind of guy. Or under, as the case may be.

"It's as good as it's going to get for right now," I said,
and that was the truth. I was living in an apartment over
Dad's art studio behind Shamrock Manor, feeding a cat
that I didn't own but who showed up every night for a bowl
of milk and a saucer of Friskies, and stalking my former
fiancé on the Internet, where I had come to find that he was
dating a Victoria's Secret model. Already. And likely
starving to death if the photos of his newly trimmed phy-
sique were any indication. It had only been two months and
he looked as if he had lost thirty pounds. He was on his
way to becoming the celebrity chef now, sought after and
desired. And I was the maid of honor at my cheating cous-

in's wedding. Maybe it wasn't as good as it gets and it could get better. Time would tell.

"Fair enough," he said.

Realizing I had finished my beer, Declan went to the bar and came back with two more. "Thanks," I said. "So are you that close to Caleigh that you made the trek from Ireland?" I asked. "She and I are pretty close. Kind of like sisters. How come this is the first time we're meeting?"

"First time I've been here," he said. "Caleigh came to Ireland a few times and that's how we know each other. And her ma and my ma were very close."

Being as her ma was my ma's sister and I had never heard of this guy, I wondered about that. But he had a quick smile and a very unassuming air and there was no reason for me not to believe that there was a McHugh cousin from Ireland I had never met. That and he seemed to know my dad pretty well. Then again, the whole crew—Mom, Aunt Helen, Dad, Uncle Eugene—all came from the same little village in the north and stayed together like a tight-knit circle of friends, coming to America, settling in the Landing. I wondered if Dad knew Declan's ma, too, and that's why they were talking at the bar. After Caleigh and Mark had said their "I dos" I had noticed Dad and Declan at the bar, deep in conversation, my dad's hands on Declan's shoulders in a paternal gesture that suggested that this was not the first time they had met.

"Where's your mom now?" I asked. I recognized almost everyone here.

"Oh, she stayed back home," he said. "I'm representing the family today."

"And my dad? How do you know him?" I asked.

"Trip to Ireland in the seventies," he said, his attention diverted by a buxom guest in a strapless gown.

I looked around the hall, noticing that after a short break the dance floor had filled once again.

"You fancy a dance?" he asked, holding out his hand. No ring. Good sign.

"Oh, thanks. You're sweet. But no." Truth was, I was only a good dancer with half a bag on. I pointed to my feet. "Aching dogs."

"Ah," he said. "Too bad. Maybe a pint when all of this," he said, waving a hand around the room, "is over?" He flashed that smile again and, I'm sorry to say, I was becoming kind of a sucker for it.

"Maybe," I said, and downed my pint. Caleigh and Mark were headed back from the great lawn and it appeared that despite having suffered through one round of toasts, we were going to suffer through another.

I watched my brothers reassemble on the stage after a short break, the tension between Arney and Feeney palpable as they argued about which song they would now play now that some of the Irish-dancing stuff was out of the way. A line of people queued up to toast the happy couple. I noticed Declan Morrison somewhere in the crowd and he gave me a little wave, making a gesture that suggested we would be drinking another pint together when all of this was over.

Caleigh returned to the hall and I watched her dance with my father, the old guy sobbing like he was sending her off to Afghanistan rather than a five-bedroom house down county in Bronxville, complete with a full-time maid and groundskeeper. When they were finished, she grabbed me as she exited the dance floor, holding on to my arm to steady herself. Caleigh could never hold her liquor; I knew that from experience. My car had been detailed more than once after a night spent with my darling cousin, a trip to Eden Island in the middle of the Foster's Landing River to party ending with a crying, nauseated Caleigh in the backseat.

"Why don't I get you a glass of water, Caleigh?" I asked, extricating her hand from my arm. She had the brute strength of someone who was a devotee of my mother's legendary Pilates classes. Around Foster's Landing, there was a cadre of women who looked more fit than a team of Navy SEALs thanks to Oona McGrath's torture sessions. "Oona" means "Queen of the Fairies" in Gaelic, but for my mother it meant "Queen of the Biceps." At sixty-five, the woman could bench-press her body weight and then some.

"Cute, right?" Caleigh slurred, accepting the glass of water I had grabbed from a nearby table and slurping noisily.

"Who?"

"The guy you were talking to."

"Yes. Adorable," I said. "Apparently, you're related?"

She didn't answer, spilling the rest of the water down the front of her dress, missing her mouth completely. "I love you, Bel. You are the closest thing to a sister I've ever had."

I'd seen this show before, too. This was the part where Caleigh had so much to drink that she turned sappy and sentimental. If I weren't careful, copious tears would follow, sentimentality followed quickly by spiraling depression. I chose my words carefully. "I love you, too, Caleigh." It was the second time I had said it that day, words that I had never uttered to Caleigh ever before.

"Like a sister?"

"Like a sister. Now let's get you upstairs," I said, steering her toward the exit. I looked around for Mark, but he was nowhere to be found.

"We're best friends! Right, Bel?"

"Right. Yep. The bestest."

I pushed open the door to the hall and escorted her out into the grand foyer of the mansion and toward the stairs, which hadn't seemed so daunting when I wasn't half-carrying a 110-pound bride. Now their wide expanse practically mocked me as I stood at the bottom, staring up at the Promised Land above, the second floor and the bedroom where Caleigh had gotten dressed.

"And you'll never tell Mark, right?" she said, taking each step as if she were a baby calf, just born. Behind us I heard raucous laughter as the strains of a peppy hornpipe drifted out from behind the closed doors of the ballroom.

"Never," I said. That wasn't a lie. I wanted to forget what Caleigh had told me the night before and move on. I'm sure she wasn't the first person to have a fling right before her wedding, but why did I have to know about it? I didn't know who it was, but I knew that it had happened. I couldn't unknow it and the thought of that made me queasy with anxiety that I might spill the beans one day, undoing this happy union with my loose tongue.

Maybe I was the one who would have to quit drinking, loose lips sinking ships and all.

We made it to the bedroom. Caleigh fell backward onto the plush bedding, her wedding dress flying up around her in pillow-like clouds of taffeta and silk. "I'm a good girl, Bel."

"I know you are, Cousin."

Satisfied with that, she smiled under a film of tulle veil. "I think I'll take a nap," she said, exhaling a piece of it off the front of her face, her snores immediate and labored.

"Good idea," I said, hearing her phone, left on the dresser, trill merrily. I picked it up to silence it but ended up staring at the screen, a message from the man involved in the tryst letting her know how great a time he had had. As

I looked at his words, I wondered why, of all the people in the world, Caleigh had to have slept with the one guy who had shown any interest in me since my broken engagement. His name—Declan—was displayed prominently on the screen of her phone. There was no last name, but really, did he need one? The only other Declan at the wedding was an eighty-year-old cousin of Jack McHugh's, and I felt certain that Caleigh hadn't slept with him.

It didn't take me long to figure out her security password, unlocking the phone. "Caleigh922"—September 22 being her birthday. I texted Declan back as my recently betrothed cousin.

Please don't text me again. I'm married now.

And then I proceeded to delete every piece of evidence that existed on her phone—photos included—of what happened two nights before Caleigh McHugh married Mark Chesterton.

CHAPTER *Three*

If all weddings were going to have this much drama, I was never getting married.

I had had my fill of my own drama, and now that I was home again I eschewed it like the plague. I had come home to be invisible, to live a life without anyone mentioning what had happened at The Monkey's Paw in Tribeca, to be seen around town without anyone mentioning Francesco Francatelli, otherwise known as the guy who had won the Oscar for playing the North Dakota farmer with the secret CIA past.

I left Caleigh napping, closing the bedroom door behind me and bumping into Declan Morrison, who, if I didn't know better, seemed to have followed us up the stairs. Why else would he be standing in the second-floor hallway, close to the room where I had just put Caleigh to bed? The handsomeness I had seen earlier, knowing what I now knew, had drifted away and in its place was an oily suaveness that I hadn't noticed before.

"She's sleeping," I said, keeping my hand on the door, him at arm's length.

"Ah, just looking for a place to put my feet up," he said.

I started toward the staircase, turning to ask him one last question. "How do you do that?"

"Do what?" he asked, still lingering by the closed bedroom door.

"Take advantage of someone right before her wedding and then actually attend the wedding?"

A smile spread across his face. "And how do you know it wasn't the other way around?"

I thought about that for a moment. I didn't. Although I liked to think of Caleigh as innocent and simple in her approach to things, I'm sure in the years that had passed since we graduated from high school and then college, the years where I had been cast in the role of her protector and de facto sister, she had matured into her own woman, someone who was completely capable of doing something like having a one-night stand with a mysterious wedding guest, someone I had never heard of and now never wanted to see again. My family had changed—heck, I had changed, too—the individual members turning into people I would have to reacquaint myself with over time, it seemed.

Caleigh's third cousin once removed, my ass.

I didn't answer him, making my way back to the wedding. I ran into Mark on the dance floor, dancing stiffly with his grandmother, Jonesy, a tiny dynamo in a St. John suit who had told me last night at the rehearsal dinner that the key to staying slim was a secret fifty-year smoking habit.

"Marlboro Lights. Best way to keep your weight down," she croaked. "Every girl in my sorority smoked them."

You know what also keeps you thin? Cancer. But I wisely kept my mouth shut and nodded gratefully for that sound piece of health advice. And the secret of her smoking habit was not so secret, I wanted to mention. A cloud of smoke followed her everywhere she went.

I pulled Mark to the side. "FYI, Caleigh is upstairs sleeping off the bottle of champagne she drank."

He grimaced. "She can't hold her liquor," he said, some kind of indictment in his voice. Behind us, Feeney was revving up and a loud song with a cha-cha beat began, complete with accordion accompaniment. Thanks to Derry's interest in diversity, The McGrath Brothers, my siblings' unoriginally named quartet, now seemed to cover every ethnicity known to mankind, so much so that I wondered if Feeney would switch to a sitar right after a musical trip to Cuba.

"She's all yours now, Mark," I said, reminding him that his vows just a few hours ago made it so that I was no longer her caretaker and that he was.

"I know, Bel," he said. "And that makes me the happiest man in the world." His face broke into a smile so wide and sincere that my heart almost broke, knowing what I knew. Sure, Mark Chesterton wasn't a guy I found attractive, but in that moment—more than any other moment so far—I saw that he adored her. And that was enough to make me feel better about the union.

He walked off, leaving me among a sea of dancers all hell-bent on making "Besame Mucho" seem like a new Siege of Ennis, the intensity of their cha-chaing rivaling my relatives doing their favorite dance. There wasn't an Irish-Catholic person among them, leading me to believe that the Protestants at this wedding had all attended the Arthur Murray Dance Studio at some point and learned well.

I decided to get a breath of fresh air, choosing the front of the historic mansion for a little sojourn before the cutting of the cake, if that would even happen, given the bride's inebriation. Although I should have been more interested in the goings-on in the kitchen, Goran was in charge and I had been warned to leave him alone, even if I thought his knife skills rivaled those of Jack the Ripper.

Out on the front porch rocking chairs faced a grand lawn that also had a view of the Hudson, and that was my destination. I had one foot in the foyer, its marble floor gleaming in the afternoon sun, when my attention was diverted by commotion overhead, somewhere in the vicinity of Caleigh's slumber.

Not my business, I thought, as I heard what sounded like two men speaking in hushed but angry tones. My first thought was that a worker was getting reamed by my father for letting the Chesterton/McHugh schedule get out of hand—where was that damned cake anyway?—or for letting Jonesy Chesterton smoke in the ladies' room. (It had to be her. No one smokes anymore and I had seen her face when her filet mignon—a big, honking piece of meat— was served. It was utter despair followed by steely resolve. And a hasty exit to smoke presumably.) I looked up just in time to see the former man of my dreams, Declan Morrison, take a swan dive over the second-floor balcony, hitting the large resin bust of FDR that incongruously sat in the center of the foyer, breaking it—and his own beautiful head—into a million little nasty pieces all over the polished stone.

CHAPTER *Four*

Let's look at the bright side. There has to be a bright side, right? I'm a McGrath; we were taught from a young age that whatever you were going through, someone had it much worse. At least I wasn't thinking about my own broken engagement or the end of my very promising career anymore. No, I was thinking about death and blood and all of the horrible nightmares I was likely to have after seeing someone die.

I hadn't signed up for this, standing to the side of a dead body in the grand hall of a beautiful historic mansion, blood everywhere, ruining what appeared to be a very well-made shirt on a very dead guy. And being the only witness, except for whomever Declan had argued with prior to his dive over the balcony railing. I stifled a gag. There was no way I was letting Kevin Hanson, otherwise known as "the wanker" in my family, see that I was feeling a little under the weather and that if I were a different person, one who didn't have complete control over her wonky digestive tract, I'd have spewed all over the place, ruining his precious crime scene.

"Bel?" Kevin said, looking at me as if I had just beamed into the crime scene, as if I had no place being in my parents' place of business at my cousin's wedding. "What are you doing here?"

Not much of a detective there, are you, Hanson? That's what I wanted to say, but instead I smiled. He was probably the last person in Foster's Landing to know I had returned and that didn't bode well for the investigative skills the badge he displayed so proudly seemed to connote. "Just passing through," I said, and that was true enough. I had just been passing through when I heard angry whispers and then the sound of wood shattering, along with one very handsome guy's head. FDR was smashed to smithereens. And so was Declan Morrison.

Kevin read my mind. He always could. He tried to affect some kind of nonchalance that he didn't have the chops to pull off. He wasn't excited to see me. Indeed, he seemed a little bothered by my appearance in his crime scene. "I'll want to talk to you again," Kevin said, still looking, in the final approach to middle age, like the boy he had once been.

"That makes sense," I said, my last word punctuated by a gag that stuck in my throat.

"What's that supposed to mean?" he asked. "I know what I'm doing," he said, the implication being that I—or someone else—didn't think he did.

"Of course you do," I said, swallowing hard, but I wasn't so sure. Kevin wasn't exactly what you'd call a brain trust, but he sure was cute. That's what had gotten him over several academic humps in high school, his ability to charm his way into a passing grade.

"Stay put. You're our only witness," he said as he gave me another once-over, still in my really uncomfortable raw-silk bridesmaid dress. He smiled even though the words sounded curt, insensitive, like I was the worst witness ever to see someone die. I was. Beyond the actual dying part, I could offer nothing more about what had happened prior to that event.

Hard to believe that I once loved Kevin Hanson so much

that I almost agreed to drop out of the the Culinary Institute for a stint at Ulster County Community College. So glad I listened to my mother, just that once. After I left, he started dating Mary Ann D'Amato, the Lieutenant's daughter, and had been with her for years. She was someone whom I wanted to hate but couldn't because she had been nice always, a real gem. A nurse. She volunteered at a local soup kitchen as often as she could, given her schedule, a regular Mother Teresa with long legs, gorgeous hair, and a heart of gold. Mom had filled me in on the details of Mary Ann's endeavors and her and Kevin's courtship over the years, often closing with the observation that everyone in the Landing—everyone!—wondered why Kevin had never proposed, never made Mary Ann an "honest woman."

It was like going back in time, coming here.

Of course he had left me for her. He couldn't leave me for a harridan, some harpy. Nope. Mary Ann D'Amato had been class valedictorian, a Peace Corps volunteer, and an all-around wonderful girl. Just ask anyone. She took my mother's Saturday morning Pilates class, one of the first things Mom told me when I moved into the apartment over Dad's studio.

"She's as gorgeous as ever," Mom had said. "Lovely girl."

I know, I wanted to say. She always had been. Even though Kevin had picked her over me, I couldn't hate her. She was just that wonderful.

"You're lucky to have me as a witness," I said, unable to turn my face away from the dead body on the floor. RIP, Mr. Hot Stuff, I thought. You were a lovely fantasy while you lasted. I looked up at the broken banister, so wrecked that I wondered at the strength of the person who had thrown Declan through it.

Kevin ignored me, getting down in a crouch in front of the body. As if he knew what he was doing. Which he didn't. Kevin Hanson was a Foster's Landing boy and now a Foster's Landing cop. "Detective," as he reminded me. Not much difference, in my book. He looked around the foyer, taking in the stunned expressions of the two uniformed cops who had responded after Goran had called 911 after hearing me scream. "You two," he said, throwing his investigative weight around inside his Men's Wearhouse suit, "go inside and question everyone who spoke to this guy, served him a canapé, or maybe had a one-night stand with him." He looked at me pointedly as if I were the painted whore of Babylon, smiling again to lessen the impact of his words. He stood up, shoving his hands in his pockets. "That happens at weddings," he said, keeping his eyes on me. "One-night stands." He offered a chuckle to cover the fact that what he had said was insulting—albeit accurate, unbeknownst to him—but the damage was done. He was being an ass and I wasn't sure why.

"Jealous?" I asked. I don't have as much control over my bloodstream as I do my digestive tract, so I knew I blushed red, telegraphing to the entire room that even if I hadn't had a tryst with dead wedding guest number one, I had thought about it. I also knew that the blushing bride, not the innocent she pretended to be, had made good on that thought. "You should call the county cops," I said in the most helpful tone I could muster. "I think we're all a little out of our league here." I wondered why I was the only one who saw that. Kevin responded by turning his back on me. He had already asked me what I had seen, heard. I told him everything, except for the part where I had deleted all evidence of Declan's rendezvous with Caleigh on her phone. That I was keeping to myself, at least for the time being.

I stepped back and waited for Kevin to take control of the scene, something that would have required him to do more than clear the area and stare at the body like it was a mermaid who had been dropped into the middle of a bar mitzvah. Tired of watching him consider the gaping hole in the guy's head, I moved into the main dining area, where two hundred silent people greeted me, one old lady pointing mutely at my shoes, blood splattered and ruined. I stripped them off and threw them in a waste can before going to find my parents in the crowd. The shoes had been the wrong size and definitely the wrong color, a fuchsia gone so wrong that it would never be right. I was happy to be rid of them, my toes cramped and stiff after a day in those suckers.

I passed my brothers, still on the stage and standing at rapt attention, holding their instruments as if to say, We all have alibis! They did. They had been playing some mash-up of "The Girl from Ipanema" and what sounded like Lady Gaga's "Born This Way" and everyone in the room had had their eyes trained on them. They had then segued into a version of Elvis Presley's "Suspicious Minds," which made me wonder if I was the only person who knew about Caleigh's transgression. But then I re-membered how Feeney had used to dress up as Elvis when we were kids, inking long sideburns down his chubby face, and it all made sense.

I walked around the head table, where Aunt Helen was sobbing loudly into one of the linen napkins, her boyfriend, Frank the Tank, as we liked to call him, with his arm around her shoulders. Frank was a former firefighter and his size and shape indicated to me, at least, that he was the guy to call if I was ever trapped in a fire. I gave Aunt Helen a quick hug. Frank grabbed my arm, his hand shaking.

"This. Is. Awful," he said in a halting tone, his face pale. Poor guy had seen his share of death and destruction, but his reaction to the day's events pointed to a sensitive nature his size and normally silent demeanor didn't make apparent.

"It is," I said.

He shook his head sadly. "And at a wedding."

There was nothing to say to that so I drifted off, looking for my parents. When I reached them finally, my mother threw her toned arms around me. She has never known quite what to do with a short, chubby daughter, wondering how she—a five-foot-ten lithe beauty—could have given birth to someone like me despite having the genetic capacity to wear the same jeans over a twenty-year period without the benefit of an elastic waist and an intrepid tailor. "Oh, honey," she whispered into my hair. "That poor fella. What happened?"

I broke the embrace and shrugged, trying to act like I saw accidents—or, worse, murders—every day. "He came over the balcony." That was one way to put it. "Not sure how it happened without somebody seeing something." Me, in particular. I didn't want to go into too much detail because I wasn't sure what I heard or what I saw besides his lifeless body on the floor.

My dad leaned in, his arms crossed over his chest. "Maybe it was one of them," he said, raising an eyebrow in the direction of Mark's family. He dropped his voice to a whisper, which for him, on a scale of 1 to 10, is about a 15. "It could happen," he said.

Maybe. Probably not. Something told me that Mark's family was incapable of that sort of violence, looking as they did, as if they had turned to stone, a phalanx of wedding guests pressed up against the windows at the back of the room. This looked a little more like a crime of passion to me, but what did I know?

"Do you know what this is going to do for business?" my father asked, drawing a hand across his balding pate. "A murder at Shamrock Manor?" He shook his head sadly.

Mom put a hand on his arm. "Let's not go there yet, Mal. We don't even know what happened."

"Officer Hanson on the scene?" my father asked, no love lost between my old boyfriend and my father.

"Sure is," I said, the three of us sitting down at the table. "And it's Detective Hanson now."

"We were told we couldn't leave," my mother said. "By that officer over there," she added, pointing to a trembling cop who looked like he had just graduated from high school. "He looks like he's about to faint. I think I changed his diaper once at a church picnic."

He did look like he was about to faint. It wasn't every day that you went to work thinking that you'd be answering calls related to shoplifting at the local grocery store only to find that you were now part of a team investigating a murder. Suicide was ruled out relatively quickly because, really, who tries to kill themselves by jumping off a second-floor balcony, the danger of the FDR bust notwithstanding? The word "murder"—as well as the rumor of an argument on the balcony—floated through the crowd like the sound a crow makes on a spring morning.

Murder.

"He says that they're going to interview every single one of us," my father added, looking chagrined.

I looked around the room. "That will take a while." Three cops plus two hundred guests equaled a long night ahead. "Where's Caleigh?" I asked, not spying the bride. "Mark?"

"Kevin gave them permission to leave," Dad said. "He had a quick word with them and then let them take off."

A "quick word"? In a murder investigation? Interesting. I wondered what their alibi was or if they even had one. I had gotten Kevin through sophomore-year geometry, so I wasn't all that impressed by his ability to incorporate logic into his thinking. Presumably, Caleigh was still sleeping when all of this happened, but that little voice in the back of my head was telling me that maybe she wasn't. Maybe she was on the balcony. Maybe she had seen something.

"Kevin looks good?" Mom said, throwing it out there like it was some innocent question, something that wasn't fraught with emotion, years of recrimination.

"He does," I said. I looked at my father, squirming uncomfortably in an oxford shirt, the collar of which circled his size 17 neck in a way that suggested it was a wee bit too tight. "Dad, did you know the dead guy? This Declan character?" I said, trying to make it sound like I didn't know him, didn't think he was the most attractive guy I'd seen around these parts in a long time, and that I hadn't daydreamed that we might see each other without clothes sometime later in the evening.

My dad pulled at the collar of his shirt. In addition to owning Shamrock Manor, he is also a painter, sculptor, and creator of "installations" that use random pieces of wood and metal as their foundations, so he's more comfortable in a paint-covered T-shirt and jeans than the formal wear he's required to wear when there is an event at the Manor. I looked at his hands, little bits of blue paint dotting his freckled skin. No blood, not a speck. I don't know why I went there in my mind, but I had. I quickly looked away while I waited for his answer.

"Just met him at the wedding," he said. A thin sheen of sweat had appeared on his forehead.

"He said you had met in Ireland," I said.

Dad looked up at the ceiling, either trying to remember or formulating a lie. "No. Nope. I don't think so."

"Dad, take off your tie," I said, reaching over and loosening the knot. "You look like you're going to have a heart attack."

Mom poured Dad a glass of water from the one pitcher that the frantic busboy hadn't taken away. "You do, Mal.

You look like you're going to have a heart attack," she repeated unnecessarily.

Dad took the water and greedily gulped it. "Thanks, Oona." He wiped his brow with his napkin and looked a little bit better, the color fading from his cheeks, his breathing returning to normal.

"You just met him here?" I asked again. "And Mom, you didn't know him, either?"

"Never saw him before in my entire life," she said. And how did I know that that was the truth? Mom has a "tell" when she lies; immediately after uttering a falsehood, she licks her lips. This time, she locked her jaw and just stared straight ahead, looking as if she was trying to tune out the chatter behind us, the group coming to their own conclusions about who had killed Declan Morrison.

"He said he was Caleigh's cousin," I said. "Third once removed."

"Nope," said Dad.

"Maybe?" said Mom.

Caleigh had once confided in me that Mark and his family thought our clan was a little "rough around the edges." Charming in our own way, but not really like the country-club set he and his people were used to hanging out with. They reluctantly accepted Caleigh, but they never would embrace the rest of us. We were just a little bit different. Too different.

Nothing like a dead guy at a wedding to confirm their suspicions.

CHAPTER *Five*

The body was carted off by the county's Medical Examiner, an amiable guy named Mac McVeigh, who looked like retirement was just around the corner for him but for whom this line of work seemed incredibly fulfilling. He gave us a wave as he drove off in his old station wagon and we waved back, just as we would have if we had had the opportunity to see Caleigh and Mark drive off in his vintage Mini Cooper, the one on which Feeney had tied the requisite tin cans to the back.

My parents, my brothers, and I stood in the foyer and looked at one another. What had started out as a supposedly happy occasion had ended on a bloody note, drama surrounding the entire event. The boys—as we all still called my adult brothers—looked too spent to fight, each one looking droopier than the rest. Feeney pulled off his tuxedo jacket and threw it onto the banister. "I'm outta here," he said, going into the ballroom to get his equipment.

Off to the side, police tape outlining the spot that still held the bloodstains from the earlier event, Goran stood by the kitchen door, his apron in his hands. He thrust it at my father. "Here! Take it! You people are crazy!" he said. "Death at a wedding? Who hears of such a thing?"

Dad looked at the apron in his hand, unable to speak. He took off his tie and wound it around his free hand, and for a brief moment I wondered if he was going to hang himself or strangle Goran with it.

"I quit!" Goran said.

"Aren't you overreacting just a bit, Goran?" I asked, pushing past Dad, my remaining brothers having fallen mute.

"This place is cursed," Goran said, narrowing his eyes. "You're all cursed. I'm leaving here before I become cursed, too."

Cursed? That might have been overstating things just a tad.

Goran started for the door and I grabbed his arm. "Goran, wait." But he shook me off and kept walking, his black clogs squeaking on the polished marble.

"Bel, let him go," Dad said as we watched the tall, thin man in the black-and-white-checkered pants and chef's jacket stride past the police tape—uttering some kind of whispered prayer as he did—and out the front door, gesticulating wildly and talking to himself as he strode down the gravel path that led to the employee parking area.

Derry's face flamed red and he looked at my father; he's always been the most excitable in the bunch. Of course he immediately regrets his outbursts and then goes to confession. These days, confession only happens on Saturdays, right before the 5:00 Mass, so I guess he has private moments with Father Pat. How do I know this? Mom has been trying to get me to go since I have come home "just to have a chat with the padre." No, thank you. I think he has his hands full with Derry and his list of non-sins. I think lusting after Pamela Anderson came off the sin list somewhere around 1996. "Well, that's just great. What are we supposed to do now?" he said.

Cargan, solemn and serene to the point where some-times I wondered if he had a pulse at all, looked at my father dolefully. "We have three weddings this month. And it's not like we have a bunch of chefs waiting in the wings."

God bless his little heart; it was almost as if he had for-gotten who I was, what I did. I think Mom must have waited a few seconds too long to get to the hospital with that one. He wasn't exactly the sharpest tool in the shed. But then again, neither was I, because it never dawned on me that they would all turn, in unison, and look at me like I was just the person to save the day. Right on cue, they turned their attention to me like I was a steak dinner and they were all death-row inmates.

"Ah, no," I said. I held my hands up. "No."

Cargan stared at me, his eyes anchored by deep pock-ets that were in stark contrast to the rest of his youthful appearance. "You, Bel. You're the chef. You're home now. You have to help Mom and Dad."

Derry upped the ante, so far that if I weren't so beaten down from the turn my life had taken I would have decked him like I used to when we were kids and I wasn't cowed by the fact that he was six-feet-three in the eighth grade. "It's not like you're doing anything else."

"But I have plans!" I said. "Dreams!"

Arney, who had remained silent thus far, chose his words carefully but not carefully enough. "I think your plans and dreams changed the minute you served the for-mer president a red snapper bone."

I waited exactly ten seconds before speaking, breath-ing in and breathing out, something I had been taught in the all-day anger-management class I had been forced to take to avoid charges in my horrible display of behavior in Francesco Francatelli's restaurant. "Nice, Arney. Real nice. Like I needed a reminder."

There was still the smell of blood in the air, like a bunch of pennies that had been dredged up from beneath a fetid pool of water. My head swam and I felt my father's strong hand around my upper arm, his fingers hitting the same place where Caleigh had gripped me so tight the night before. "Take some time, Belfast," Dad said, giving me a little squeeze that made me wince in pain, as much affection as I was likely to get from the guy.

Mom gave me one last look before she drifted off to the second floor, taking a hard right at the top, the left cordoned off by police tape, marking the spot where Declan Morrison had come crashing through the antique banister that Mom and Dad had reclaimed from a farmhouse in Quebec. I didn't have time to tell her that she was missing an earring, lost somewhere in the Manor with all of the hullaballoo that had taken place. Her high heels made no sound on the plush carpeting and I heard the door to their bedroom, way at the other end of the hallway with the rest of their living quarters, close with a thud, its heavy oak providing a necessary seal between her and her emotional progeny.

Derry and Cargan went into the ballroom to collect their instruments, leaving me with my father and my oldest brother, once an ally. Arney stared down at me, a lock of his jet-black hair—a throwback to some Spaniard who had invaded northern Ireland, or so my mother always claimed—hanging over his eyes, his cheekbones high and not covered with the pudge that even the thinnest McGraths are saddled with. "It's your turn now, Bel," he said not unkindly. "It's your turn to help out here."

"We've missed you, honey," Dad said, and although I am not one to shed a tear, preferring anger to sadness like the rest of this dysfunctional clan, the tears were pushing at the backs of my eyes, threatening to make an appearance.

One thing I had learned from growing up with four brothers is that once you show them that—the tears, the crying, the femaleness—they knew you were weak and that would be the end of everything.

CHAPTER *Six*

I didn't want to go back to my dank little apartment over the garage, not after the day we had all had, but I begged off my father's suggestion that I join the lot of them at a local restaurant for a burger. Our appetites had returned after we realized that we had passed the dinner hour, but we didn't want to use the kitchen either in the Manor or in my parents' living quarters, the smell of the place, even if it was just all in our minds, putting us off my whipping up a dinner fit for a family of starving hosts and musicians.

Truth be told, I was hungry, too, but I needed to get away from my family. Dinner would turn into something else, some other activity, and I was pretty sure I'd end up with one or more of my nieces and nephews, probably Arney and Grace's horrible toddler twins, Eddie the puker and Audrey the wailer, while my brother and his wife grabbed a nightcap before going home. Date night. Alone time. Whatever they called it, they never got enough of it, according to them.

There would also be more strong-arming and name-calling about me becoming the chef at Shamrock Manor, a job for which I was perfectly suited and that I surely didn't want.

Taking that job would mean that I was staying and I was definitely *not*.

I peeled off from the boys and my parents, my mother having emerged from the bedroom after a few minutes, the promise of a burger too much for her to resist. I got a pair of flip-flops out of the back of the old Volvo wagon that my dad had procured for me and which was serving its purpose for the time being and prepared to drive off.

I ended up in the center of the village, back to a place I had avoided up until now. Even when I was driving around with nowhere to go, I took care not to drive past it so as not to be tempted to stop in. Too many memories. Too much heartbreak. So, I wasn't sure why, on this day, the sun starting to set over the Hudson, the memory of the guy's face as he realized he was going over the balcony and likely to his death lingering in my mind, I ended up at Oogie Mitchell's place, The Dugout, somewhere I hadn't been in almost twenty years. In my maid-of-honor dress and flip-flops, my previously coiffed hair hanging in crazy corkscrews around my face, I entered the bar, and while I didn't expect a hero's welcome, I didn't expect total silence to be the greeting.

The smell of the place brought me right back to that time, melting away the years and making me feel like a teenager all over again.

And not in a particularly good way.

Hot dogs on the grill. Peanut shells on the floor. A half century of beer, sticky at first and eventually absorbed into the pine floor, yeasty and organic.

This place hadn't gone the way of the other bars in town, the ones that used to be filled with the guys from the railroad and the old guys from the original part of the village. Those bars now served beer with a hint of lilac, a note of ginger, and were empty of anyone with who had the hint of old Foster's Landing on them, their stools now populated with a younger, hipper set. Microbrews had found the village, and now it was hard to get a beer that tasted like a beer.

No matter; I liked the cheap wine here anyway. It reminded me of my best friend, Amy, gone all of these years, of bottles purloined from her father's place and stowed in the tips of our kayaks for a trek out to Eden Island lit only by the moon above.

I looked around before taking a seat at the bar, mildly amused at its denizens, the regulars, guys who looked as if they had been there for years and probably had. There was a guy snoozing in a puddle of beer sitting next to me; he's the one I started a one-sided conversation with, letting off some steam after the day. I recognized him as the janitor who worked at the elementary school when I went there what seemed like a hundred years ago; he was also the guy who had held my chin together with his undoubtedly germ-riddled hands after I had taken a header off of the jungle gym in the playground when I was in the third grade. Ten stitches, right to the kisser, Mom in her infinite wisdom asking for the best plastic surgeon the hospital had to offer. All I had to show for that day was a little, tiny divot on the right side of my face, a dimple. Nothing else.

"Come here often?" I asked, his face firmly planted on the bar, a snore escaping. "Me either. Great hot dogs, though," I said, looking around for a bartender. I wondered what one had to do to get a drink around here. Back in the day, all you had to do was flash a couple of dollar bills and someone would magically appear out of nowhere. "I saw a dead guy today."

The guy mumbled something unintelligible and turned his face to the other side. If I wanted to continue this conversation, it would be with the back of his head.

"Right. No big deal," I said, spying Oogie Mitchell coming out from behind the swinging kitchen doors. He hadn't spotted me yet.

The last time I had seen Oogie, he had said, "Happy graduation, princess," on what was my departure from high school. Amy, his daughter, was my best friend and constant companion since kindergarten. It was she who gotten the janitor when I had fallen and she who had convinced me that Kevin Hanson wouldn't break my heart, that even though he wasn't as into school as I was, he was cute and nice and worth a chance. I was a lot older than that now and I certainly didn't feel like a princess anymore, but as I sat on a stool I had occupied a number of times as a teenager part of me hoped that someone would recognize me, welcome me home, even though this was the last place I wanted to be. I had kept a low profile since arriving back in Foster's Landing, spending the first few days of what I considered my "exile" in the apartment, going through the detritus that had accumulated there, making myself almost believe that what I was doing was not preparation for an extended stay. But over the last few days, I had made some sort of peace with the fact that I was going to be here for a while and because of that I needed to redecorate. I got stuff out of storage and painted the bedroom. I adopted the feral cat, even though the cat wasn't aware of this new arrangement. I started to make a home for myself, back where it all started a long time ago, in the place I never wanted to return.

I looked around The Dugout. The last time I had been here I had been wet, cold, and hungover. I had eaten one of the hot dogs and drunk one of the beers, even though it was barely eleven in the morning, but I had felt better instantly, pushing aside the fact that I couldn't remember a lot from the previous night except that I had said something not nice to Amy, not knowing that I would never see her again. I had never figured out how I had ended up on an island in the middle of the Foster's Landing River by myself or why I had been alone. But coming into the bar that morning, finding Oogie, made everything all better. For a little while, at least.

The longer she was gone, the more frantic he became. It was clear, soon after that, that she wasn't coming back. To me, anyway.

Now, with the place frozen in time, the guys around me focused on their beers, it felt like the right time to come back. No one paid me any mind. Those railroad shifts were long and it was getting warmer, so all these guys wanted to do was drink their beers before going home to shower the smell of metal and solder off of themselves so that they could settle, clean, into their old recliners and drink a few more beers before drifting off to sleep and starting another day. When I thought about it, there was not a soul in this bar, except for one maybe, wondering why I had been gone for as long as I had.

The same knotty pine adorned the walls and the pool table still had a slit by one of the side pockets. Over the bar, there was still a shrine to Oogie's daughter Amy, gone a long time now, her disappearance something it seemed he had never gotten over.

Me either, I wanted to say. But saying so might indict me, if ever so slightly, in her disappearance and that was something that had hung around me a long time, like a stench that had settled in and clung to every fiber of my being, the main reason I had left as quickly and suddenly as I had, hoping never to return.

"Ran away," Oogie told everyone, touching the picture lightly when he said it, Cargan told me, even though everyone suspected that that wasn't the truth. "I don't know why." But people like Amy Mitchell, popular, smart, going places, didn't run away; rather, they jetted off in spectacular fashion, coming back to let everyone know that they had left and when they had landed they had arrived.

On the jukebox, Journey played, bringing me back to

that time. Oogie eyed me from the end of the bar. "That you, Bel McGrath?"

I attempted a smile, but a pang of guilt traced my gut. I had nothing to feel guilty about, at least not when it came to Oogie, but I still felt it, deep inside like a heavy weight pressing on my diaphragm. "It's me, Oogie Mitchell." His name was Augustine, but he was and always had been Oogie. I wasn't sure why and neither was anyone else. Like a lot of things in Foster's Landing, it was just the way things were.

His wariness was reflected in his slow saunter to my end of the bar. As unprepared as I was for this visit, it seemed he was even more so. "What are you drinking?"

"How's your Cabernet?" I asked, half-kidding.

He shrugged. "Tastes like dog piss. Probably is." He reached under the bar. "Probably been under here since you left. We don't get too many red-wine drinkers in The Dugout." He poured me a glass, pushed it toward me. "But you'd remember that, I bet." He gave me a hard stare and I expected a tough question. "You in a bridesmaid dress?"

"Maid of honor," I said.

"Not your color. Redheads shouldn't wear pink." He winked. "You're still a beauty, though."

I ignored that. It felt weird to have a man old enough to be my father compliment me. "Caleigh got married."

"That little pissant found a man?"

"Yep. A good one. Handsome. Rich. She's moving to Bronxville."

"Well, well. La-di-da," he said. "She still can't hold her liquor?"

"You could say that."

Oogie had turned a blind eye to the fake IDs of our teenage years, and as a result I drank at Oogie's most of my junior year and all of my senior year, the drinking age a few years beyond my eighteen and a forgery costing all of fifty bucks. Mine had been a doctored license that had once belonged to Jessica Ramos, someone I didn't resemble in the least, but that hadn't mattered to Oogie. I suspect he had a cop or two on his payroll, the Landing's police inexplicably not all that concerned with underage drinking. Back then, Oogie knew I didn't drive—the brothers always had one of the various cars that sat in my parents' driveway—so after every evening my friends and I spent drinking cheap beer and eating bad hot dogs he would call out a helpful, "Walk safely!" to us as we navigated the dark streets of the tiny village where everyone knew everyone, but kids were brazen enough to do their underage drinking right in the middle of town. I still wondered if my parents really thought that I spent every Friday and Saturday night "in the library." Maybe they had too many kids to care, the youngest getting the longest leash.

"Heard you lived in New York City," Oogie said.

"Used to."

"Like it there?" he asked.

"I guess," I said. I did. I loved it. Every single minute.

"Heard you're a chef?"

"Was."

"Wouldn't have pegged you for that," he said. "You look like you'd be married by now. With a bunch of kids. Taking care of them." He smoothed back his snow-white pompadour in the dingy mirror over the bar.

Thank you? "You have any grandchildren, Oogie?" I asked, thinking about Amy's older brother, Jed, and her younger sister, Elaine.

Oogie didn't answer, asking me another question instead. "Going to the candle lighting tomorrow?" he asked. "I'm giving a speech. Nineteen years tomorrow."

I shrugged. I wasn't sure I'd be welcome.

"Suit yourself," he said, repositioning some liquor

bottles behind the bar, in front of the dusty glass. "How's the wine?" he asked. "Want a hot dog?"

"Wine's good," I said. "No hot dog." I looked into the wineglass, magenta liquid with a few specks of something unidentifiable floating on the surface. "How you been, Oogie?"

He picked up a rag, ran it over a sticky spot on the bar. "Good, I guess." He started away from me. "Wine's on the house. If you stick around, don't be a stranger," he said over his shoulder.

I'd try. But these days, I wasn't sure who I was, where I belonged. The past could do that to you, make you a stranger to yourself.

CHAPTER *Seven*

"I brought you a cheeseburger."

My mother was waiting for me when I walked in, having mounted the rickety stairs to the apartment over the garage in her high heels and dress before I got back home. She had a key and wasn't above using it. How did I know that? Well, first, I always lock the door, my life in New York City and some sketchy apartments I'd lived in convincing me that the world wasn't a completely safe place. Also, I now had a toilet brush and cleaner in the space where I had put a makeshift litter box, hoping that the feral cat would settle down and become mine completely, even though I was still at a loss as to what to call him. Or her. I could never get close enough to find out. My refrigerator was regularly stocked with salads and things made with lentils, otherwise known to me as "lentil crap." Sometimes, even though I never made my bed, it was all arranged, new throw pillows at the head, when I returned home at the end of the day. Other times, my living room smelled like Febreze.

I made a mental note to change the locks the next day and then remembered that in order to do so I'd need to make money. And ask my Dad's permission. With Caleigh off on her honeymoon, probably bemoaning how "her day" was ruined by a guy dying and how it "just wasn't fair," I couldn't ask my cousin for a loan, even though, all told, she probably owed me close to a grand from her borrowing money over the years. Talk about "not fair." Not being fair was the story of our childhoods, her rallying cry when she didn't get her way. (Which wasn't often.) I got a new bike while she rode last year's model? It wasn't fair. I got an A on the Geometry Regents and she had to repeat the test in August? Not fair. Everyone was paying attention to me because my best friend was missing? Totally unfair. Amy had been Caleigh's friend, too. Had everyone forgotten how she might feel?

You know what wasn't fair? Getting fired for something you didn't do. That was the unfairest thing of them all. Knowing your fiancé had cheated on you repeatedly and lied to your face. Not having the wedding you thought would be the best day of your life.

All not fair.

Mom was sitting on my Ikea sofa, picking disconsolately at the fabric, her makeup still flawless even after the Siege and everything that had happened at the wedding, her thin legs crossed at the ankles. "Hungry?"

I opened the Styrofoam container and inspected its contents. With blood leaking out of the sides of the burger and ketchup covering the fries, all I could see was Declan Morrison's busted head and not one of the best cheeseburgers the Landing had to offer. I closed it and thanked Mom. "Maybe later," I said, kicking off my shoes and climbing onto the couch, finding myself curling up into the crook of her left arm, something I was much too old to do. "Did you meet Declan during the wedding?" I asked.

"Declan who?"

"The dead guy."

"Oh, him," Mom said. "I guess during the cocktail hour." She kicked off her pumps, a beautiful pair of black sling-backs that never would have supported my thick ankles. Irish ankles, the kind that you get from taking ten years of Irish-dancing lessons, or that you were just unfortunate to inherit from your father's side of the family, Aunt Finnoula the likely culprit. Mom had the legs of a Thoroughbred, but even that wasn't enough to convince me to get me hooked up into one of her Pilates machines for a spell.

"He's supposedly Caleigh's third cousin or something?"

"Or something?" Mom murmured, a question mark at the end.

"But Dad knew him."

"He did?" She shifted slightly, redistributing my weight. "I don't think he did."

Being as I was nestled in the crook of her arm, I couldn't see if she had used her "tell," licking her lips nervously. Turning around to see would have taken too much effort and I was exhausted.

She changed the subject. "Where have you been, honey? Work?"

"The Dugout," I said, and could immediately feel her tense beside me.

"You didn't eat one of those horrible hot dogs, did you?"

"No, I didn't eat a hot dog." I wondered why that was her only concern. I hadn't been there in nineteen years and for one specific reason: I had been with Amy the night she disappeared. For a while, that made me persona non grata in town, as if I were hiding something. I wasn't. I had no idea where she went but couldn't seem to convince a lot of people of what was the God's honest truth. "I did have a glass of crappy wine, though."

"Just not the hot dogs, Bel. Those things will kill you," she said. "Sorry. Bad choice of words."

"It certainly wasn't a hot dog that killed Declan," I said. But what was it? I had replayed that scene over and over in my mind, trying to re-create the sound of the two voices I had heard—one of them certainly Declan's but the other so muffled I couldn't even tell if it belonged to a woman or a man—and the events leading up to the point where he landed at my feet, his head cracking open with a sound I wasn't going to forget anytime soon.

My mind kept going back to Caleigh, spread out on the bed with the canopy, inches from where all of the action was taking place. Had she woken up? Had it been me, even totally inebriated, I would have come running when I heard the commotion, but the door to the bedroom at the top of the stairs never opened.

"Did you see Caleigh before she left?" I asked. "After Kevin questioned her?"

"I didn't," Mom said, and I was able to turn my head slightly, catching a glimpse of her tongue touching her upper lip.

Liar.

"Where's Dad?" I asked.

"Painting," she said, moving from in back of me and getting off the couch. She stretched, the top part of her dress coming up and exposing a sliver of belly that would rival a twenty-year-old's. "I guess I'd better go find him and see how he's doing. He was pretty unnerved by what happened."

More unnerved than he should have been? I didn't ask. Maybe I didn't want to know. They were both acting strangely, and I knew there were things they weren't telling me. "Thanks for the cheeseburger."

She leaned over and kissed my head. "See you tomorrow?"

She'd see me every day unless there was some kind of miraculous event that spirited me far away from Foster's Landing and back into the culinary world of New York City. Maybe that was a good thing. Maybe it would leave me with plenty of time to figure out just what I was going to do with my life, where I was going to go.

Or what I would be when I finally grew up.

"Did you give any thought to what you discussed with Dad?" she asked.

"Yes and no."

"It would be a tremendous help, Bel. To us." She smiled at me. "To you."

"Let me sleep on it," I said, knowing that there was really only one answer to the question. A vision of Mom from long ago, her hair tied up in a green scarf, stirring a huge pot of potatoes on the stove in the Manor came back to me. Although she wasn't the best cook and didn't profess to be, in the early going of the business she was always there, adding butter to this and salt to that, and smiling merrily the whole time. Those times were in the days before she became the "hostess" and steered the events of whatever wedding the Manor was having, a job she took to with steely determination, with less of the genuine happiness that had accompanied her kitchen duty. She seemed at home there. I guess the apple didn't fall far from the tree after all.

After Mom left, I downloaded the snippets of video I had on my phone into my computer, and it was a lot of footage, more than I remember. I scanned it for any view of Declan Morrison. There he was, dancing with Bridie McKay, one of Mom's cousins. And there he was again, a few minutes later, talking to a busboy about something. And still again, glad-handing a guy with his back to the camera but who was clearly one of the Protestants. (Don't ask me how I knew. I just did.) And finally, there he was, the time stamp showing that it was moments before I spirited Caleigh up to the bedroom, talking to the new Mrs. Mark Chesterton, their noses practically touching, a tear running down Caleigh's flushed cheek.

I saved the entire raft of footage into a folder called "Recipes." Anyone who knew me well, like Amy had once, would know that this was a dummy file. I don't use recipes. I'm too good for that. Then, I edited out any footage that included Caleigh talking to Declan and saved the file as "Raw Footage."

I stared at the computer screen for a while, the picture of Caleigh talking to Declan a shadow on my retinas even when it wasn't on the screen. I was good at a lot of things, I determined, but I was getting especially good at forgetting the past.

CHAPTER *Eight*

I hadn't planned on going to the candle lighting for Amy in the village square the next night, but that's where I found myself, moving wordlessly among a sea of people for whom the disappearance of Amy Mitchell was a singular focus, at least for one night every year. I had pushed my red hair up under a baseball cap and wound a gauzy scarf around my neck, taking out my contacts and putting on my glasses before leaving the house; maybe no one would know who I was and maybe no one would realize that I may have been the last person to ever see Amy.

Earlier that day, I had attempted to go back into the Manor to see what awaited me in the kitchen should I take the head chef job, but the place was swarming with Foster's Landing finest, led by Kevin and Mary Ann D'Amato's father, Lt. Daniel D'Amato, our village's chief of police and keeper of the peace. I was shooed out by a uniformed cop who I recognized as a classmate who had thrown up on me during one particularly laborious bus ride to a local farm when we were in the fourth grade and so, knowing about his delicate constitution, I made haste back to the apartment. Lieutenant D'Amato had caught up with me outside.

"Sorry for your loss, Bel," he said, referring to what I

thought was my broken engagement and lost job. "Poor guy. A cousin of Caleigh's?"

"Oh, you mean the dead guy?" I said. "Yes, a shame," I said, sounding far less troubled than I actually was. I was preoccupied by the thought that exactly nineteen years ago Amy Mitchell and I had had our first and only fight, after which she had disappeared, and that the event would be commemorated, as it was every year, with a candle lighting that night.

"Anything else you want to tell me, Bel?" the Lieutenant asked, looking down at me, his bushy black eyebrows two question marks over his kind eyes.

I thought about it. "Nope. I told Kevin everything."

"Are you sure?" he said, and in that question, asked in a kind voice, was the memory of a similar question he asked me a long time ago when Amy didn't come home. "Are you sure there's nothing else you want to say?" he had asked then.

"I have a habit of being in the wrong place at the wrong time, Lieutenant." I looked up at him, the kindly officer who had been a part of this town, my life, for as long as I could remember. "You know that," I said, giving voice to the fact that I knew what everyone thought: I knew more than I let on.

They'd be wrong.

He rubbed his hands together even though it wasn't cold. "Yes, Detective Hanson filled me in."

I did have something to ask him, though. "Why did he let Caleigh and Mark leave?" I asked. "You know, go on their honeymoon? Shouldn't they be forced to stay around in case there's anything else that comes up?"

Behind him, I saw Kevin poke his head out of the Manor's front door and then, seeing that I was talking to his boss, quickly disappear again. "Well, Mark was on the dance floor with his aunt," Lieutenant D'Amato said, "and Caleigh was in the bridal suite."

"Alone," I said.

He frowned and it occurred to me that while I was only speaking the truth, I had just implicated my cousin unintentionally. I don't know why it mattered to me that she was on her honeymoon and we were all here; that was the way it was supposed to be even before Declan had died.

So, she and Mark had alibis. It got me wondering who didn't.

I don't know what made me go to the candle lighting, but I was here now and took a look around. I recognized several of our old classmates and Amy's brother and sister in the crowd, as well as some of the parents of people I had grown up and gone to school with. The McNultys. The Blakes. The Cozzastanzas. They were all there. It seemed like the whole town had come out.

When Amy first disappeared, I had lain low, my sadness over the loss of my best friend turning me into a hermit that summer before I left for college. Not to mention all of the people who thought I should have known more about what happened that night. My parents had hovered and worried over me until it got to be too much and I took leave of my self-imposed exile and spent too much time out and about, drinking and carousing, looking for any way out of the deep pit of despair in which I lived.

People hadn't been kind, alternately trying to insert themselves into the tragedy by becoming nicer to me than they had been before or shutting me out, not wanting to be associated with one of the last people who had seen Amy. Kevin—and no one else really, if memory served—hadn't had the same experience, seeming to rise above all of it, remaining as popular as before, as normal in his dealings with the people in town. Maybe it was me. Maybe I had become different in my mourning and that's why people treated me the way they did.

My parents sent me to Ireland later that summer, hoping that a change of scene would do me good. It had. It was so great that I hadn't wanted to return, but return I did.

As I looked back, it seemed as if every decision I had made, every place I had run, had been as a result of that night, the night my best friend had looked at me and heard me say the words "you'll be sorry" without feeling a bit of remorse.

I left the crowd and went and sat on the hill behind the Bleeding Heart of Jesus—or BHJ, as we proudly wore on our Catholic Youth Organization's basketball uniforms—a huge Gothic church, too big for this little village, looking out over the crowd that had assembled in the square below. Amy's father, Oogie, spoke, beseeching his daughter to return. Jed, her brother, stood next to Oogie, and next to Jed was Elaine, his and Amy's younger sister, looking exactly as she had when we were kids. She was the one who tagged along with us in that annoying fashion that younger siblings had. The candles bobbed and danced in the encroaching darkness until that was all I could see, hundreds of lights blending together into one.

"She's dead," I whispered to no one, knowing that that statement would be received with gasps. Sad sighs. But to me, it was the truth. I didn't know it for sure, but it had to be. People like Amy Mitchell didn't just disappear into thin air.

I sat there for a long time, long after everyone else left. I hoped that wherever Amy was—whether she was dead or alive—she wasn't sorry but very happy, bobbing and dancing in the darkness like the candles that were lit in her memory.

I got up finally after an hour or so and began my trek home. I passed all of my old haunts, purposely staying on the opposite side of the street from The Dugout as I made my way through my hometown, stopping to look in the window of what used to be a five-and-dime and which was now a fancy coffee shop. I caught my reflection in the window and, behind me, the silhouette of someone else, someone a little stooped, thin, with a shock of white hair, his appearance startling me. I turned.

"Oogie," I said. "I didn't hear you come up."

"Sorry, Bel," he said, reaching out to touch my shoulder, to steady me. "Didn't mean to scare you." He backed up a bit, taking his hand from my shoulder. "I thought you said you weren't going? To the candle lighting?"

"Changed my mind," I said. Behind me, the interior of the coffee shop was full of activity, people having streamed in there after the ceremony in the village square, grabbing cups of decaf, specialty coffees with steamed milk floating on top. "I hope that's okay."

"It was fine," he said. "Listen, don't be a stranger. In The Dugout. There's no hard feelings. Just so you know."

I bristled. "Why would there be? Hard feelings?"

"Because of that night," he said as if I would know. "Because you were the last one to see her." He paused. "You were, weren't you?"

"That was a long time ago, Oogie. I don't know what to say about that," I said, taking a step in the direction of the Manor. "I'm still really, really sorry about everything that happened. About Amy not coming back. I hope you know that."

"Everyone is sorry, Bel. Not just you," he said.

I didn't know what that meant, but I let it go. I drifted farther away until he grabbed my arm, this time more forcefully than the touch on my shoulder had been.

"If you remember anything . . . ," he started.

"I don't," I said. "Whatever I remember I told you and the police that next day and the day after that and the day

after that. There's nothing else, Oogie. There never was."
But that wasn't completely true; my version of the events
was sanitized to keep everyone blameless and without the
hint of scandal surrounding them. Doing what I had done
then reminded me of what I had done recently by deleting
the texts from Caleigh's phone.

I left him standing on the street in front of the coffee
shop.

Only time would tell if anything I had done was right.
Or wrong.

CHAPTER *Nine*

The next morning, I started the day clearheaded and with a plan. All those years ago, when my parents had sent me to Ireland, I had met a bunch of girls. All distant relatives but a lifeline for someone so adrift in an ocean of grief and anxiety. One of them—Annie O'Dell—had taught me how to laugh again after so many months spent in abject sadness. I looked in a box that I had stashed in the closet when I moved in and found a recent Christmas card she had sent me, which contained two things: one a photo of the two of us in front of a pub and the other her phone number. It was late enough in Ireland to call, so I dialed her number, hoping she was home in Ballyminster, a place she had wanted to escape but had never left.

"Annie? It's Belfast. Belfast McGrath," I said when she didn't immediately recognize my voice.

"Belfast!" she shouted, not out of surprise but to be heard over the din in her home. "Frankie, put that down! For the last time, Jaysus save me, I will put you in your room and you will never come out!" She moved to a quiet place, the sounds of a herd of boys disappearing in an instant.

"Where did you go?" I asked.

"Toilet. It's the only safe place around here," she said. "Five kids, three of them boys. It's not for the faint of heart." I heard the lid of the toilet close. "I'm happy to hear from you, Bel. What's the occasion?"

I gave her the Reader's Digest version of what happened at Caleigh's wedding and heard her sharp intake of breath. "A murder?" she asked. "That's awful."

"It was horrible. I saw the whole thing," I said.

"The whole thing?"

"Well, not exactly," I said. "I saw him die, though."

"Oh, good lord, Bel. That's terrible."

"It was," I said. "But listen, Annie, you grew up in Ballyminster. Do you remember anyone named Declan Morrison?"

"Ah, let me think. It's Ireland, Bel. Lots of Declans. And Dermots. And Donals." Someone banged on the door to the bathroom. "Don't make me come out there!" she hollered. "There's Declan McDonough and Declan Scurry and Declan Martin and Declan O'Keefe," she said. "That last one was a bit of a rogue," she said, chuckling.

"But no Declan Morrison?" I asked.

"Not that I remember," she said.

I gave her my e-mail address and promised her a lengthier chat in the future, one that would encompass what I had been doing since the last Christmas card that I had sent, five years previous. I looked around the quiet apartment and thought that maybe a week here, away from what seemed like a brood of unruly kids, would be just what the doctor ordered for my old friend Annie.

That phone call was a dead end, so I got dressed and set out for a little wander. I wended my way through the train station parking lot and headed toward the water, something I had done time and time again when I lived here as a kid. Those were the days when we all had kayaks and would spend hours on the river, traveling to a little place called Eden Island where we really weren't supposed to go but did anyway. In those days, the local police didn't have a fancy boat—or the staff—to cruise up and down the river and disperse crowds of teenagers who pulled their kayaks up to the edge of the island and decamped for the better part of the weekend. When I was a teen, everyone decorated their boat as they liked and eventually they were all banged up from going out at low tide, when rocks poked through the water's surface and scuffed the bottom of your boat.

I pulled the car into a spot normally inhabited by kayakers and noticed that you could now rent them there, something that wasn't possible when I was a resident. Oh, that's right, I thought: I *am* a resident. Again. As much as I tried to convince myself that I was just visiting, the two months I had been here told a different story. I had a resident parking permit for street parking and a village ID. Yep, I was a Foster's Landing resident again, despite my protests to the contrary.

I got out of the car and walked to the water's edge, which was farther in the distance now, a months-long drought making its presence known here. I watched a group of swans float slowly toward me from the north end of the river, the spot right before it dumped out under the trestle bridge of the train and into the Hudson. I looked for other people, but all I saw was a smooth expanse of water, a couple of geese, and nothing else.

I walked around, looking for signs of my old life. The initials we carved into the tree when Kevin and I first started dating. The old picnic table that was used by the local fishermen, its top splintered and worn. It was all still here, just like it had been years before, and in that was a small measure of comfort, the familiar wrapping itself around me like a warm blanket.

Here's where I was now. Maybe it was time to think of an exit strategy. But the only things I could think of were the sad faces of my brothers and my parents as they watched Goran stride down the gravel path, carrying on about Shamrock Manor being cursed along with the rest of us.

It's just temporary, I told myself.

I can leave any time I want.

I would never make Dad cancel an event because he didn't have a chef when a perfectly good one lived in the apartment over the studios.

I walked away from the porta-potty and over toward the water, my decision made. Heck, that was easy. And before I could change my mind, I pulled out my phone and sent a group text to my family that was comprised of one word.

Yes.

I waited for a response, but none came. Dad thought texting was the Devil's handiwork, and while he read the ones sent to him, he never responded, afraid to touch the keypad with his response. "Where does it go?" he would ask and while no one could really tell him the answer, we laughed nonetheless. As for the other ones, the boys, I wasn't sure why I didn't hear back immediately, but after a few minutes the pinging on my phone indicated that they were responding, the messages revealing that they were happy. The breeze that lifted the hair from my neck felt like a collective sigh of relief from the entire family.

The ground was damp from the tide, but I sat down anyway, holding my shoes in one hand, my knees bent. I was surprised to see that even though there had been no rain, the drought prolonged now, there was still some water in the normally shallow parts of the river, a few birds pecking below the surface looking for fish. Out past the highway overpass was Eden Island, the place where I most wanted to be right now. My last visit there was full of unanswered questions, while my visit here today was filled with different questions, one of them already answered. I looked around, noticing a pair of eyes staring at me from the other side of the put-in area. A man now, he had been a boy when I had first met him. When Kevin stood, I could see that he still had the loose-limbed physicality of a teenager, scrambling over the rocks, a sandwich tight in one hand, a bottle of water in the other. He looked far more anxious to see me than I was to see him, probably because he knew that he had acted like a pompous jerk two days earlier. Or, after all these years, alone with me, he was still a little afraid of me after what he had done.

"Bel?" he asked, making his way over. "What are you doing here?"

Even though I knew that he was a detective now, since I had followed his ascendance from afar, it still surprised me. If there had been a category in the yearbook—"Most Likely to Become the Village Detective"—he would have been my last pick; he was more of a musician/stoner type than law enforcement, but the same could be said of me and my creative pursuits. I had won the math award in high school—much to Caleigh's chagrin—proving that I could effectively use both sides of my brain, something she always contended wasn't possible, a myth. I pointed over my shoulder. "Just thinking." I looked out to the water. "You?"

He hoisted the sandwich. "Lunch." He sat down next to me, careful to keep his shoes out of the water. "I can't stand lunch in the station. It takes Loo about twenty minutes to decide on what he wants and then he usually sends one of us out to get it. I'd rather come down here and be by myself for a few minutes."

"I hear you," I said. I kept looking straight ahead, still a little sore from our encounter at the wedding, when he acted like me not seeing enough of what had happened prior to Declan's dive off the balcony was a supreme inconvenience to his detecting skills. No time like the present to clear the air. "So, the wedding. The way you acted. Was that for the other cops' benefit or did you really mean to humiliate me in public? In the middle of a crime scene?"

He blushed deeply, something I remembered from our time together. His old sensitivity, a trait that I would have thought had disappeared over the years of him being a small-town cop, making itself known. His red cheeks. His shaky hand, palming his face. The last time I had seen him blush like that was when he told me that he had fallen for Mary Ann D'Amato, the Lieutenant's gorgeous and lovely daughter. "I'm sorry, Bel. I get around those guys and . . ."

"You turn into an asshole?"

"You should be a detective," he said, smiling. He held out the sandwich he had brought. "Hungry?"

I shook my head. Although it looked delicious, there was no way I was going to share a sandwich with Kevin Hanson, the wanker, the guy who broke my heart until the next guy broke it all over again with a different form of duplicity.

"You sure?" Kevin asked, taking a bite of his sloppy sub, oil and vinegar running down his arm. He switched the sandwich to the other hand and knelt down, rinsing his arm off in the little pool of clear water that inexplicably remained. He smiled at me, letting me know that he still thought we were kindred spirits, the onetime swim team captain (me) and the former standing bass player in the school band (him). Truth is stranger than fiction, they say. I guess enough time should have passed that seeing him in this casual setting should have been just that: casual. But after everything that had transpired in my life over the course of half a year, seeing him again felt like just one more sucker punch. "You sticking around?" he asked.

"I think so." Saying it aloud made it seem more likely. I didn't have anywhere else to be, in truth.

"Want to grab a pint at The Dugout sometime?" he asked. "Well, maybe not The Dugout," he said, remembering that I might not like to go there. "I owe you one."

You owe me more than one, but who's keeping score? "Maybe."

We stayed at the water's edge for a while and I finally took a bite of his sandwich, two old friends for whom no time had seemed to pass. "Where are you living?" he asked.

"My parents'. Over the garage. Behind Shamrock Manor."

He looked at me out of the corner of his eye. No comment.

"Still scared of my mother, huh?"

"She's terrifying," he said, laughing. "All those muscles on a woman that age. It's unnatural." He took a swig of water. "What does she bench-press? A buck fifty? Two-ten?"

The easy banter almost made me forget that I hated him once, but maybe it was the old him, not the guy sitting next to me. "Probably two-fifty."

"What about you?" I asked.

"Apartment in Mystic Bay," he said, referencing a pricey condo complex. "Before you get any ideas, I live on the side that faces the train station. No river view for me."

"I see. But you're close to it and that's good enough."

"I guess," he said. "Where have you been since you got here? Why haven't I seen you before this?"

"My parents'. Over the garage." You could have found me if only you had looked.

"Hiding?" he asked.

"Maybe."

"Glad you're out in the open now."

I wasn't so sure about that, if I was as glad as he was. "So, the dead guy at the wedding," I said. "What do we know about him?"

Kevin hesitated.

"Heck, I'm your only witness," I said. "You can trust me."

"It's a weird thing," he said. "We think maybe he crashed."

"The wedding?"

He nodded. "Not on the guest list. Mrs. McHugh didn't know him."

Oh, but Caleigh did, I thought but did not say. I wondered again where they met up, what made her decide that two nights before her wedding was the best time to get to know him. "He was Irish. Said he was one of Caleigh's cousins, albeit a really distant one." I decided to keep my mouth shut for the time being, my mind going back to the messages I erased from her phone.

"I got that. The Irish thing," Kevin said. "And it wouldn't have been hard to figure out anyway. Wasn't everyone at the wedding Irish?"

"Just about. My cousin Seamus married a woman from Scotland. She was there, too." I watched a bird swoop in and grab a little fish out of the water, flying away with it in its mouth. "And Mark's family is . . ."

"Protestant?"

I nodded.

"And the guy with the one leg?" Kevin asked.

"You mean Uncle Eugene?"

"Was there more than one guy there with one leg?" Kevin asked.

He had a point. "Uncle Jack's cousin." He still looked confused, so I elaborated. "Caleigh's dad. Uncle Jack McHugh's first cousin. So, he's Caleigh's uncle."

"Aha," Kevin said. "You McGraths, McHughs, et cetera, are hard to keep straight."

"He used to live here, but he's been in Ireland for years." I splashed some water on my feet; it was getting hot. "Why?" I asked. "And how did you know he had one leg?"

Kevin didn't have an answer for that, or if he did he didn't want to share it with me. Maybe he was a better detective than I gave him credit for. "Really. We should grab a drink," he said.

I pulled a pen out from his shirt pocket and took his hand, just like I had done when we were kids, writing my number on his palm. I folded his hand over and held it tight. "Call me."

"Oh, and if you remember anything else, let me know," he said.

I licked my lips, remembering something else: the texts from the phone. I prayed that Declan's phone had been destroyed in the fall, realizing at that moment that while I had deleted his texts to Caleigh, the originals were still on his phone. I licked my lips again. Jesus, I was developing Mom's tell. "Got it."

"Why'd you come back?" Kevin asked after a few moments of silence, the implication being that once I had escaped the Landing I should have stayed escaped. "You were always the one who wanted to get away from here."

"Had to." I didn't want to go any deeper than that; that was the truth. Where do you go when you're out of money, out of a job, and practically left at the altar? Out of your world, the world you thought you knew? You go back home. "I guess you don't read the paper. The *Times*?"

"Nah, I'm a *Post* guy myself. Something happened?"

he asked, concern crossing his face. Although it was impossible not to know, or so I thought, he didn't seem to have a clue. This was a village that loved its gossip, loved the tale of the fall. But then again, maybe I was only the center of my universe and what happened sixty miles south in some pretentious restaurant with an even more pretentious name was no one in Foster's Landing concern. Something told me, however, that Kevin hadn't lived under a rock, that he knew exactly where I had been and why I was home.

"I'll tell you when we get that pint."

I looked over at him, seeing the boy I used to love, the one who had a different idea of success, who thought that staying in Foster's Landing and making good—showing everyone just what he was made of—was the definition of "making it." For me, it was leaving and never coming back. Well, one of us had achieved their goal. In his smile was the memory of the fun we used to have, why I would have left everything for him at one time in my life. "You have a job?"

"Funny you should ask." I held out my hand. "Nice to meet you. Bel McGrath, the new head chef at Shamrock Manor."

"Really?"

"It's a job," I said. Technically, it was. But I still didn't know what I was getting paid, if I was getting paid at all.

He nodded as if he understood, but I knew he didn't. If what he had shown me at the Manor was indicative of his character, the person he had become, part of him probably thought that I was there because he was. Rather than disabuse him of that notion, protesting too much and all that, I got up, dusting off the back of my pants, dislodging a few loose stones from the fabric. "Oh, and Kevin?"

He looked up at me, squinting into the sun.

I said something I hoped I wouldn't regret. "I kind of missed you. This guy. Not the other one, the cop," I said.

I shoved my hands into my pockets and walked away. It was true. I did miss him. I just hadn't realized it until now.

CHAPTER *Ten*

After my visit to the river, I climbed the stairs to my apartment, hearing what sounded like a chain saw when I passed my dad's studio. He really was getting into what he called installations now—he had just done one for the river walk at the end of our street commemorating 9/11, his second since the swordfish—and was using pieces of old scrap metal and fallen tree limbs to create "art." I knew that art came in many different forms and was subjective, but my dad's installations were just plain weird. For instance, the swordfish had a face. And not just a face, a face that looked like Aunt Finnoula's—she of the "cankles"—husband, Gerard. Made no sense. Made me wonder if he was starting to lose it, if just a little bit.

In the apartment, no sign of my feral cat, a guy (or gal) who really needed a name, I sat down at my computer and poked around, seeing if there was any information on the mysterious Declan Morrison. Turns out that there were lots of men with that name on Facebook, Twitter, Instagram, and the like, but none were my Declan Morrison.

If I hadn't seen him with my own eyes, heard him say his name, I would have thought he never existed. Then again, Declan Morrison may have made up his name, in which case he could have been anyone.

I stared at the computer screen for a few minutes, finally

pushing away and taking out a leftover container of lo mein from the refrigerator, not bothering to heat it up. From beyond the sliding glass doors at the back of the house I heard a meow, and I found the cat—name unknown— standing on the deck, the one that was two stories above the ground.

I glanced into the living room before going out onto the deck, noticing that there was a pillow on the floor, a stain on the white slipcover of the couch. Looked like ketchup that someone had desperately tried to clean up, but the mark was there nonetheless. I didn't take Mom for the type who would eat a meat-loaf sandwich on my couch, but that's what the place smelled like and the ketchup stain in- dicated. I couldn't look a gift horse in the mouth—I was living here rent-free—but why my mother felt the need to spend so much time in my living space was beyond me. I looked at the stain and decided to deal with it later, head- ing out to the porch and the cat.

"How did you get up here?" I asked, bending down to pet him/her and losing the container of lo mein in the pro- cess, the noodles spilling out onto the deck. The cat dove into the old Chinese food and made a meal of it, me won- dering how far I had fallen when the thought crossed my mind that I could scoop up whatever hadn't been touched by his sandpaper tongue and salvage it for my lunch.

I decided that as low as I had sunk, as depressing as my life had become, I was still one step above eating cat- saliva-tainted Chinese food.

I had been avoiding my dad, pretending that I didn't know that he was right below me every single day, but I couldn't pretend any longer when he appeared at the side door of the apartment, a napkin-wrapped sandwich in one hand, a can of Diet Coke in the other. The look on his face, the one that said you are so pathetic but I love you anyway, seemed to reside there permanently, hence my avoidance. I was happier here than his expression suggested, and to prove it I plastered a smile on my face and gave him a big hug in greeting, breathing in the scent of citrus thinner and the soap he used to clean his paintbrushes. Smells of my childhood still here now that I was an adult. It was a comfort to me knowing that despite everything that had happened throughout my life, things here would still, solidly and without a doubt, remain the same.

"Hi, Dad," I said into his T-shirt. He was covered head-to-toe in some kind of fine silt that made what remaining red was in his hair look silver. I opened the screen and let him in even though he owned the place and could come and go as he pleased, something that my mother had already decided was her right.

"I saw that you were home, so I brought you a sandwich," he said, offering the tuna on wheat like it was a precious gift from the gods. "Oh, and here's a soda."

The last time I had had a tuna on wheat with a Diet Coke, I had been sixteen and living in the Manor, a magical place to grow up with four brothers, its hidden staircases and long hallways the perfect place to run and yell and be boisterous. In the intervening years, I had stopped roughhousing with my brothers and had also developed more of a taste for the exotic foods one could find in my East Village neighborhood. Ethiopian. Thai. Moroccan. I never thought I would eat tuna again, really, unless it was prepared tartare or found in a sushi roll, but staring at the sandwich in my dad's hand, smelly and a little crushed from being in his huge paw, brought on a wave of pleasant nostalgia, a feeling that I hadn't had since I was little and this snack greeted me when I came running in from school to regale Dad with stories of who did what and when during the day, his face lighting at my vocal impressions of everyone from Sister Dolores Regina, our principal, to

Father Morse, our pastor. I wouldn't go so far as to say I was a "daddy's girl," though the boys might beg to differ. But whereas they considered Dad a nuisance and sometimes nothing short of an idiot for his old-fashioned ways, his adherence to a code of honor that hearkened back to a time long ago, I remembered the father whose blood, sweat, and sometimes tears made Shamrock Manor a place that was popular for a long time and that afforded us a rather nice life.

"Thanks for the sandwich, Dad." I dug in, the taste of soggy bread and warm tuna just what I needed, though I hadn't known it until now.

"Any thoughts on what we discussed yesterday?" he asked, leaning over onto the counter and resting on his elbows. Today, as with any day he worked in his studio, he was wearing an oversized dress shirt that had been deemed a "rag" by my mother and pants he called clamdiggers. They were baggy, shortish, and had assorted pockets, like capri pants that were worn mostly by woman over the age of fifty. I was used to his look. My ex-fiancé? Not so much. The first time I had introduced Ben Dykstra to the McGrath clan and my dad appeared in his usual getup, I knew it was probably the end of the relationship. Ben Dykstra was nothing if not concerned with appearances. The first time he commented on my weight, a comment that took me so by surprise that I felt sure that I must have not heard him correctly, I should have known that the relationship and the subsequent engagement were doomed from the start.

"You didn't see my text?" I asked. "Mom didn't tell you?"

"Devil's handiwork, that texting," he said. "And Mom has a client, so we haven't spoken."

"Yes, Dad," I said. "I'll do it." How bad could it be? I would make money. (I think. That detail still remained a mystery.) I would leave in a few months. They'd find some-one else. I would get back to my old life. I had a plan.

Dad didn't respond one way or another, just adding a little "hmmphh." To me, it was the closest we were going to get to "thanks."

That decision made and articulated, I lifted my head from the counter. "Hey, Dad, I want to ask you some-thing."

"Aye?"

"That guy that died at the wedding. Declan Morrison. You knew him. How?"

Dad was shaking his head negatively before I even got the first sentence out. "No. Never saw him before in my life."

"But I saw you talking," I said. "At the bar. At the wed-ding. It looked like you knew him."

"Nah, just met him at the wedding." He ran a hand through his hair, leaving a layer of dust on my kitchen floor. "Never saw him before in my life."

"So, why were you talking? If you just met him? He told me he was Caleigh's cousin." I had that same feeling I used to get when Ben professed a late-night prep when really he was prepping the vagina of another sous at a compet-ing restaurant. Dad didn't have a tell like Mom; he didn't need one. He just got nervous and jittery when the truth wasn't forthcoming, making him possibly the worst liar—and poker player—in the world. He got louder and more expansive, if that was even possible. Dad took up a lot of psychic energy when he came into a room and even more when he felt ill at ease.

"Wanted to let him know that we McGraths are friendly! Accepting! Nice!" he said, sputtering. "Jaysus, Bel, can't a guy share a pint with a new friend?"

I cracked open the Diet Coke. "Sure, Dad. Of course." I changed the subject. The last thing I needed was to be responsible for my father's imminent heart attack. "Aunt Helen okay? You know, after everything that happened?"

He nodded, still a little perturbed. "She's fine. Mom has been with her all morning."

"I thought she was with a client?"

"She was with her before Pilates and she will be with her after Pilates."

Of course. Nothing stands in the way of Pilates. Ever. Mom had even had clients, prior to Caleigh's wedding.

Dad walked to the door, his work here done. Sandwich and soda delivered, me on board at Shamrock Manor a done deal, we had nothing left to talk about. He slid a key to the Manor onto the counter, the indication that I needed to get to work. I already knew that we had a wedding the following Saturday. "You ever going to be happy again, Bel?" he asked in an uncharacteristic show of sensitivity, if you could call it that.

"Yes. Definitely. Real soon," I said, my father's red hair not the only thing I inherited from him. Steely resolve and stoicism were also part of the genetic deal, the transference of DNA. "I'm happy here, Dad," I said, taking in his gloomy face. "It's great." I threw my arms out, gesturing to the apartment. "What could be better? This place is great. And if I stand out on the back deck and crane my neck really hard to the right, I can actually see some of the river." The Manor itself had the gorgeous river view; my apartment, not so much.

He smiled sadly. "Okay, honey." He put his hand on the knob. "I think it's a good sign that you're up and around, out in the world."

"Me too," I said. I closed the door behind him, waiting until I heard the muffled sound of the chain saw beneath me before going into my bedroom and taking down a box from the shelf in the tiny closet. In it were some memories that I had carted around from apartment to apartment, even overseas for that three months I had lived in Paris. I had never opened the box, not since it had been packed, but the last few days were bringing up emotions I hadn't expected to have.

Thoughts of Amy and the night she disappeared.

Coming back here had been my only option, but leafing through the pages of my old yearbook, I started to think that maybe it had been a mistake.

CHAPTER Eleven

Figures the year I move back, and the same year when I would have some free time to start swimming again, there was a severe drought but I figured that that wouldn't affect the town pool. If I wanted to go, I'd have to go by myself. I had not one friend to call on, since everyone I knew from my past lived either in the Landing with a boatload of kids or far, far away, never to return.

Yeah, right, you'll never be back, I wanted to say to those who had fled and vowed never to come back. Happens to the best of us.

I took a quick look inside the Shamrock Manor kitchen and decided there wasn't enough wine in the world to make it look better, or to make me not regret my decision to cook there. I went back to the apartment and dug around on the Internet for Declan Morrison some more and decided that he was a complete non-entity in the world, a man with an alias who had shown up, inexplicably, at my cousin's wedding. Who killed him was one mystery, but who he had been was another.

I jotted down the number of the Ballyminster police department, which was housed in a building that I was unfortunately familiar with after a night out with Annie ended up with her car hitting the front of a tree. Turns out Annie's lack of driving skill was well-known in the little village. She had hit just about everything that didn't move and, sadly, once, a cow. After the incident that had us seeing the business end of a large oak, we were taken to the station, Annie being stripped of her license and us awaiting the wrath of Mr. O'Dell, a blustery fellow who was prone to flights of anger.

Everyone we knew was from Ballyminster, so the chance that Declan was, too, was not exactly a long shot even if Annie couldn't summon his name immediately. I rang the police station and spoke to a cop who was more than willing to engage in a conversation with someone in the States. Slow day in Ballyminster, the cows all penned, the kids all in school.

"Hi, my name is Belfast McGrath and I am inquiring about a man named Declan Morrison, who I believe resides in Ballyminster."

"Belfast McGrath? Malachy McGrath's daughter per chance?" Sergeant Donvan asked. "You live in America, yes?"

I looked at the phone in my hand. How did he know that? "Um, yes, sir."

"I remember when you visited a few years back," he said. "What was it? Ten? Fifteen years ago?" He went silent, thinking. "Probably more, now that I think about it."

"At least," I said. "I was wondering—"

"You were with that O'Dell girl most of the summer, if I recall."

"Yes. So—"

"Got into a little mischief."

"True again." I waited for him to conclude the walk down memory lane before I got into my real purpose for the call. "So Sergeant, we had an unfortunate circumstance here at my parents' business. A man named Declan Morrison passed away unexpectedly. Does that name ring a bell?"

"Declan, you say? It's Ireland, Belfast. Can't shake a stick without hitting a Declan."

"So I've heard."

"But Morrison? No. No Morrisons in Ballyminster."

"Not one?" I asked.

"Well, you've got Declan Martin and Declan Scurry and Declan McDonough, and Declan O'Keefe. That last one is a bit of a rogue."

"So I've heard," I said. His list matched Annie's to a tee. "Thanks for your help, Sergeant."

"My pleasure, Belfast. Don't be a stranger, you hear me?"

I thanked him, hung up, and looked around. Declan Morrison really was a cipher, a guy whom no one knew. So just what had impelled him to attend Caleigh McHugh's wedding? I thought about that as I made my bed, an old habit from growing up in the Manor that I never lost.

I had some other thoughts while hanging around the apartment, thoughts that went to the old days, to Amy, to the life I used to have here, my visit to The Dugout, Oogie's horrible food and drink menu, if it could even be called that. All that thinking got me thinking about hot dogs and crappy wine. Foster's Landing was better than that. We deserved just one more place where we could rest our weary bones and enjoy a nice beverage and even better meal. I deserved to feel as if I was helping, even if deep in my heart, I knew this was a way to assuage the lingering guilt I felt over the last night with Amy. I pushed that feeling away and left the apartment. I found Oogie in The Dugout at the bar.

"Bel McGrath," he said, using the same rag that he had used a few days earlier to wipe down the bar. I kept my hands at my sides, touching nothing. "What brings you here?"

"Hey, Oogie," I said. "Turns out I'm going to be here a while, so if you need help with your menu," and I used that term loosely, "I'm happy to consult. On the house."

"I'll give you all the wine your heart desires," he said, grateful.

That really didn't interest me, but I nodded.

"I've got to get rid of it anyway," he added. "Would be a waste to pour it down the drain."

"Indeed," I said. "I'll be back in a few days, after I figure out what's going on at the Manor. Deal?" I asked.

He held out his hand and I took it reluctantly. "Deal."

I drove over to the village pool as I had planned, figuring that I could blend in with the scores of mothers tending little ones, making sure that they didn't get the debilitating sunburns that some kids I knew had gotten but which we had managed to avoid given Mom's diligence about wearing sunscreen before it was fashionable. It rains all the time in Ireland and I was starting to think that nature had a way of protecting its own.

I pulled into the parking lot, noticing that there wasn't one other car there. When I got out and looked over at the pool itself, it was obvious what was going on: the drought. No water. I was wrong and the drought had affected the pool, too. The pool was almost bone dry, a fetid puddle of green-hued water sitting in the center, covering the belly of the mermaid—the one with my mother's face—that my father had painted on the bottom so many years ago. I walked over to the chain-link fence and stared in at the vast, empty space, the concrete bottom of the pool exposed for the first time in my entire life.

"Kind of sad, right?"

I turned at the sound of the voice and came face-to-face with a tall, lanky guy, a crown of messy curls sitting atop a cute face. "Yeah. Is it ever going to open again?" I said, asking possibly the stupidest question one could ask. If it didn't start to rain in buckets, water refilling the dwindling reservoir, no, it was never going to open again.

A look crossed the guy's face, confirming that it was indeed a stupid question. "Well, I hope it opens again. Kind of boring around here without it." He leaned in, his big frame blocking the sun and casting a shadow over me. "Bel? Bel McGrath?"

I searched his face for a clue to his identity. "Yes," I said, buying myself some time before I had to ask, "and . . . you . . . are?" "Bel McGrath. At your service," I said, scanning his Foster's Landing Swim Club polo shirt for a name, any name. Zilch. Nada. Finally, it hit me, the little hint of his brogue jogging my memory. I remembered his first day of school sophomore year, the homeroom teacher mangling the name of the town from which he had emigrated: Sligo. She had pronounced it "Sleego," not knowing that it was pronounced as it was spelled: "Sl-eye-go." "Brendan Joyce?" That was a long time ago, but his intonation still held a bit of his native land, its lilting tones.

"It's me!" he said, and in that enthusiastic response, the crinkling around the eyes, the exposure of a big mouth full of straight, white teeth, it all came back to me in a rush. Brendan Joyce, the kid who had worn braces from seemingly the moment he arrived on our American shores until we graduated. Whoever his orthodontist was, he or she had had no idea of a reasonable timetable for wearing braces, just an eye for detail. Brendan Joyce now had some amazing teeth and an even more amazing smile, warm and sexy. "What are you doing back here, Bel?"

Where to begin? I kept it short and sweet. "I missed the Landing."

"You did? No one misses the Landing after they leave." He looked confused.

I shrugged, leaving it at that. He was right, after all.

"Where are you living?" he asked.

Giving someone that answer was akin to ripping off a Band-Aid so quickly that you wouldn't realize what you had done. Or, in this case, what you had said. "My parents'. Behind Shamrock Manor."

His face clouded over a bit, not at the mention of my parents but likely at the thought that I, a woman with a history and a life, was back in town and living with my parents. He moved on from that, letting out a little laugh. "My mother takes your mother's Pilates class. First time, she couldn't walk for a week." The cloud lifted and he burst out laughing. "Funny thing, that Pilates. I don't think they have it in Ireland yet. My sister would have told me."

"She's gone back?" I asked, remembering a freckle-faced girl who waited for her brother outside of school, a violin case in her hand, Irish-dancing shoes slung over her shoulder. They always walked together, Brendan and the little girl whose name I couldn't remember, him being kinder than any big brother that I had, putting his arm around her as they crossed the street, picking up her dancing shoes when the laces broke and they fell with a clatter to the ground.

"She has," he said. "She always missed the old country more than I did." He shifted uncomfortably. "Heard you had a little trouble at the Manor on Saturday."

"Yeah, and that was just my brothers' fight on the opening of the second set," I said, attempting a joke that fell way flat. He looked confused. "Sorry. This isn't really the right time for humor. Yes, a man died at the wedding. Murdered," I said, shuddering at the thought.

"Guest?"

"Sort of? We don't know," I said. "No one really knows who he is."

"So how did he get into the Manor?" he asked.

"Well, it's not like we have a crack security system. He

basically walked in, sat down, and helped himself to a pint or three," I said. And the bride. He helped himself to the bride as well, I thought, but I didn't let that part slip. I turned away from the pool to get a better look at Brendan.

"Not a clue as to who he was?" Brendan asked.

"He told me something about being Caleigh's third cousin or some shite, but no one owns up to knowing him."

"Owns up?"

"He talked to a few people and I thought they looked chummy, but no one saw him before," I said. I had said too much. Those "few people" were my family after all. I turned back to the pool. "So, no pool."

He shook his head. "No pool."

"That's a shame," I said. I had wrestled myself into a bathing suit right before coming over, never thinking that swimming wouldn't be an option. "Don't you have some pull here? Can't you use the hose when no one's looking?" I asked, even though I knew that water rationing was a state-mandated thing and not the purview of the village board. And using the hose might net a full pool somewhere around the year 20-never.

He laughed, and I got a glimpse of those great teeth again. "If only I could. I run the village's summer camp program and I'd love to have the pool available for the little bastards," he said. "But no such luck. I've been sending them to that sketchy waterpark that's north of here one day a week just to get them out of here." He pointed to the bunch of keys attached to his Bermuda shorts. "I know I look important what with the keys to everything around here in my possession," he said, sweeping out his arms, gesturing toward the snack bar, the restrooms, the picnic tables, "but I'm just the hired help."

I put up a hand, shading my eyes from the sun, which appeared behind his head, giving him a kind of halo. I didn't remember him being this much of an angel, but my return to Foster's Landing so far had been full of surprises and they were starting to become a little more positive, Brendan Joyce being proof positive of that. "Well, thanks, Brendan. It was good to see you again," I said, the spandex of my bathing suit concealed beneath a long muumuu that I had picked up on 10th Street starting to become uncomfortably warm in the summer sun. I started back up the hill toward the parking lot.

"Hey, Bel! Bel McGrath!" he said, and I turned to find him running up behind me. "Listen, I know it's kind of sudden and all, but would you like to get a drink?" he asked.

The brace-faced kid who was nice to his sister had turned into a fine specimen of a man, and besides the fact that I had been planning on becoming a hermit or maybe even a cloistered nun and was well on my toward achieving one of those goals, I couldn't think of any reason at all why I shouldn't have a drink with this nice guy with the beautiful smile. I could play just so many games of poker with my card-shark nephew, Domhnall. "Well, sure. That would be nice, Brendan."

"You know? Catch up and everything?" he said.

"That would be great. Where and when?" I asked.

"The Dugout?" he asked, realizing too late, based on history, that the place might not be the best meeting point. He didn't know that I had been there twice already and that I was trying to make visits there feel more normal. Routine. He came up with an alternative quickly. "Oh, sorry. How about Saturday? The Grand Mill?" he said, referencing a restaurant walking distance from my house. "Seven o'clock?"

"The Grand Mill it is. But make it Friday. I'm busy on Saturday," I said, crossing the street from the pool to the parking lot. I turned and called after him, "And they do, you know!"

He looked at me. "They do what?"

"Have Pilates in Ireland," I said.

"Good to know," he said. "I'll tell Francine."

"Who?"

"My sister!" he called, and turned off running at the sound of a phalanx of buses pulling into the pool area, all filled with the "little bastards" who were in his care.

I was starting to rethink the hermit thing, the staying-in-the-house-all-the-time plan. Being a cloistered nun really didn't hold a lot of appeal. And besides, getting out was proving to be a little more interesting than I would have thought.

CHAPTER Twelve

I finally stopped stalling and went into the kitchen of the Manor the next day, thinking that getting started on the preparations for the wedding might be in order. At four o'clock in a few days one hundred starving Irish wedding guests would descend upon Shamrock Manor, and I needed to be ready to knock their socks off.

Before I left the apartment, my black-and-white-checkered pants on, my chef's coat buttoned, black clogs on my feet, and my hair held back by a colorful scarf that I had picked up on Canal Street years before, I could feel that old fire start in the pit of my stomach, the need to experiment with ingredients and spices. I took the short walk from my apartment to the kitchen, letting myself in with the key that Dad had given me, and took a look around.

Inside the walk-in freezer I found frozen canapés, egg rolls, and a hundred pounds of fresh ham.

On the wire rack next to the oven I discovered eighty pounds of potatoes. In the cupboards were some paper goods and a few large, industrial-sized cans of carrots, floating, I knew, in a putrid, ginger-colored liquid if I were to be so bold as to open one up. The refrigerator held a gross of eggs from a local farm, so that was good, and the requisite Irish butter that I knew my dad had imported for his guests. The Irish are nothing if not particular about their butter. His mother, Bridgie, my grandmother, had been able to go on for hours about the proper color and consistency of butter. There had been no autopsy when she died, but I always suspected that maybe butter had played a role in the massive heart attack she had the day before Arney's Confirmation.

I stood by the stainless-steel island in the middle of the kitchen and put my hands on my hips and looked around. This, in my humble opinion, was a sad excuse for a catering-hall kitchen.

But it was my sad excuse and my responsibility to make it not so.

I heard the office behind me whir to life, the printer spitting out paper, the fax machine beeping. I went through the back of the kitchen and into the main office where I found Cargan—whom my parents had elected "catering manager," God help us all—sitting at a desk in the windowless room, staring at a ledger, a Rubik's Cube in his hand, his fingers lazily turning the sections without him looking at it.

"The Maloney party canceled."

"Who?"

"The Maloneys. February ninth."

"What year?"

"Next."

Talking to Cargan was like putting together a puzzle with several missing pieces. I had learned over the years how to communicate with him, my mind able to fill in the blanks with just a few pointed questions. We were close in age, not quite "Irish twins," being more than a year apart, but closer in age than any of the other siblings to each other. I was his protector in such a way that he always seemed younger than me, despite being two years ahead of me in school.

Amy had seen something in him, though, and they had dated his entire senior year, she wearing an iridescent purple dress to the prom that made her look like one of the girls who sang backup for Prince. Cargan had worn a matching bow tie and cummerbund, and together they had looked smashing, if purple was your thing.

"I'm worried," he said, his fingers still working the Rubik's Cube, a puzzle, like my brother, I had never been able to solve. His Shamrock Rovers soccer team jersey hung on his thin frame, wrinkled and voluminous. He played soccer on an adult team with a bunch of Ecuadorians in the next town over, his pale skin, often with a layer of unabsorbed sunscreen making him even whiter, blinding in the summer sun next to his darker teammates.

"That more will cancel?" I asked.

He nodded. "That we'll lose the business. That Mom and Dad won't have anywhere to live. That we'll have to move."

I held up a hand. "Slow your roll, pallie. Slow your roll." I leaned over and eyed the ledger. Indeed, there were cross-outs through some of the booked parties, but the O'Donnell wedding, this coming weekend, was still a go. If we could pull that off and assure our guests that all was well at Shamrock Manor, in spite of the trouble we had had the weekend before, we might be able to right the ship. "This will blow over and we'll get our footing back." I gave him a little chuck to the shoulder. "And wait until you see what I have planned for the kitchen."

He looked up at me, his eyes red rimmed; poor guy looked like he hadn't slept in weeks. "The kitchen?"

"Yes," I said, a surge of enthusiasm masking the hollow pit in my stomach at the thought of exactly what the "kitchen," and I use that word loosely, looked like. "After a few weddings, we'll be the talk of the Hudson Valley."

"Because?"

"Because of the food, silly!" I said, wondering why it was that he looked like he was going to vomit instead of embracing my plan wholeheartedly. "Shamrock Manor has an award-winning chef at the helm and wedding fare will never be the same." Geez, even the publicist I had had back in New York couldn't have made me sound as fabulous and inventive as I made myself sound to my skeptical brother.

"But we want it to be the same," he said, standing up behind the desk. I got a glimpse of his baggy soccer shorts, the socks that went to his knees. "We don't want it to be different. We want it the same as it always was." He pointed at the ledger. "These people want what they ordered. Ham. Potatoes. Shepherd's pie," he said, and stopped me before I could speak, "and not shepherd's pie with duck crap in it. . . ."

"It's call foie gras." I crossed my arms over my chest, trying to steady my breathing, the tips from anger-management class still front and center in my mind.

"Whatever!" he said, kneeling down to pull up one of his drooping soccer socks, the elastic at the top having died an untimely death in a hot dryer. "We don't want what *you* do. We want what *we* do. Simple. Classic. Irish cuisine."

That really wasn't what I had in mind. "People really want shepherd's pie at a wedding? Really?"

"It's our reputation. It's what we serve. People want to eat things that remind them of home," he said.

We weren't really getting anywhere and I had work to do. "Well, what did the O'Donnells order?" I asked.

He pushed a piece of paper toward me and I scanned the menu. Canapés. Check. We had those in the freezer. Ham. Check again. We had a lot of ham. It was decent ham and could be manipulated but it was ham nonetheless. And we had potatoes, lots of potatoes for the desired mashed potatoes. We were all set. I grimaced when I looked at the menu and maybe even uttered a little groan.

"Arney was right," Cargan said.

I arched an eyebrow in his direction. "About what?"

"About you. About how you'd come back here and want to change everything. About how you think you're better than we are because you lived in the city."

"That's not true," I said. "I don't think I'm better. I just want to *make* things better." I didn't know if that clarified my intentions. By the look on his face, I would say the answer was "no."

"It's fine here, Bel. It always has been." He leaned down and pulled at his sock, finally giving up and letting it fall to his ankle. "We don't need your help."

"Then why did you hire me?" I asked, the office now almost completely silent now that the printer had gone to sleep and the fax had ceased chirping. All I could hear was my brother's shallow breathing, a panic attack coming over him at the thought of conflict with his younger sister, and the sound of my own heart beating.

He looked at me, not wanting to answer the question but knowing that I wouldn't leave until he did. Cargan couldn't tell a lie. He was incapable of a half-truth, let alone a full truth. "Because you were our only choice," he said as if it was the most obvious answer of all.

And it was.

I knew that was the reason, but I didn't know that I was going to be hamstrung—no pun intended—by our traditionally minded clientele, my parents' adhesion to cuisine of Ireland circa 1964, by our "catering manager's" intractability, by everyone's collective inability to change.

"Well, okay then," I said, feeling stupid and overdressed in my chef's coat. Thankfully, I had left my toque at home. If I had been standing here in a high hat, a trademark of my profession, in front of my brother in his droopy socks and soccer uniform, I would have felt more foolish than I already did.

He closed the ledger with such force that a stack of papers flew around the desk before landing everywhere. I walked over to help him pick them up, but he stopped me. "Go. I'll do it. I have practice in a few minutes, but I'll be back later," he said, and I could tell he was on the verge of tears, for what I wasn't sure. For everything, I guessed. He placed the Rubik's Cube on the desk, its colors all neatly matched up and perfectly aligned.

Before the book closed, I had seen a lot of red, a lot of minus signs. Not too much black to indicate that Shamrock Manor was thriving, that everyone involved was making money, supporting themselves in grand fashion. Rather, without anyone having to tell me, it had become apparent that things were a little worse than they had seemed and I, in my prolonged fugue state, had failed to realize it.

You want ham? I thought as I walked back to the kitchen.

I'll give you ham.

CHAPTER Thirteen

I returned to the apartment after putting a long day in in the kitchen, getting it as ready as it would ever be for the O'Donnell wedding and any future events in the Manor. The door to my apartment was unlocked, as it usually was after one of my mom's visits; she always forgot to lock it and that's how I knew she had been up there. I checked around. No smell of Febreze. No lentil crap in the fridge. No Dustbusters, or new mops, or a broom I hadn't had before.

I went into my bedroom to change and noticed that Mom had been in here as well, a new development. She usually kept to the living areas. I'm not sure what she thought she might find in my bedroom, but up until now she had eschewed that space lest she come across something that didn't suit her Puritan sensibilities. My copy of *Fifty Shades of Grey* maybe. A thong that had "YOLO" affixed to the front in sequins I had bought during a drunken night while watching Home Shopping Network. The vibrator that someone had given me at a bachelorette party and that might cause the immediate death of Mom or Dad should they happen to come upon it standing proudly on my nightstand, the pink rubber phallus waving jauntily from side to side. I shoved it under my bed.

My bed had a depression in it where someone had been

sitting, my yearbook out and open to a page that showed me and Amy at a pep rally, my mouth wide open in some kind of cheer and her sitting next to me wearing a huge smile. My yearbook had been in my closet, so it had taken some searching to unearth it, but apparently Mom had done that.

I wondered why.

I put it back under the pile of chef's pants that I kept on the top shelf of the closet and made sure that it was well hidden. Mom was slipping. Usually the only signs that she had been in the apartment were the things she left behind for me. I hadn't thought she had taken to snooping, but the open yearbook on my bed led me to believe that she was looking deeper into my life by poking around. There was nothing to see here, really; I had nothing to hide. And right now I was just too tired to be angry at Mom. It just wasn't worth it.

My phone vibrated in my pocket. Kevin.

I know it's short notice, but would you like to have dinner tonight?

It took me a few seconds of nail biting and mental gymnastics before I thought, What the heck? and texted him back that yes, I could come, falling asleep moments later with the phone on my chest.

That night, after my confrontation with Cargan and my surreptitious preparations for the O'Donnell wedding, I thought about Mark and Caleigh on the beach in Bermuda, sunbathing, not a care in the world unless you count the fact that a wedding guest had come to celebrate their union and was dead before the cake cutting.

I was going so insane that I almost couldn't wait for Caleigh to come back from her honeymoon. Maybe, I thought, Mark Chesterton would reveal himself to be a really good egg, someone with whom I would bond. Be the brother I always wanted to have, not the ones I did have. Right. That was insane.

I had a few more texts from Kevin, who seemed to enjoy this mode of communication more than any other. According to him, Mary Ann had made "gravy," or what we Irish Americans call sauce, which we liberally coat with "sprinkle cheese," otherwise known as Parmesan, for her family dinner and there was a lot left over. She had also made fresh pasta. And tiramisu. All while tending to the children in the pediatric cancer ward at a local medical center.

I looked at myself in the mirror, running a comb through my red curls. "You are so not worthy, Belfast McGrath," I said, riffling around in the drawers of the vanity that my father had crafted from the reclaimed deck of a boat that was found floating, empty, in the Foster's Landing River. I found a lipstick, something I remembered wearing to dinner at Ben Dykstra's apartment for our fourth date—the one when he had said, "I love you," and I had believed him—opened it up, and then closed it. I tossed it in the garbage. A tinted ChapStick would have to do. I would never wear MAC "Razzledazzler" ever again, despite it being the perfect shade for a redhead. It landed in the bottom of the garbage can with a little ping.

My wardrobe was sorely lacking and I was at a loss as to what to wear. When you work—nay, live—in a uniform like I had for much of my adult life, you don't spend a lot of money on clothes, and my closet was evidence of that fact. I spent way too much time thinking about it, staring at my choices before finally settling on a tunic I had bought in a bazaar in Istanbul, jeans, and some silver bangles. I was a little upset to find that the tunic wasn't quite as flowy as it used to be, hugging my curves with a little more seriousness. I guess a steady diet of takeout from Happy

Life/Hunan Style wasn't a recipe for being svelte. Still, it wasn't enough for me to even consider a morning of Pilates with Mom. I still had some standards.

Mary Ann lived in the Hadley section of town, a short drive from where I had grown up and now lived again. Her house was a tiny Tudor on a tidy street with a variety of different house styles, all old, all immaculately tended. The front door was red and the lawn was manicured within an inch of its life. Everything about the place was perfect, just like Mary Ann D'Amato, whom, if I wouldn't hate myself for feeling it, I wouldn't like at all. But I couldn't go there. She was just that wonderful.

She opened the door, still in her scrubs from work, her shirt adorned with dancing bears. She wore clogs on her feet and her gorgeous mane of jet-black hair was pulled back into a sensible bun. A stethoscope hung around her neck. "Bel McGrath," she said, pulling the heavy door open wider. "So good to see you!" she added, pulling me into a hug.

I so wanted to be the woman who had an archenemy, but even I—of the vivid imagination and highly suspicious nature—couldn't cast Mary Ann D'Amato in that role. I wasn't Catwoman, after all. If I had to be honest with myself, my relationship with Kevin was over long before Mary Ann had reappeared after getting her nursing degree. She returned to the Landing after graduating, moving back in with her mom and dad and commuting to her job at the hospital. I guess during that time she, on the one hand, had saved for a house, like a smart woman would. I, on the other hand, after dickering and negotiating with Kevin about what our life would be like if we did stay together, couldn't convince him that my new job, which had crazy hours, would be conducive to a marriage. Kids. All those things that he seemed to want yet still didn't have.

That fact gave me pause. Maybe it wasn't the circumstances of my new life back then that had been the final nail in the coffin of our relationship. Maybe it was just me.

I stood in the foyer of the well-appointed house, a bouquet of flowers in my right hand, a bottle of wine in my left, and waited for instructions. So this was what it looked like to live like an actual adult. Even when I had lived in the city, my house had that just-ransacked look that someone who worked day and night could identify with. There were boxes from my move years previous and a coffee table that doubled as a bar, dining table, and sometimes seat. I look around Mary Ann's and wondered if someday I would be someone who had a cut-glass vase of gerbera daisies sitting jauntily on a polished foyer table.

I didn't think so, but time would tell.

Mary Ann excused herself to change and Kevin appeared from the back of the house, taking both of my offerings. I bit my tongue, not asking the question that seemed most obvious: Why aren't you married to this woman? And if you don't to marry her, can I?

He held the wine up to the light to get a better look at the label. "Rosé. Mary Ann's favorite." He gave me a little chuck to the shoulder with the flowers. "You done good, McGrath."

Stepping into the house was like taking a walk through a Pottery Barn catalog. A little rustic chic here, a little French country there. Kevin led me to the back deck, where potted plants and assorted greenery dotted the perimeter and tasteful wind chimes hung from the eave over the back door, signaling to me that this was a place of calm, not conflict. It was a little different from what I was used to at Mom's. For all of her "*namaste*" this and "universe" that—words she tossed around but that were at odds with her devout Catholicism—the house I had grown up and now had dinner in every Sunday with my brothers and their families was about as calm as Grand Central at rush hour.

"I could get used to this," I said, realizing, too late, that I hadn't meant to verbalize that aloud, looking around at the lush expanse of garden, the water falling gently from a rock formation. Maybe I was the one who should have taken up with Mary Ann D'Amato. Maybe she was actually the catch and he had partnered "up."

Mary Ann emerged a few minutes later with three glasses of the wine that I had brought on a silver tray, bending over to hand me one. Not only was she gorgeous and nice, but she smelled like a newborn baby's breath, just a hint of something sweet and lovely. Her hair was now down, swinging behind her as she walked. Whereas I felt like I had been rode hard and put up wet, as they say, she looked like the teenager I remembered from growing up, the first female altar server at our church, someone for whom piety came easy. I, sitting in the pews sandwiched between my brothers, prayed that church would be over in under an hour; that's how I rolled back at BHJ. "Thank you," I said, resisting the urge to add, I love you! I just hadn't realized it until now!

She sat across from me on an Adirondack chair, sipping her wine. Finally, after several minutes of uncomfortable silence, during which time the back of my fancy tunic became soaked with my sweat, she leaned in, a concerned look on her face. I was starting to worry. Was it natural to sweat this much at my age? Was I entering perimenopause? "Did you go to the candle lighting, Bel?" Mary Ann asked.

"For Amy," Kevin added unnecessarily.

"No," I said, lying. "You?"

"We go every year," Mary Ann said, taking Kevin's hand. "It's beautiful. The whole Landing coming together.

Supporting Oogie and Margaret. Just candlelight. And silence."

Sounded like a whole lot of weird to me. And it had been.

"Where do you think she went, Bel?" Mary Ann asked, studying my face for an answer.

"Amy?" I asked.

Mary Ann nodded. The solemnity of this occasion, one that I thought might include some laughter in addition to amazing spaghetti sauce, was throwing me off my game a little bit.

I didn't want to say what I thought had happened to Amy, because if I did it would be out there and I'd never be able to take it back. She'd been taken and murdered. That was the only answer, because I had been her best friend—her sister from another mother, really—and she would have told me where she was going if she had left on her own. All I said, an unsatisfactory answer at best but the same answer everyone else gave, was, "I don't know."

Over dinner, Mary Ann's sauce living up to its reputation, I asked Kevin what he knew about Declan Morrison, if the investigation had turned up anything else about the mystery guest.

"You've heard nothing, Bel?" he asked, going back to one of the first questions he had asked me after he had come into the crime scene. "Now, after a few days, you've got nothing that would help me with this?"

I thought that was *his* job. I sincerely hoped that what I heard in his voice wasn't accusatory, like I was holding something back—which I was—or I was so addled that I had forgotten everything until this very moment. I was still sitting on Caleigh's interaction with the handsome Celt, but other than that, I had nothing to offer. "Just some muted voices on the landing, Kevin. Nothing else." I told you, I wanted to say, but sitting here at this beautiful, candlelit table, with the beatific Mary Ann sitting across from me, it didn't seem appropriate to get snippy. I wanted to ask if Kevin had Declan's phone and, if so, what might be on that phone, but I didn't want to tip my hand in that direction.

Mary Ann shook her head sadly at the idea that I couldn't help with the investigation, my mind so full of holes that it was just a crying shame. "Maybe you should be hypnotized?" she said, brightening at the thought.

I felt the pasta in my mouth turn to a grainy paste at the thought. "Hypnotized?" I asked, choking down the once-delicious food. I had been hypnotized once to quit smoking, so I knew that I was highly suggestible, because I no longer bought cigarettes. But I also had developed an inexplicable aversion to onions, once a staple of all of my recipes and now gone from my culinary repertoire, the mere thought of them making me gag.

Kevin looked at Mary Ann as if she had discovered the cure for cancer. "Brilliant! That's a great idea."

"That's not a great idea," I said, putting my napkin to my mouth. "That's not a great idea at all." A Vidalia onion, all papery and yellow, popped into my head.

"Why not?" they said in unison, studying my face for an answer.

How would I tell them that if they were going to hypnotize me to see if I could remember anything the likelihood was that I would spill what I really knew: that Caleigh had not been the gorgeous, blushing bride everyone thought they saw but a two-timing woman who wasn't sure that the guy who adored her was the right man for her. That before walking down the aisle and pledging her troth to Mark Chesterton she had given Declan Morrison—if his texts to her were to be believed—the night of his life.

CHAPTER *Fourteen*

I didn't go back home right away, making a left out of Kevin's street and heading toward the train station, at the end of which was the kayak put-in that I had visited two days before. Rather than sit at the water's edge, I elected to take a seat, carefully, at a weather-beaten picnic table, hoping that I wouldn't add insult to injury and put a butt splinter on the list of complaints I now had related to my life.

The last thing I needed or wanted to do was go back to Kevin's to have Mary Ann play find-the-splinter-in-Bel's-butt.

I hadn't planned on coming here, but I felt like Amy's name had come up more in the past few days than ever before, her presence like a whisper in my ear. This is where we were last together, where we had had the first, last, and only fight we would ever have, me leaving in a huff, she standing by the water's edge, her own car parked in its usual spot by the trees. How could I have known that that was the last time I would see her? That my last words—"you'll be sorry"—were words I had never strung together since and that I wished, daily, that I could take back? Like the footage I had left on the cutting-room floor, so to speak, from Caleigh's wedding, I had left those words out of my statement to the police when they came to my house, questioned me, and insinuated I knew more than I was telling.

I didn't know more. I knew less than they thought. But I had said those words and they could have been some of the last words she had heard.

Sometimes I wondered what her killer had said to her before he took her life, because I was sure she was dead. We had a kind of telepathy, a two-hearts-beating-as-one connection, and a few days after she went missing I was convinced that it was so, that my heart had started to beat alone.

I had left my car back by the train station, under a street-light, walking the short distance to the water. More rocks were visible at the put-in now, the water having receded to the lowest point that I could remember. This drought was no joke, the real deal. Even in the dark, lights from the train tracks the only thing illuminating the area, I could see that this was serious. If we didn't get some rain soon, there would be no water at all in the small river.

Behind me, I heard a car driving over the gravel that separated the paved train station parking lot from the sandy area where cars parked at the put-in. Its lights off, the driver drove slowly over the uneven ground, pulling right up to what was once the water's edge but was now exposed rock and silt. At the picnic table, in relative dark-ness, the lights from the train station not extending as far as the area I was sitting, I was protected, hidden from view. I sat perfectly still and waited, wondering why I now had company, who it might be, and what he or she had planned.

Just out for an evening swim? I've got news for you: no water.

The car stayed at the edge of the put-in, the motor running, the lights off. I couldn't see what kind of car it was, but it looked like a small SUV, a Honda CRV or a Toyota Rav4, something of that ilk. The driver's side door opened and someone got out, someone tall, thin, and who moved like a teenager, scrambling more than walking over the rocks and into what remained of the river, many feet in the distance. Whoever it was, and it seemed to be a man, wasn't wearing shoes; that was evident by the way he picked his way gingerly over the rocky ground and into the water. There was nothing to suggest that another person was there except for my shallow breathing, something that sounded loud to my ears but which I suspected couldn't be heard in the still night. I couldn't see much except for the outline of a figure out in the water, the gentle waves lapping at his ankles. He stood and stared out at the dwindling river, the phragmites bending in the breeze, a duck or two gliding by, not realizing they might have to migrate sooner than they thought if the drought continued.

Minutes passed and the person continued to stare. A train barreled north, chugging by the trestle bridge that spanned the Foster's Landing River and the adjacent Hudson, its headlamp casting a glow over the whole area. I ducked back, not wanting to be seen.

But just before the light faded, glancing over me to light up the tracks going into the station, it lit up the person standing in the river and I finally saw who it was.

I wondered why Kevin was staring out toward Eden Island.

CHAPTER *Fifteen*

On Thursday, I did more prep for the wedding on Saturday, still dismayed by the sad stock of ingredients that I was presented with in the underwhelming kitchen. But I was a chef and it was my job to make it wonderful for the happy couple, their guests, and my parents, who would be the harshest judges of all.

After putting in a tray of bacon-wrapped scallops that I would serve to Mom and Dad for their take on them before putting them on the menu, I took a few minutes to poke around the Manor, seeing what had changed since I had last been here. Heck, who was I kidding? I wanted to go upstairs and see what the crack detective squad—aka Kevin—had missed in his investigation after Declan's death. There had to be something. I knew it wasn't the right thing to do, but I did it anyway, making sure no one was around, slipping under the police tape that was still draped across the door to the bridal suite and letting myself into the room where I had last seen Caleigh draped across the bed, passed out drunk. I closed the door behind me, stepping over a mess of police tape in a pile by the floor, all wadded up and waiting to be disposed of.

I had a pair of plastic gloves in my coat pocket and slipped those on as I poked around the bridal suite. I got on my hands and knees and pulled up the dust ruffle around the four-poster bed, making a mental note to tell Cargan that whoever he had cleaning the guest rooms was doing a piss-poor job of it and that in addition to getting rid of the police tape, they needed to acquaint themselves with a vacuum and its purpose. I ran my hands under the bed and came out with a face full of dust but not much else. I opened every drawer of every dresser in the room, finding nothing, and pulled open the armoire to see if there was anything in it or behind it.

Nothing.

I stood in the center of the room with my hands on my hips and surveyed the space. The windows were spotless; that was something, I guessed. But if we were going to up our game around here—something I wasn't convinced the rest of them wanted—then we were going to have to do a massive overhaul of the place to bring it into at least the twentieth century, if not the twenty-first. Baby steps.

I covered every surface of the room visually before crawling around and seeing what I could find beyond the dust bunnies that were stuck in every corner, behind every piece of furniture. I stifled every sneeze, knowing that Mom, Dad, and Cargan were lurking in the Manor somewhere, preparing for the next wedding by taking stock of the chairs, overseeing the ironing of the tablecloths and napkins, and making sure the dining hall was in good shape after Saturday's debacle of a wedding. I was on the other side of the bed, my ass sticking up in the air, my torso under the bed frame, when someone entered the room. Along the wall under the headboard, taped to the molding, was a long wire. I couldn't figure out where it went or if it was attached to the landline on the nightstand, but I didn't have time to find out, my brother's voice interrupting my investigation.

"What are you doing?" Cargan asked, his voice recognizable despite my burrowing in under the bed.

I slithered out, bringing a trail of dust with me. "Has this place been cleaned in the last five years, Car?" I asked, showing him my gloved hands, filled with under-bed detritus and nasty fluff.

"Why are you wearing gloves?" he asked.

I stood up and wiped my hands on my pants. "I was in the kitchen. Cooking." In the distance I heard the timer go off that I had set to alert me when the scallops were done. "And I have to go," I said.

My brother blocked my path to the door. "What are you doing?" he asked again.

"I was looking around."

"Did you see the police tape?" he asked, pointing to the yellow tape hanging listlessly in front of the open door.

"How did you know I was in here?"

"This is a crime scene, Bel," he said. "You shouldn't be in here."

"You always were the rule follower, Car," I said, starting for the door. My eyes landed on the pile of police tape discarded outside the door, something glittering in between the adhesive and elastic. I picked it up on my way out. "I'll get rid of this," I said, my hands burrowing into the tape and feeling for the shiny object that had become stuck in its web.

"I don't know if you should," he said, but I was already headed down the stairs, the tape in my hands.

In the kitchen, I took out the scallops. They were perfect. I would bring a tray of them into the office and show Cargan that my mind really was on cooking and nothing else. I pulled the tape from my pocket and, making sure no one was around, unspooled it as quickly as I could, looking for the thing that was buried beneath all of that caution tape.

There it was. I held it up to the light.

I wondered where Mom's earring had fallen off, when, and how. And why, up until this point, it had gone undiscovered.

CHAPTER *Sixteen*

The next night, I stopped in Dad's studio before starting the short walk to the Grand Mill Saloon to meet Brendan Joyce. All I could hear when I entered was a banging coming from one of the side rooms, this one with a door that never closed tightly, the frame slightly bent from one or other of the times Dad had failed to measure one of his paintings or installations before trying to stow it in the room.

"Measure twice, cut once," Feeney used to say to Dad, a statement that was met always with my Dad's face flaming as red as his hair.

It was like being back in high school. I was going out for the night and had to tell my father where I was going, what time I would be back. And the weird thing? I was getting kind of used to it. No, this would never do. I couldn't get comfortable here. I had to remind myself that I wanted to get out, to not be beholden to eating with my parents every Sunday, another day with the whole clan, pushed together in the kitchen, still fighting over the last drumstick, the last piece of pie stuck in the tin and misshapen.

I'd tell them after I got things up and running at the Manor that they should start looking, with seriousness, for a new chef, a new Goran. Or maybe the old Goran. Maybe enough time had gone by that he had forgotten his blood oath to never return to the cursed catering hall.

I walked over to the door and pulled it open. My father was bent at the waist, drilling nails into the side of a large wooden box that had "ART" stamped on its top, as if it would be anything else. When he heard me, he stood up quickly, hitting his head on a low beam in the A-shaped overhead space, staggering backward, the drill still operating at top speed, Dad waving it around wildly as he grabbed at the top of his head.

I ran to the outlet and pulled out the plug, watching the drill whir its last revolution. "Dad, are you all right?" I asked. I took the drill from his hand and placed it on top of the box.

"Bel! You scared the bejesus out of me," he said. "What do you want?" But his angry tone was a result only of the blow to the head, the consternation at his pain. He rubbed his head vigorously, hoping to rub it into a painless state. "I'm fine!" he said even though it sounded like he was anything but "fine."

I pulled his hand away from his head to check the knob that was forming. No blood. That was good. "I just wanted you to know that I'm going out. Please tell Mom that the apartment is clean and that she shouldn't take my absence as an invitation to go up there and vacuum."

He stood next to the box, his hand on the top, an almost protective gesture. "She's just trying to help."

How did my letting my father know that I was going out turn into a defensive conversation about my apartment, my dust bunnies? "I know, Dad. I just don't want her to go to any trouble."

"You just don't want her to invade your precious privacy," he said, his hand going back to his head.

This wasn't going the way I had hoped. All I could hope for at this point was a hasty getaway with no further damage done to my father and his sensitive head.

"We're all set for tomorrow," I said. "All of the potatoes are peeled and I created a few new canapés for the cocktail hour."

Dad raised an eyebrow. "What kind of canapés?"

"Nothing fancy. Just your standard wedding fare," I said, and it was the truth. I didn't want to rock the boat too much, not with what I actually had planned.

"Good."

He moved his hand across the top of the box. "What's in the box, Dad?" I asked.

"Art!" he said. "See?" He ran his hands across the letters stenciled on the top. "*A.R.T.* It's art!" It sounded like the same response he had had when the local paper called the mural he had done at the library "disjointed" and "sadly reminiscent of something one would do with colored markers." It took him a long time to recover from that one.

I held my hands up. I surrendered. "See you later," I said. "I hope your head is okay. Have Mom put some ice on it." I walked out of the room, running into Frank, Aunt Helen's paramour, outside the studio.

"Bel, hi," he said.

"Hiya, Frank. How goes it?" I asked.

"It goes well," he said. "Your dad in there?"

"He is," I said. "How's Aunt Helen?"

"Okay." He moved his mouth around, looking for the words. "I hope Caleigh is enjoying herself," he said finally.

"On her honeymoon?"

He nodded.

"Is there a reason why she wouldn't?" I asked. I couldn't help myself, adding, "Besides the fact that a guy died at her wedding?"

"Well, that," Frank said.

"Yeah, that," I said. "Terrible thing. What do you think?" I asked.

He chewed on that for a minute and shook his head. "I think nothing."

I believed that. It was probably the best course of action when dating Aunt Helen; she could do all of the thinking for both of them. I stood for a minute and looked at him. When it was clear he had nothing else to say, I said good-bye. He let himself into the studio and made some positive noises about Dad's installation. God bless you, Frank, I thought. You're a better person than I.

The Grand Mill had been here since the beginning of time, or so it seemed. When we were kids, it was called Trixie's and was home to the town's most dedicated alcoholics, the ones for whom a nip at eight in the morning was not an uncommon occurrence. Dad and Uncle Eugene had been regulars, though they didn't order their first pint until after five in the afternoon, having what they called standards. A few years ago, it had been taken over by a couple who had moved here from trendy Brooklyn and who had turned it into more of an upscale eatery, even while retaining the "charm," if you could call it that, from its days as Trixie's. So, bead board, now clean and white, adorned the walls, and the tin ceiling gleamed overhead. Still, the guys left over from Trixie's hung at the bar that sat at the far end of the dining room, their hoots over a Yankee home run or a Red Sox loss filling the space where diners came to enjoy a good burger or a bowl of mussels. I didn't see Brendan when I walked in, so I took a seat at the far end of the bar, close to the kitchen, and studied the numerous taps that were now on display. All microbrewed with the exception of two domestic selections, many with names I didn't recognize. The Grand Mill had changed even more than I thought, judging from the drink list that was put in front of me. French Kiss? Pometini? And the dreaded Green

Apple Martini, the bane of every bartender in New York. It was as if I had left the city only to have the city follow me right here. Was that what Foster's Landing was becoming?

I didn't have too much time to mull that over, because Brendan and his dynamite teeth walked in the front door of the place, striding toward the bar with a confidence he hadn't had when he was fourteen and then fifteen and so on. At eighteen, he hadn't been much different than he had been at thirteen, so to see him walking with purpose toward me, not one feather ruffled, was refreshing.

Maybe all of that orthodontic work had boosted his self-esteem in a way no one could have anticipated.

He slipped onto the barstool next to mine and fingered the drink menu. After greeting me with a quick peck to my cheek, he said, "Hard to get a good old-fashioned cold one around here. Everything is microbrewed within an inch of its life." He pushed himself up onto his elbows and surveyed the bar taps. "Ah, Coors Light. Nothing better." He looked at me, smiled. "And for you?"

After I had eaten a farm-to-table meal at Mary Ann's, Brendan's lack of gustatory sophistication was welcome. I do enjoy hanging with people who enjoy a good old burger every now and again, for whom Jerusalem artichokes are anathema. Oh, who was I kidding? I do not. But if they come in the Brendan Joyce package I can overlook a lot. "Same."

He greeted the bartender warmly, a small woman with a prodigious backside I remembered from high school. Mandy or Mindy or something like that. I had blocked out her name because I remember her being particularly cruel after Amy had disappeared, intimating to me more than once that summer that I knew more than I was letting on. I watched her carefully for signs that she recognized me, but it was the same old girl whom I remembered checking out her reflection in every reflective surface available; this time, she had the big mirror behind the bar to make sure that her black eyeliner stayed put, that the height of her perm was just as it had been when she had styled it that unfortunate way before coming to work. "You remember Bel, Sandy?" he said to the woman behind the bar.

Sandy. Sandy Greer. How could I forget? That girl had worn a perpetual scowl from the first day of kindergarten until this very day.

"Bel McGrath?" she asked, putting the beers down in front of them. "Yes, I remember Bel McGrath," she said before sauntering off, her jeans making a whispering noise in her wake. She remembered me and what she remembered she didn't like.

Brendan looked at me. "She remembers you," he said before bursting into laughter. He stood and walked over to the waitress, asking if we could have a table in the corner, beckoning to me when he got her approval.

I grabbed my beer and followed him, remembering that this table was not the one you wanted at sundown, light streaming in from the big window, blinding me as I felt around for my chair. Brendan reached over and took hold of the cord over the window shade, dropping it and draping the table in a more comfortable shadow. Once across from him, I took the opportunity to get a better look at him now that he was out of the village-mandated shorts and polo shirt that he wore for his job at the camp. Please God, I thought. Please make him have another job besides camp counselor, because as evolved as I am, I do like my paramours—and I hoped that Brendan Joyce would be in the running to fill the bill—to have a steady paycheck, a life plan, not just a summer job until the next thing came along.

Too bad I hadn't been thinking about that as I had stared into Declan Morrison's dreamy brown eyes. That,

I concluded, had been a minor hiccup in my usual practical personality.

Brendan wasn't wearing his village-issued clothes tonight, though he was sporting a nice polo shirt and khaki pants so that he looked like he was still on the clock, if just a little bit. He had tried to tame the mop of chestnut-colored curls atop his head, but to little avail; a few sprung loose and danced around the top of his head as he talked, animated and funny, a twinkle in his eye indicating that this was a happy person who enjoyed himself.

"Don't worry," he said, perusing the menu but seeming to read my mind. "I only work at the camp in the summer. You're not on a date with a part-time summer camp counselor."

I feigned relief. "That's good to know." I studied his hands; they were paint covered and looked suspiciously like my father's.

Good God. He was an artist.

"Art teacher," he said, reading my expression of horror, the one I had failed to suppress. "At the high school. Drawing and painting. Advanced drawing and painting. Advanced Placement art." He smiled that toothy grin again. "All of the biggies."

"And your own art?" I asked.

"When I can. Usually on the weekends. I do watercolors of the Foster's Landing River mostly. Sell them at craft fairs. I can usually pull in a couple of hundred extra bucks on a weekend, which is a nice way to make ends meet. Big craft fairs are even better." He polished off his beer. "People love watercolors. Particularly of landscapes."

"You mean your salary as a public-school teacher doesn't keep you in caviar and champagne?" I asked.

"Hardly," he said. "I'm saving up for my own studio so I can move the paints out of my house. I think the smell of turpentine keeps me in a permanent state of light-headedness."

You and my father, I thought.

"How is it going with the investigation?" Brendan said, his eyes still on the menu.

"You mean the death at the Manor?" I said. "Nothing as far as I can tell."

"Was he drunk?" he asked. "You know, crashing through the banister like that?"

It had all been detailed, right down to the broken FDR bust, in the local paper.

"Hard to know," I said. "I don't think so."

"Accident?"

"Definitely not."

"Murdered?" he asked, looking at me.

"Definitely," I said. "I was the only witness, if you could call it that. I was just wandering through the foyer when it happened. When he fell."

Brendan winced, making a whistling sound through his clenched teeth. "Oh, geez. Sounds awful."

"I didn't know the guy at all, but it was still pretty bad," I said. All I knew was that I had once found him attractive until he turned into an oily gigolo. "Seemed like a pleasant guy, though." And cute. But not as cute as you, Brendan Joyce.

"Anybody at the wedding who might want to kill him?" Brendan asked, putting his menu down on the table.

My mind flashed on a few faces: Mark Chesterton's. Caleigh's. And, for some reason, my own father's. Mom, licking her lips as she told her latest lie. I quickly shook the thought of that aside and didn't answer, except to give a little shrug.

Over dinner, I got to know a little more about my date. He had never married and at thirty-seven, exactly my age, was the talk of his mother's friends, his elderly aunts. His reason—he hadn't met the right person, anyone who excited him enough to give up the life he had now—didn't sit well with them. There had to be a girl out there. He was just too picky. He couldn't make a decision. And on and on and on. Did he like women who brandished broken wine bottles with wild abandon? I wondered. If so, I was his girl.

"So, I've been on more blind dates with more former Roses of Tralee than I can count." He smiled, signaling for a third round for the two of us to the server. At this rate, I'd still be half in the bag by the time the O'Donnell wedding started, and I was notorious for being able to hold my liquor. I had a lot to do, given my thoughts about how the ham would be cooked and was starting to think that I was in over my head with this whole thing, the preparation I had in mind. But this was the most fun I had had in ages and I wasn't going to let a hundred hungry Irish guests—and a pig—stand in the way of my having a good time.

"Not a good one in the bunch?"

He must have been a little drunkish himself. "Not as good as you."

Well, hello there.

CHAPTER *Seventeen*

Four o'clock in the morning comes quickly.

Especially after three beers and a bourbon nightcap.

But memories of an excellent make-out session with the sweet Brendan Joyce put a smile on my face when I awoke and made the effort it would have taken to get out of bed a little easier, a bed that was slightly rumpled when I got home, even though I remembered making it and fluffing the pillows that very morning. But that didn't matter. I had had a date with a nice guy and that made 4:00 a.m. not quite as difficult to face.

I was so glad he had gotten his braces off.

I tiptoed down the steps of the garage and down the gravel path where I waited, in the dark, the full moon overhead the only light to see by, for the truck that would bring me the most succulent pig I had ever tasted.

You want ham? I'll give you ham.

It takes about twelve hours to roast a hundred-pound pig and after I had come home the night before, Brendan acting as my partner in crime, we drunkenly cleaned out an old pit that Dad had once built behind Shamrock Manor and away from the old structure where I could place the animal for roasting. This was always going to be a clandestine affair and I was glad to have an accomplice, someone who had a lot more upper-body strength than I did and who could help me make the pit usable. The truck pulled up a few minutes after four, and I directed them to the space where I would roast the pig, hoping that the telltale signs of going in reverse—the *beep, beep, beep* of Javier's large truck—wouldn't wake up my parents. Mom, I hoped, was using her noise machine, and Dad, his own noise machine, was probably dead to the world as usual.

The truck backed up to the riverside of the manor and Javier and his guys jumped out. Javier, an old contact from my days in the city and the first guy I had thought of when the plan entered my mind, gave me the once-over. "Late night, Bel?" he said, taking in my rumpled jacket and pants. I had put them on when I got home, afraid that in my addled state I'd end up out here in my pajamas with the guys. Behind him, a couple of guys whom I would never see again and couldn't describe to anyone given the darkness, opened the back of the truck. "Is that a hickey?" he asked, leaning in to get a better look at me under the one light that shone from the manor.

I grabbed my neck. "No."

"Just kidding, *chica*. Just confirming what I already knew: you had yourself a booty call," he said.

"A date, Javier. It was just a date. Nothing more," I said, peering around him to get a look at what was in the truck.

"A date, a booty call, whatever. You say 'tomato' . . . ," he said, trailing off. "Glad you're away from that Ben guy. What a . . ." He searched for the right word.

"Wanker?" I provided helpfully. That was the closest approximation of what my former fiancé, a Brit, Ben Dykstra was. He was a liar, and a cheater. In other words, a wanker. It had only been two months since I had been home, a little more than that since we had broken up, and already I was over him, going on dates. What did that say about me? Did I care?

"I was thinking of something worse, but I'll keep it to myself," Javier said. He blessed himself. "My mother up in heaven would strike me down," he said, kissing a medallion around his neck. He turned around and in a shouted whisper told the guys to hurry up.

One of the guys jumped off the back of the refrigerated truck and brought down the lift gate. Another guy wheeled down what I was waiting for: a one-hundred-pound pig, raised for the express purpose of providing "ham" to the O'Donnell wedding guests. Neither he nor his former owner knew that at the time he was living peacefully on a farm somewhere, but today he was a feast fit for a family celebrating the wedding of their only daughter, the lovely Patrice.

Javier waved a hand with gravity. "And there he is."

The team made quick work of getting the pig all ready for the roasting. A half hour after they arrived, the pig was smoking away, turning lazily on the pit, Javier's guy Fernando getting two hundred bucks in cash and a tryout as my new sous chef as his reward for making sure that Henry, as I had dubbed our pig, was not getting too brown on any one side at any given time.

As the dusky morning light turned to soft sunlight, the smell of roasted pig filled the air around the Manor. I prepared myself for what my father would say when he saw a pig roasting a few hundred yards from where the cocktail hour would take place—under the same tent where Caleigh had not eaten enough canapés to soak up the booze in her stomach—but I was resolute. If I was going to be the chef at Shamrock Manor, things would be done my way, not the way some thickheaded groom or unsophisticated bride wanted. Roasting a pig was casual but just retro enough to be elegant.

At least that's what I told myself.

"Make sure you put on sunscreen, Fernando," I said,

tossing him a tube of something that I had in my jacket pocket. Mom had been vigilant about keeping her own skin protected and ours, too, years before it was considered the norm to lather up in the sun. Fernando looked like he wanted to object but, seeing the look on my face, wisely kept his mouth shut.

In the Manor, I grabbed another chef's coat, left over from Goran's tenure, and brought it outside to Fernando as well. I had never asked about staff; I knew that Goran had had help, but I wasn't sure of their caliber. And now I wasn't sure where any of them were. None of them had shown up for work during the week and Dad had been evasive, leading me to believe that they had either all quit or been deported in the days since Caleigh's wedding. Hence, Fernando. Fortunately, the O'Donnell wedding was a later-afternoon affair and on the small side, so I had plenty of time. I went to work making several trays of shepherd's pie the way I wanted—with short ribs, not the foie gras that Cargan had accused me of slipping in there—and preparing a host of beautiful hors d'oeuvres with just the right amount of whimsy for a bride such as Patrice O'Donnell, a young woman who had come in for a tasting weeks before and thought she was getting Goran's specialties of the house or the Shamrock Manor "special": the aforementioned shepherd's pie, ham of some kind, mashed potatoes, carrots, and a wilted salad drenched in a crappy dressing. Dad said that Mr. and Mrs. O'Donnell had been very happy with the fare and maybe they were. But Patrice deserved better.

How did I know that? I didn't. But after Googling her announcement and finding only one in the local paper that went on endlessly about her groom, one Keith Damscott of the Poughkeepsie Damscotts, and his incredible career as a budding novelist and only one line about Patrice— that she "taught math at a local high school"—my heart broke just a little bit for her. Implicit in that announcement was that Mr. Damscott didn't have a visible means of employment and that Patrice was supporting her husband with his non-existent writing career. It was all right there on the page, right down to the dark circles under Patrice's limpid eyes, the ones that she clearly had tried to cover up before the photo was taken but had failed.

I had stared at the picture a long time, maybe recognizing myself in Patrice's optimistic face, thinking that maybe, like me, she was talking herself into something that would turn out not to be a very good idea. I thought about her as I carved out little centers in tiny potatoes and filled them with caviar, topping them with a dollop of crème fraiche.

No, Patrice O'Donnell, you will not have "ham," at least not the ham of your youth, the kind of ham that came in a can and that your mother studded with cloves for a special occasion. You deserve better.

CHAPTER *Eighteen*

Turns out Patrice O'Donnell didn't deserve better. But Keith Damscott did.

The not-so-blushing bride and shell-shocked groom arrived at Shamrock Manor just after six o'clock, pretty much right on schedule, and Patrice, in a wedding dress that cost more than the last renovation of the Manor, demanded to see the chef. Her attitude made me wonder if she had ever really been to Shamrock Manor, because clearly she had higher hopes for her wedding day that went beyond a down-on-its-heels catering hall that boasted a spectacular view and not much else.

Oh, but there was the great chef now. There was that even though Patrice didn't know that when they had booked the place.

The pig, roasting in the hot sun, had been a better idea when I had originally come up with it. Now it just seemed like folly, Fernando having looked as if he were one of those rowers in a Charlton Heston movie about slaves in ancient Rome. Fernando was rethinking becoming a sous chef at Shamrock Manor and he hadn't even seen the kitchen yet.

Mom and Dad had seen the pig before the wedding started and hadn't said a word, Mom just looking at me silently and shaking her head, Dad putting a paint-splattered mitt to his face and rubbing vigorously, their own versions of abject disappointment in their only daughter.

I met Patrice O'Donnell in the foyer, the bust of FDR having been replaced with a bust of Bobby Sands, the most famous of the Irish prisoners who had led the 1981 hunger strike in a British prison. Where my dad had gotten a Bobby Sands bust on such short notice was anyone's guess, but there he was. My guess is that Dad had been working on this for years and Declan Morrison's destruction of the FDR bust was just an excuse to bring out this new creation, one that bore the hallmarks of Dad's late-night work. The crooked nose. The asymmetrical eyes, the squiggly mouth. So how did I know it was Bobby Sands? The plaque affixed to the bust gave helped me figure it out.

"Who's that?" Patrice asked, pointing one gloved finger at the bust.

"Bobby Sands," I said.

"Brother?"

"No," I said, smoothing down my chef's coat. "Irish martyr."

"He wasn't here a few weeks ago. FDR was. I prefer FDR."

She said it as if old Franklin had really classed up the joint. "Yes. Unfortunate incident," I said, wondering how Patrice O'Donnell had missed the news that a man had died in the Manor just a week earlier or if she had chosen just to ignore that little fact. Or if Dad had cut the price per person and the O'Donnells were getting a bargain. "We lost President Roosevelt and replaced him with a great figure in Irish history."

"Right," Patrice said. "The murder. The only reason we're still here is that your father cut the price in half."

I knew it. But we'd have to talk, Dad and I. We'd be closed in a month if word got out that Mal McGrath was slashing prices on weddings.

Patrice crossed her arms. "Hmmm. What's for dinner?" she asked.

"Just what you ordered," I said.

"And where's the sexy foreign chef?" she asked. Next to her, Keith Damscott remained silent while he should have bristled, even just a bit, in my opinion. Their official union was only hours old and already she was talking about another man in a way that suggested that she had a wandering eye. What was it with the brides at Shamrock Manor? I had only met two so far and both were lacking in both the morals and fidelity departments.

"He got promoted," I said. "He's now the chef at the Ritz-Carlton in New York. But he did all of the prep on your meal tonight, so I think you'll be happy." The lie fell off my lips so easily that I almost believed it myself. Behind me and through the doors to the banquet hall I saw my brothers testily setting up their equipment, Cargan looking as if he was on the verge of tears. That could mean one of two things: his soccer team had lost that morning or the brothers were in all-out war with one another about one of his arrangements. I suspected the latter.

She regarded me coolly, the only sound in the foyer the whir of the air-conditioning, now working after two days of Dad tinkering with the wonky system. I had encountered some tough customers in my time, but Patrice O'Donnell was a force I hadn't encountered in a long time. She was bitchy. Tense. Unhappy. On edge. That didn't mean that I was unprepared for her; she couldn't hold a candle to some of the customers I had served throughout my career.

"The only reason we're here is because you're cheap," she said, hitting the one button that I knew I had to address with Mom and Dad. We were cheap and even cheaper when you factored in that they were paying half of cheap. At a good twenty dollars per head below that of our chief rival—Le Chateau in Monroeville—we needed to up our game. This place was falling apart, and even though I wasn't staying that long, I could help make some changes that would elevate the standards, if only a bit.

"And your father is friends with Mal," Keith said, reminding her of the connection. Keith looked at me and smiled, accustomed to using his pearly whites to smooth over whatever tenseness his wife brought to the interpersonal communication in which he was involved.

"Yes. My father is friends with Mal." She handed Keith her small handbag. "Well, it just better be good. The last guy promised me the world." She hooked a thumb in Keith's direction. "Just like this guy over here. Still waiting for the proof on that one."

"And what a lucky man he is," I said, affecting what I hoped was a sincere tone. The "limpid pools" that I had thought described her eyes previously really just indicated a lack of soul that I hadn't been able to ascertain from the photo. Whereas Keith had looked smug and arrogant in the wedding photo, the man before me was anything but, attending to his bride and her lengthy train like a bridesmaid himself.

"And was that a roasting pit out there?" she asked before leaving the foyer and entering the anteroom to the banquet hall, where guests were starting to assemble after getting half a load on at the cocktail hour. She didn't wait for an answer and I didn't give one, wondering if she had gotten a glimpse of the butchered animal in our kitchen, fine roasted pork ready to be served to fifty starving guests of the O'Donnells.

I had texted Brendan Joyce earlier in the day when it was clear that the "staff," the existence of whom Dad had danced around, really had been deported. Or something.

If they had even ever existed. Brendan ran into the kitchen, breathless, a smear of yellow paint across his handsome mug, and put on the apron I handed him.

"I don't know how to cook," he said, blurting out the one thing that I knew for sure about him. The way he had devoured his food at the Grand Mill last night, as well as asking for a meal to go, was an indication that the guy had a tremendous appetite and probably didn't cook for himself.

"I just need hands," I said. "You're my expeditor."

"If that means 'love machine,' " he said, burying his head into the hair that was falling out from beneath my head scarf, "I'm your man."

"No," I said, extricating myself from his welcome embrace. "It means 'food handler.' Or guy that makes sure what I plate gets into the servers' hands." I let him give me a kiss, glad that Fernando and the servers were otherwise occupied. "That's it. That's your job."

The servers who remained were a bunch of girls who had come over from Dad's hometown and who were staying in the United States for no more than the summer, ostensibly. Dad still had friends in Ballyminster and, hence, an ability to hire girls who wanted a little adventure but not at the expense of their safety. They lived around town in various rented rooms, something else Dad had a bead on as well. He paid them well and the tips were not insubstantial, making it so when they weren't working the girls could go to New York City if they wanted and shop at the outlet malls a few miles up the river, snapping up last year's styles at bargain prices. Working at Shamrock Manor was a boon for girls from the small village in the north of Ireland. Although their visas allowed them a certain time to work and after that they would return home, that wasn't always what happened, many of them disappearing into the weeds after their stint here and joining the hordes of illegals who stayed on after their approved tenure. The three working today—Colleen, Eileen, and Pauline— entered the kitchen and awaited my instructions. They had already served a round of hors d'oeuvres and were back for more.

"Like a nest of hungry vipers," I heard one of them say when they entered en masse.

I leaned on the stainless counter and peered under the warming rack at the three of them, nearly identical in their Shamrock Manor black vest/black pants/white shirt combination, their hair all pulled back into tight ponytails. "How's it going out there?"

Colleen, or it could have been Pauline or Eileen for all I knew, made a sad face. "The thingies with the caviar? Not a hit, Belfast."

One of the other raven-haired servers underscored the point. "There're a bunch in a garbage pail."

Beside me, I could feel Brendan brace for a histrionic display from a temperamental chef. But there was none. Those days were over. Anger-management class had brought me this far and my own self-control would take me the rest of the way. "Okay. So, what do they like?"

"The crab cake canapés," Eileen said. I now remembered that Eileen had a pronounced, and adorable, lisp, one of the things that had Fernando's eyes trained on her since she had introduced herself to him earlier.

And Colleen had the long legs and a prodigious bosom. Pauline was very skinny and, according to Dad, a "runner." Whether that meant she was a flight risk for INS or just into jogging I never could figure out. Maybe both.

"Fine," I said. I pointed to the other two. "And you two? Did you crowdsource the hors d'oeuvres? What's going well?"

"The pigs in the blankets," Pauline said. "They love them."

Fortunately, suspecting that my more ambitious creations would fall flat, I had put in a few more trays of the old standbys. With Brendan's help, I loaded up the girls' trays and sent them back out, taking time to check the butchering I had done on the pig. Perfection.

"Fernando!" I said, spying him in the refrigerator. "What's going on in that walk-in?" I asked.

"Nothing, Miss Bel," he said, emerging finally. "I was just hot."

I could imagine he was. All of those hours in the sun, roasting a pig, had taken their toll. Fernando was shaky and pale. "Sit down, brother," Brendan said. "I'll be right back."

When the doors opened, I could hear my brothers tuning up, the sound of the drums, lots of cymbals, the most prevalent. Feeney was singing in a half whisper, something about how much he hated Arney set to the tune of "The Fields of Athenry," but since his half whisper was amplified by an impressive sound system everyone could hear what he was saying. A few guests laughed while others stood in openmouthed horror. I leaned into the dining hall and when I got Feeney's attention drew a finger across my throat. *Cut it out,* I mouthed. Cargan really was on the verge of breakdown now, his lips white and set in a grim line. Boy could never handle the drama of being a McGrath, having a pathological aversion to conflict. I looked at Feeney and pointed at Cargan, staring disconsolately at his fiddle as he plucked at the strings, and Feeney turned off the mike, turning around to clap a hand on our brother's shoulder in an attempt to calm him down.

Feeney came into the foyer. "What?" he said, his whining not attractive on a grown man.

"I get it. You want to be a rock star. You want out of this one-horse town. You want a life separate from the extended family on whom your livelihood depends." I gave him a little slap to the cheek and held a finger to his lips when he tried to protest. "Take a number, Brother," I said before going back to the kitchen where Brendan was doing a great job tending to the potatoes bubbling in the giant pot of water. I'd mash them within an inch of their starchy lives and add a lot of butter and, with the roasted pig, would serve a dinner the likes of which no one at Shamrock Manor had ever eaten. The guests were working their way through the salad course, after which there would be some dancing and speeches, and then the entrée would be served.

Mom and Dad had been conspicuously absent from the kitchen since I had arrived and I wondered if that was standard operating procedure, given that Goran had been such a diva, or if they were afraid of meddling too much in my business and driving me out of the place as well. Everything under control, I went into the office, where Dad was having an animated discussion with someone over the presence of a bouncy castle at an upcoming wedding—Dad didn't want the liability, but the customer was demanding it—so I backed out noiselessly and looked around for Mom, wanting to see if, from her vantage point, everything was going well. She was, after all, the hostess—the grande dame, as it were—of Shamrock Manor, the gorgeous face of a mansion that was starting to show its wear and age, unlike its female proprietor, who, for all I knew, had a fountain of youth in the basement. Or just great genes.

Or a great plastic surgeon.

Upstairs, the last of the police tape hung limply from the doorknob of the bedroom where I had last left Caleigh during her own wedding. A smudge of something—blood maybe or just red wine?—was on the doorjamb, which was slightly ajar. I got a whiff of Mom, Chanel No. 5, and knew that she was on the other side. I knocked gently.

"Just a minute!" she called out. "One second!"

I stood outside the door, but I didn't have a lot of time to kill, what with the potatoes in the pot and the hungry guests and Brendan, a lovely art teacher but not a cook, helping out in the kitchen. I pushed open the door and found Mom at the mirror, dabbing under her eyes with a tissue and reapplying some under-eye concealer. On the bed was an imprint and a wrinkled comforter, the telltale signs that she had been sitting on the bed before I entered.

"Mom?" I said, taking a step into the room.

"Yes, Belfast?" she asked, turning to face me, the only sign she had been crying her red-tinged nose. "Everything okay in the kitchen? And who is that tall man in there with you?"

"Brendan Joyce," I said.

"Paddy and Fiona Joyce's boy?" she asked, adjusting her spine so that she was standing as straight as she could, her pageant-girl posture returning.

"One and the same," I said.

"He was always a nice boy. Always carrying his sister's hard shoes before dance class."

"Were you crying?" I asked.

I could see the wheels turning in her head. "Well, yes," she said, deciding not to lie. "I'm just a bit overwhelmed. Today's wedding, what happened at Caleigh's party, the state of the Manor." She paused and crossed her arms over her chest, her voice catching a bit when she said, "That poor boy."

"What poor boy?" I asked.

"Declan. Mr. Morrison."

"That poor *man*," I said, correcting her. "He was a man." And not a very nice one at that, but I left that out.

"You're right. He was a man."

Behind her, outside, I could see the smoldering pit where I had roasted the pig, the river in the distance. "You lost an earring that day, Mom. The day of the wedding." I watched her carefully. "I forgot to mention it."

She touched her ears reflexively, making sure the earrings she had donned that morning were still there. "Yes. Thank you, Belfast. They were cheap. Plastic, really. I don't care."

"Any idea where you may have lost it? Did you retrace your steps?" I asked.

"No need," she said. She sighed. "I'll get more earrings."

"We'll get this place back on track, Mom. Don't worry."

"Yes, we will," she said. "You're here now, Bel, and that will help things tremendously."

I didn't know about that, but I let her indulge the fantasy. After all, she was upset. And I couldn't bear to think of her, the rock of the family, feeling off her game or upset about the events of the past few months and last week. The Manor was in trouble and she felt as if she were to blame. It was written all over her smooth, unwrinkled face.

"Shouldn't you go back to the kitchen?" she asked.

"Yes, I should," I said. When hugging or any kind of emotional display of affection isn't in your family's repertoire, there's not much else to do but move on, so that's what I did. But before I got to the door, I turned around. "The man. Declan Morrison. Did you know him?" I asked for not the first, or last, time.

She did her best not to lick her lips, but she couldn't help herself. "No. Never met him before in my life."

CHAPTER *Nineteen*

The next morning, the cat, whom I had named Taylor after the lovely Ms. Swift, made an appearance on the back porch. Mom had left me a pouch of salmon during one of her clandestine cleaning trips to the apartment, and even though I was starving when I got home the night before the smell of it gave me another idea.

I sniffed. "Cat food!" I put it on a paper plate and let the feline chips fall where they may.

It never occurred to me that leaving out the contents of a pouch of salmon would also attract an intrepid raccoon, his or her eyes glistening merrily as I walked past the glass door on my way to the bathroom in the middle of the night. He or she scarfed up most of the salmon before I shooed him or her away by shoving a broom handle between the door and the porch. I had lived in the city long enough that I had forgotten about raccoons. Rats, no. Pigeons, not them, either. But raccoons were denizens of the suburban rural environment and made their presence known, particularly when food was around, even if it was in the form of garbage.

The cat smelled the oil that had soaked into the paper plate, though, and that was enough to bring him or her up the steps, once the raccoon had retreated when daylight broke. I stood in the hallway, not daring to make a move, and got a glimpse of the animal I had been hoping to make my pet. Big, fluffy, white, with an orange spot on her mouth—I decided an animal this beautiful could only be a female—she regarded me from the other side of the glass door before loping down the steps to parts unknown. I made a mental note to buy more crappy salmon in a pouch and to research how to keep raccoons from arriving at your back door. I wondered if she liked her new name and if she would ever settle down and become a part of my life for real.

For the past few Sunday mornings since I had come home, my parents and I went through the same charade. They would creep up the stairs and rap lightly at the door and ask if I was going to Mass, to which I would reply that I couldn't, citing "work" I had to do. I don't know why we persisted in pretending that I would actually go to Mass—I was a grown-up and could tell them that Sunday Mass was not part of my routine anymore—or why they accepted my contention that I was so busy. It was easier that way for everyone, I guess. I had no friends—well, I sort of had Brendan Joyce, our bond stronger now that he had come to help at Shamrock Manor the day before—and I had less of a life. It was me, this apartment, and the phantom cat. Regardless, church was not part of my plans.

But making breakfast for Brendan, snoring loudly on my couch, was. Fortunately, the door to my apartment is at the back and as far away from the living room as you could get. Mom would surely paint me a harlot if she knew that I had a man in the place, even though the man hadn't laid a single hand on me the night before, the two of us, exhausted from the O'Donnell wedding and its attendant messiness, sharing a bag of microwave popcorn before going our separate ways in my four-hundred-square-foot space. I didn't have a team of cleaners to come in after me and make sure the kitchen was shipshape; that was all on me, so we spent several hours making the kitchen at the Manor spic-and-span so that the next time I came in it would look more like a professional kitchen and less like an Army mess hall.

But today Mom and Dad didn't come up to ask me to go to Mass that Sunday and I was relieved. Maybe they had seen how exhausted I had been after the O'Donnell wedding. Cooking at the Manor was different from cooking in a restaurant kitchen and I was unused to being the sous chef, the line cook, the expeditor (Brendan, bless his heart, did his best, but it wasn't good enough), and the manager of the waitstaff. I was glad my parents were going to Mass because with them occupied for an hour at the service and then again at the Cub Scouts' pancake breakfast, something that Dad never missed in thirty-five years in Foster's Landing and as a parishioner at Bleeding Heart of Jesus, I could make Brendan an omelet that would make him fall hopelessly in love with me in peace. Our plan the night before had been to share an exceptional bottle of Bordeaux that I had in my wine rack and that I had purloined from The Monkey's Paw that night I left, but after one glass and a bellyful of popcorn Brendan was sound asleep, his big feet resting on my Ikea coffee table, and I headed to bed as well, feeling as if I had been run over. I had covered him with one of Mom's crocheted afghans, one of an army of blankets that seemed to be recklessly reproducing, a new one appearing in my apartment practically with each passing day. This one was an homage to her beloved New York Mets, an off-center blue-and-orange logo the centerpiece of this particular monstrosity.

Before he fell asleep, a little punch-drunk, he said, "Is it my imagination or does this place smell like meat loaf? Or hot dogs? Or both?"

I couldn't get rid of the smell or the ketchup stain on the couch, so I had given up. No amount of Febreze helped and Mom, when confronted, denied ever having been in the place.

I stared at Brendan on the couch, his mouth hanging open, his hair even more unruly than usual. He was cute. And sweet. A deadly combination for someone like me, someone truly on the rebound. Go slow, McGrath, I cautioned myself. You're not that long out of a relationship.

His eyes closed, he spoke. "You shouldn't stare at sleeping people. They may get the idea that you're some kind of psychopath or something."

"Not a psychopath," I said. "Just your normal, everyday chef with amazing knife skills."

"Oh, that's heartening," he said, opening his eyes. "Thanks for the blanket." He pulled the afghan up to his chin and craned his neck to get a better look at the Mets logo. "A Mets fan?"

"Mom is."

"Mom likes to suffer, eh?"

"Mom *loves* to suffer," I said. "Don't all Irish moms?"

"Good point," he said, pulling himself into a sitting position. "Mr. Met looks like he's had a stroke, though."

"Mom is still learning the finer points of crochet." The kitchen was attached to the living room, so I kept up my end of the conversation while I assembled the ingredients I would need for breakfast: a slab of pork belly that I had brought home from the Manor the night before, some eggs from a local farmer's market, a loaf of store-bought bread. Milk. Cheese. All of the good stuff. I pulled some bowls down from the cupboard and recognized them as the free stoneware we used to get at the grocery store when we were kids, saving Mom's receipts and figuring out which items we'd be able to get with our next order. Cargan was the last to get his own dinner plate and never let us forget it. I got the first full set because I was the only girl, the youngest, and, according to my brothers, the "most special" and "Dad's favorite." I wasn't sure about that, but being the only female and younger than those hellions did accord me some privileges that they didn't receive. Eating the last Oreo. Being believed when I said "he hit me first." Or not having to sit in the way, way back of the Vanagon because I professed a profound car sickness that could rear its ugly head at any time, particularly when we were going over a particularly windy road that led to the bridge out of town.

I wasn't carsick. Just spoiled. The boys were right, but I would never tell them that.

Brendan lumbered over to the counter and took a seat, watching me as I started to cook. After a few minutes, minutes in which he was awed by my skill, or so I told myself, he asked me a question.

"So what really happened?"

The fork that I had been using to beat the eggs slipped from my fingers and sank into the deep stoneware bowl, disappearing beneath a pool of viscous yellow fluid. I didn't have to ask what he was referring to; the look on his face told me that he was asking about my former job and life and that he instantly regretted bringing it up.

"The Monkey's Paw?" I asked. "How much do you know?"

"Just what was in the paper. You were the head chef. President Moreland was there. You left."

"I was fired."

Brendan dipped his head so that he didn't have to look at me. "Okay. You were fired."

I leaned on the counter. "It was a Tuesday night. Pretty quiet. A nice couple, a cop and his professor wife, were celebrating his fiftieth birthday with his partner and his wife. I knew the partner's wife because she's a cable bigwig and had been talking to me about doing my own reality show."

Brendan's eyebrows went up.

"I said no," I said, putting to rest any thoughts he might have had of me being a cable star. "It was just them and the reporter from the *Times*." I grimaced. "Unfortunately."

"I'll say."

"Anyway, the president was a late reservation, but being as it was a Tuesday, we had plenty of room to spare. Secret Service came in and swept the place. All clear." I dipped my fingers into the eggs and extricated the fork. "He ordered the snapper."

"Ah, the snapper," Brendan said, his own memory of the story jogged.

"It had a bone in it."

"Yep. I read that."

"That's basically it," I said.

He smiled. "But it's not really, is it?"

I thought about how much to tell him, how much to reveal. "You want the true story?" I said. "You want to know what really happened?"

"I do."

"Are you trying to decide whether to cast your lot with a crazy chef?"

"No," he said. "I already think that I want to. But I have a feeling there's more to this story because I've known you, what?" he said, counting on his fingers. "Twenty-two years with a long hiatus thrown in there? So, seventy-two hours at most? I don't see crazy. I see passionate. I see smart. I see kind." He looked at me, the fork in my hand dripping egg onto the counter. "I see beautiful."

I didn't want to blush, but I couldn't help it. "I was engaged to my sous chef, Ben. He's what my parents would call a wanker."

"I thought wankers were British."

"They are, but my parents love the word, particularly when it applies to my former boyfriends. And he is. British, that is. But that doesn't matter. That's what they call Kevin Hanson, too."

"Detective Hanson?" Brendan asked. His sunny demeanor clouded for a moment, leading me to believe that he and Detective Hanson—Detective *Wanker*—had a history of which I wasn't aware.

"One and the same." I put the fork in the sink and got a new one out of the drawer. Only two remaining. Just right for our breakfast a deux. "Anyway, Ben was in charge of deboning the fish, making sure it was ready to go from the grill to the plate and to the president's table."

"So, not you?"

"Not me."

The realization dawned on his sweet, concerned face. "You took the fall."

"And Ben never said a word," I said, choking back a sob with a little, rueful laugh. "Francesco didn't like that I was becoming bigger than the restaurant, that my star was rising. He had been looking for a way to get rid of me for months because I didn't want to do the show. People loved my food, so he didn't just want to out and out fire me. This was his out. This was his way to get rid of me, promote Ben, and bring the spotlight back to him and his ownership rather than a celebrity chef who could have had her own television show but who chose not to." Brendan looked at me, his expression a combination of pity and pride. "It was all about the food with me. It always has been. I didn't need some television crew following me around, watching my every move. I am not in this business for the fame or the glory."

"Well, that's good, because now you're the head chef at Shamrock Manor," he said, and the sound of his laughter was welcome after going back in time to The Monkey's Paw and Ben the wanker and Francesco Francatelli. "The broken wine bottle?" Brendan asked. "Saw something about you threatening Francesco with a broken wine bottle?"

"When Francesco came into the kitchen to tell me about the president's snapper, he picked up my chef's knife and was going to throw it at the wall behind me, so I picked up the closest thing I could find and made it into a weapon." I shrugged. "You don't grow up with four older brothers and not figure out ways to defend yourself."

"He was going to throw the knife? This story is just ridiculous," he said.

"I wouldn't believe it myself if it hadn't happened to me. Maybe he would have thrown it, maybe not. But my line cook was coming out of the walk-in and if Francesco missed his target, well, that would have been the end of Lucio." I looked at the bowl of eggs. "Remember. Francesco was nominated for an Oscar for *The Thrill of the Sierra Madre* and supposedly learned knife throwing. But that was in the seventies, so I didn't trust his skills."

Brendan rubbed his hands over his face. "You can't make this stuff up."

I began to beat the eggs again. "No. You can't." I got a skillet out from the drawer under the stove and lit the burner. "So there it is. The unvarnished truth. Did I lose my temper? Yes. Did I threaten my former boss with a wine bottle? Indeed. Did I serve the president red snapper with a bone in it? No, I did not. Was it my responsibility to check? You betcha."

Brendan spoke softly. "Do you love Ben?"

I answered quickly and without reservation, "Not any-more." Thinking about it, I wasn't sure I ever had, and that troubled me even more than the fact that I had fallen for his lines, his charm. If everything had stayed the same, I'd be engaged still to a wanker who had no second thoughts about betraying me to save his own hide or make his own star rise.

"When were you supposed to get married?" Brendan asked.

"This Christmas," I said.

"I'm sorry," he said.

"Don't be. It's the best thing that ever happened to me." And I was starting to believe that.

The butter I put in the pan turned a lovely golden brown, and when the eggs hit it they smelled like a little piece of heaven. I shaved some sharp cheddar onto the eggs, lift-ing the edges when they were brown, and flipping one half over the other. I put some toast under the broiler and grabbed a couple of plates from the cupboard. I pulled the toast out just in time, slathering it with butter and putting it on a plate. "Oh, the pork belly!" I said, looking at the slab of meat on the counter. "I forgot to make it."

Brendan waved his hand. "No worries. The eggs will be enough." He leaned around the corner of the kitchen, looking down the hallway that ran the length of the apartment to the back door. "Someone at your door," he said.

I wiped my hands on a rag and peered around the same corner, wondering who would be visiting me on a Sunday morning. By my accounting, the pancake breakfast hadn't even started yet; if Father Pat was through the homily I'd be surprised. When I saw who was at the back door, though, I pulled myself back into the kitchen, hoping they hadn't seen me.

It was like the Ghosts of Boyfriends Past, both Ben Dykstra and Kevin Hanson standing there, eyeing each other suspiciously.

I looked at Brendan Joyce, the nicest guy any girl could ever hope to meet, and said, "Jelly on your toast?"

CHAPTER *Twenty*

They let themselves in, having seen me peering around the corner. Ben sauntered into the room as if no time had passed, nothing had ever happened.

"Hello, love," he said, giving me a kiss on the cheek, taking a bit of toast off of Brendan's plate, and shoving it into his mouth. Whereas Brendan's Irish brogue made him adorable, Ben's British accent made him sound pompous. Arrogant. And sort of like an extra in *Mary Poppins*. I shuddered to think that I had once found that attractive and wondered if it was even real.

He was in last night's work clothes, his short-sleeved chef's jacket—the kind that only wankers wore—a little dirty, a lot wrinkled, suggesting that maybe he had slept in it for a spell. Kevin stood at the edge of the kitchen, his hands shoved into the pockets of his dress pants, taking in the scene. The thought of him standing in the Foster's Landing River the week before came back to me, his posture the same as it had been that night.

"Ben, what are you doing here?" I asked. I could smell the bourbon on him from a mile away. "You didn't drive here, did you?"

"Took the train, gorgeous," he said. "Great little town you have here. Hung out in a place called The Sandlot until it was time to visit." He looked around the apartment. "Old guy who owns the place said you're consulting on the menu?" He twirled a finger by his forehead. "A bit of the dementia?"

"The Dugout. It's called The Dugout. And the owner is not suffering from dementia," I said. Behind Ben, Kevin's eyebrows shot up. I didn't know what he was doing here, but being here with Ben was not something Kevin had bargained for.

Brendan stood. "I'd better get going," he said. "Bel, thank you for breakfast."

Now it was Ben's turn to raise his eyebrows.

"No. Stay," I said, but hearing the desperation in my voice, my reluctance at being left here with these two, I stopped myself. "Thank you for your help yesterday, Brendan. I really appreciate it." I walked him to the back door, his shoes hanging from his hands, his feet bare. I guess he couldn't wait to get out of here.

He looked down at me. "That guy *is* a wanker," he said, smiling. "I'll see you later."

I watched him go, taking the rickety back steps at such a fast pace I was afraid he would slip and fall. I hoped that my former association with Ben—both personal and professional—didn't color me in a way that Brendan found unattractive, but his haste in getting to his car certainly didn't serve as a rebuttal.

Ben and Kevin were sitting at the counter when I came back in. "Francesco says 'hi,'" Ben said, not a touch of sarcasm in his tone. Francesco had wished me dead the last time I had seen him. I doubt he had taken the time to say "hi."

"How's the restaurant, Ben?" I asked. "How are you enjoying your head chef status?"

"Oh, are you still sore about that?" he asked.

I turned off the broiler; no one else in this strange threesome was getting breakfast. "Yes. I'm still sore about that."

Kevin looked from me to Ben and then back at Ben again.

"Hey, Kevin," I said, "I don't know why you're here, but obviously Ben and I have some catching up to do. Can we reconnect later?"

"Afraid not, Bel," Kevin said, standing and opening his jacket wide enough so that Ben could see the gun on his hip. He no longer carried the badge of his teenage masculinity—a football that was with him all the time when his standing bass was not—but a gun was better than that. Ben gave it a cursory glance and looked back at me. "I have some things to talk to you about with respect to the Morrison murder."

That got Ben's attention. "The Morrison murder? What in the hell is that?"

Kevin turned to him, officious. "It is the murder of one Declan Morrison who met his demise at Shamrock Manor last week."

Kevin must have gotten a word-a-day calendar. His vocabulary had improved considerably since we were in high school and I had had to explain to him that "flatulence" meant the same thing as "fart." I turned and looked at Ben. "In that case, you should go. This is something I need to discuss with Kevin. Alone," I said as I rounded the counter and pushed Ben toward the door. Outside on the back deck, high above my father's studio, where the sounds of banging and cursing had ceased while Dad contemplated life and Catholicism at BHJ, I guided Ben toward the stairs.

"Wait," he said, his chef's coat moist beneath my hands from sweat or something else, I couldn't tell.

"What, Ben?" I asked. "I've been gone for over two months and that life, the one we had together, is over. You made that perfectly clear when you didn't come after me. When you didn't call."

"To here?" he asked. "To this hellhole? You hate it here. You told me yourself."

"It's not a hellhole," I said, and I was surprised to admit that. Foster's Landing had wrapped me in its warm embrace, the one where it was not unusual to awaken to the sounds of the train in the distance and, on a really clear night in the summer, the sound of a local band playing at the riverfront park. "I needed a break from all of that. From The Monkey's Paw. From New York." I looked into his eyes and seeing nothing that would ever draw me back in—and wondering why he ever had that power—said, "From you."

"From me?" he said. "Baby, you've got that all wrong."

"No, I don't," I said. "And don't call me baby."

He leaned in close and I got a good whiff of booze, sweat, and something else that smelled like dehydrated shiitake mushrooms. I wondered what in God's name— and yes, I took it in vain—I ever saw in this guy. Had the accent been enough? The good sex? The common goal of becoming top chefs, working at competing New York City restaurants but always remembering that we were one unit?

I decided, after I thought it through, that it had been two years of temporary insanity.

"What happened to you?" he asked. "You used to be fun. Now you're cooking at a bougie wedding hall and living in a dump."

"At least I didn't serve a life-threatening piece of snapper to a president," I said. Behind me I heard Taylor, the feral cat, let out a howl of approval.

"So there it is."

"There what is?"

"You blame me," he said. "For everything."

"And why wouldn't I?" I said. "You let me take the fall. You let Francesco treat me like garbage. You never said one word to defend me."

"One word: 'head chef,'" he said. "You were responsible for what left that kitchen."

"That's two words." I turned my back on him. because if I looked at his face any longer I would start crying and that would ruin everything. "Why are you here?"

"You never gave me the recipe for the bordelaise."

"You don't know how to make bordelaise without a recipe?" I asked. Any chef worth their salt—heck, any home cook worth their salt—knew how to make a bordelaise from scratch and memory. "Have you ever heard of Google? Allrecipes.com? You needed to come up here via train to ask me what the recipe is?"

"Max doesn't want to do the show anymore," he said, finally revealing why he was really here.

"Of course she doesn't," I said. Max Rayfield was the reason there had been any discussion at all about a reality show about The Monkey's Paw. She was a cable honcho and the restaurant was her favorite. It all came together except that it didn't; I didn't want to do the show. "She wanted to do the show with me, not some guy who can't make a bordelaise."

"She wanted a female chef," he said, spitting the words out with a venom they really didn't deserve.

"Well, that makes sense," I said. "Male chefs are a dime a dozen. She's no dummy."

He got red in the face. "What did I ever see in you?" he asked.

"Beauty. Brains. Talent," I said. "I thought that was obvious." It sounded better and more confident than I felt, but that was okay, given the circumstances.

Kevin appeared at the back door. "I think you'd better go," he said, and I wondered how anyone took him seriously. He looked like a kid playing dress up in his blazer and pants, his tie tight around his neck.

"You got it, Barney Fife," Ben said, hustling down the

steps. "You're done in New York, Bel. You know that, right?" he called after himself before disappearing out of sight.

I leaned over the railing. "And you need to know how to make a decent demi-glace to make a bordelaise, something you could never do!" I called after him, but he was gone.

I didn't look at Kevin until we were inside the apartment again, him assuming his position at the counter. I knew I was officially finished in New York. Thing was, I didn't know if I cared.

CHAPTER *Twenty-one*

Kevin was in cop mode when we finally got down to the business of why he was there. "So have you heard from Caleigh since she went on her honeymoon?"

"What kind of question is that?" I asked. "Would you call me if you were on your honeymoon in Bermuda?" He looked a little stricken, whether at the thought of being on a honeymoon or the thought of calling me while on said honeymoon I wasn't sure. "Let me rephrase that. Do you think Caleigh would call anyone while she was on her honeymoon? Why would she?"

"So, you haven't heard from Caleigh?" he said, jotting notes down in a little pad that I had seen on sale at the CVS for twenty-nine cents.

"No. I haven't heard from Caleigh."

"Mark?"

"Mark Chesterton has even less of a reason to contact me than my cousin. What's going on, Kevin?"

He toyed with the idea of not telling me anything; I could see it on his face. But in the end, he probably realized that there would be no harm in telling me, Bel, the disaster, where the investigation was headed, and he spilled it. "We found Declan Morrison's phone . . ."

Uh-oh.

". . . and discovered that he was texting Caleigh during the rehearsal dinner and the wedding."

I put on my best I'm ready for my close-up, Mr. De-Mille, face and gasped. "Really? On his phone?"

"On his phone," Kevin said, my overacting lost on him. "Did you know him?"

"Never saw him before the wedding," I said. Finally, back to the truth.

"But Caleigh knew him?" Kevin asked. "How could that be? You two are close. She never mentioned him? Never mentioned having a relationship with someone other than her fiancé? Her"—at this he started flipping through his CVS notebook—"third cousin once removed?"

"No, she never mentioned it."

He looked at me and the years melted away and we were back to where we started: me, Kevin, and Amy, a trio of friends, one of whom went missing and never returned, the other two trying to forge new lives in her absence. "What, Bel? What is it?"

"It's nothing, Kevin," I said. "I didn't know this guy and I didn't know that Caleigh knew this guy." My eyes went to the sugar jar on the counter, the one with the big shamrock painted on the front and the earring shoved deep down into the granules.

"Does she love Mark?"

That was a weird question, coming from Kevin. I thought about that for a moment. "I would say yes, but we have evidence to the contrary, don't we?" I looked at the pork belly, pink and flaccid on the plate in front of me. "Is she a suspect? Caleigh?"

"Everyone is a suspect," Kevin said.

"Well, Caleigh and Mark sure weren't when you let them go to Bermuda."

His face turned dark at the suggestion that I didn't think

he was good at his job. He wasn't. Yes, they had had alibis, but maybe there was more to the story. Heck, there *was* more to the story and now one of the key characters in that story was sipping champagne and getting her feet rubbed at a five-star hotel somewhere in the Atlantic. "Everyone is a suspect," Kevin said, his teeth clenched. "But they had alibis."

Hers was rather thin, if you asked me. Passed out and alone. How convenient.

"Even me? I'm a suspect?" I asked.

He thought about that for a minute. "Well, probably not you. You heard voices. You saw him come over the balcony. You saw him die." He studied my face. "At least that's what you told me."

It was the truth and I told him so. "I've never lied to you, Kevin," I said, the unspoken words indicting him. He had lied to me, more than once, and all these years later it still hurt, though I wasn't sure why. Lies. I thought about my mother, her lie about knowing Declan Morrison. The earring in the sugar, found right where the man had last been. "But everyone else?"

"Pretty much everyone at the wedding is a suspect," Kevin said.

I started naming the least possible suspects. "Jonesy Chesterton?"

"Suspect."

"Mark's mother?"

"Suspect."

I threw one out just to see Kevin's reaction. "My mother?" I don't know why I went there, but I did. Mom had been acting weird since that day, whether from the tragic event that had occurred or something else I wasn't sure.

He didn't answer, closing his notebook and standing. "Let me know if you talk to Caleigh before she comes back. Suffice it to say that we will be waiting for her upon her return." He grimaced; he wasn't supposed to tell me that. "But don't tell her." He rubbed a hand over his face. He was still getting used to this detective thing, obviously, finally realizing that the element of surprise would come in handier than the gun on his hip.

I walked him to the door. "Thanks for coming by, Kevin. I'm here to help in any way I can," I said, even though I didn't have a lot to offer in the way of information. What information I had once had and that I thought no one else knew was now in his possession. I hoped Caleigh was having a good time on her honeymoon, because it seemed like she was coming back to some unpleasantness, something that would make her little heart-shaped face crumble, her eyes fill with tears. Somehow, I imagined, she would get away with this, too. Just like she always did.

Kevin paused on the back deck. "One question, Bel?"

"Shoot."

"What did you see in him? That guy. Ben."

I chose not to answer, giving Kevin a little shrug instead. When he was gone and the only sound in the neighborhood was that of a dog barking in the distance I told Kevin the truth, even though he wasn't there.

"He wasn't you."

CHAPTER *Twenty-two*

Sunday dinner at my parents' house was a standard affair, with the entire clan coming together for two hours starting at five. We had missed last week's, for obvious reasons. I hoped everyone was in a good mood; the comments from the Damscott/O'Donnell wedding guests had been incredibly positive, bordering on glowing when it came to the food. One guest did remark that Feeney had sung off-key all night, but I hadn't heard any evidence of that. There hadn't been any events at the Manor that day, so after some basic maintenance—Dad hung a new painting in the foyer, a weird take on Vincent van Gogh's *Starry Night* but with the faces of various relatives dotting the sky instead of stars—and another sweep through the kitchen to make sure we were ready for the McCarthy wedding the following Saturday, we all assembled at the big handcrafted table that Dad had built during a snowstorm from two boat hatch covers and some leftover wrought-iron legs that he had purloined from a junkyard.

I had gotten a text from Brendan Joyce right before going downstairs; apparently, he hadn't been that put off by the morning's events and asked if I was free for dinner the next night. I offered to cook at my apartment, the breakfast I had promised him that morning not having gone as I wanted. "It's a date!" he had cheerfully replied, and I wondered if the guy was ever in a bad mood.

Before I went to dinner, I stopped by The Dugout and looked over Oogie's menu. Amy's brother, Jed, a local cop, was at the bar, eating a hot dog and drinking a pint of beer that was half foam.

"Hey, Bel," he said. "I heard you came back."

It wasn't the friendliest of greetings, but Jed had never been much of a wordsmith or a conversationalist.

"I'm back all right," I said, leaning against the bar. "Is your dad around?"

"In the back," Jed said, nodding toward the kitchen door. "You're helping him with the menu?"

"Sort of," I said. What Oogie was capable of from a culinary standpoint would severely limit the changes I was able to make. I was hoping to get him up to speed on your basic BLT, maybe a turkey burger, some sausage and peppers if we ever got to the point of combining ingredients.

"Menu doesn't need any help," Jed said.

Here we go again, I thought. Just like the conversation I had with Cargan about the Manor's menu, so would this conversation about The Dugout's menu go. "Nothing big," I said. "Just a few tweaks."

Jed hadn't looked at me up until this point, preferring to stare into his pint. "Doesn't matter, Bel."

"What doesn't matter, Jed?" I asked. I was losing the thread of this particular conversation.

He swept his hand around the bar. "This. Food." He turned and looked at me. "You. Your guilt."

I could feel the flush starting at my feet and moving up my body. "I'm not guilty," I said, but even to my ears it rang hollow, a little false.

"Sure you are," he said, draining his beer and getting to his feet. "We all are."

"I've got nothing to feel guilty about," I said.

He smiled, but it wasn't cheerful or pleasant, more of a grimace with some sarcasm laced into it. "Sure you do, Bel." He walked out of the bar and onto the street, stopping in front of the bar and looking out at the village for a few moments before moving on.

I was unsettled most of the day but tried to put it out of my mind as I ventured into my family home. Walking into the part of the house in which I grew up, I was assaulted with the smell of red cabbage bubbling away on the stove. Cabbage of any kind had had a kind of resurgence a few years back, becoming the new kale, which had replaced arugula as the hot veg, but it was still one of my least favorite foods. I felt as if I had eaten more cabbage in my lifetime than any one person should. Mom always added too much vinegar and not enough salt, and the effect was briny and mouth puckering in intensity. The only thing that saved the meal was the way that Mom roasted meat and I could also smell a fresh ham in the oven, which mitigated my disgust at the prospect of the red cabbage.

Your perfect summer meal. If you were Irish, of course.

Cargan was mashing potatoes with a hand masher, no electric mixer good enough for this task. "Hiya, Bel," he said. He was in his home jersey, his droopy shorts grass stained. "Great job on the O'Donnell wedding," he said, as if we had never had the conversation about my fancy food and how it would be a disaster to serve. "Everyone loved it."

I already knew that, having eavesdropped on the comments from the departing guests.

"And we won today," he continued. "Eduardo was amazing in goal."

"Excellent, Car," I said. "You'll have to let me know when your next game is so I can go."

His face lit up. To the best of my knowledge, not one of my brothers had taken the time to see Cargan play soccer, so engrossed in their own lives and squabbles that they couldn't focus on anyone else.

On the screened-in porch, which faced the back forty, as Dad called it, or the lawn that he tended to with the precision of a surgeon, were Arney and his wife, Grace; Derry and his wife, Maria, or the Eye-talian, as Uncle Eugene called her; and Feeney, with his latest conquest, a girl barely out of her teens and covered in tattoos with the bizarre moniker Sandree. "Her ma named her Sandy, but she didn't like it, so she sexed it up," Feeney had told me the first time we had met the lovely Sandree, she of the tattoo that ran up the length of her arm and was tribal in nature. When I had commented that she seemed a little young and perhaps "unfocused," Feeney had let me know that she had a thriving career as a manager of the local Old Navy and that was she twenty-one, "almost twenty-two." In eight months. Her birthday was in February, I had come to learn. That made her closer to twenty than twenty-two, but I let it slide. Feeney looked as happy as he could look when he was with her, and she certainly provided hours of entertainment, what with her "original guitar compositions" that she played for us after the first dinner we had together. She had Feeney's punk sensibilities, the ones he had to tamp down when he sang the standards at the weddings. "Your Tats Are Sick" was my favorite composition of hers followed by "My Pit Bull's Name is Red."

Aunt Helen also arrived shortly after I did, Dad handing her a gin and tonic with a squeeze of lime, her signature drink, as she walked in the door. Frank the Tank was by her side, but if history was any indication we wouldn't get much from him in terms of lively conversation. Helen collapsed heavily onto the wicker settee on the sunporch.

She wasn't as beautiful as my mother, and I suspected that had haunted Helen for her entire life by the way she sometimes behaved around her older sister. It also informed Helen's treatment of Caleigh—the "pretty one" as she liked to refer to her when I was around and probably when I wasn't—helping my cousin become someone who spent an inordinate amount of time on grooming. "Is this what it's like, Oona?"

Mom was placing a plate of cheese and crackers on the round, glass-topped coffee table, and the boys and Sandree descended on it like a pack of vultures. "Is this what what's like, Helen?"

"Marrying off your children. Being alone," she said. I looked over at the old Tank, wondering how he felt about this proclamation of solo-hood. She wasn't completely alone, obviously, but as my father liked to say, "Caleigh didn't lick it off the grass"—meaning that any character traits Caleigh had exhibited had come straight from her parents—when it came to high drama. Like mother, like daughter.

"You have me," Frank said.

Helen treated Frank like a doddering old man when, in reality, he was a robust fifty-eight. "Oh, yes, dear," she said. "I do."

"You're not alone, Helen," my father said, his booming voice filling the space. He had arrived from his studio in one of his patented studio outfits: paint-splattered clamdiggers and an oversized shirt, Adidas slides on his feet. One toe was completely covered in yellow paint, an inexplicable phenomenon. "You have us!" he said, sweeping his arms out to encompass the boys and their significant others, the kids playing outside on the back forty. His hand caught the ceiling fan with his grand gesture, twirling lazily above us, and a blade broke off, clattering onto the plate of cheese and crackers. Feeney swept it off and continued eating, handing Sandree a Triscuit with a slab of cheddar and a splinter from the blade, which I'm not even sure she picked off before putting the whole thing in her mouth.

"You've gained a son," Mom said, but that did nothing to mollify Aunt Helen, who was in a complete swoon over Caleigh's marriage. Nothing about the guy who died at the reception, but everything about Helen's new life as the mother of a married woman. "And a fine man, a wonderful provider and husband, at that." Mom looked over at me and I couldn't tell if she was telegraphing that I should keep my mouth shut about Mark or I should get on the stick and find my own Mark.

Sandree brought up the "troubles," as I had come to think of them. "That poor guy! The one who was murdered? That was awful!" she said to a cacophony of "oh, yes" and "we don't want to talk about that" and "let's focus on the positive!" coming from Mom, Dad, and Aunt Helen. "But really. A murder at a wedding? If it wasn't so horrible, it would be kind of cool," she said, Feeney poking her in the ribs. She looked at him, aggrieved. "Well, it is. Cool, that is. No one will ever forget it."

"A man is dead," Cargan said, having left the confines of the kitchen, his potato masher in his hands. "And I don't think that's 'cool,' Sandree."

"Shut it, Cargan," Feeney said.

"Make me." Cargan brandished the potato masher, ready to fend off whatever assault Feeney had planned. Yes, Feeney. My forty-year-old brother.

And we're off, I thought. I was surrounded by grown men with the intellectual and emotional capabilities of a bunch of fifteen-year-olds. Derry stood and took his wife's hand. "I think we'll see what the kids are doing."

Arney and Grace took their leave as well. "Yes, the kids. Make sure they aren't getting into any trouble."

I was left with Cargan, Mom, Dad, Helen, Feeney, and Sandree, wondering how a nice Sunday dinner could take such a nasty turn. Oh, right. It was my family. We had two emotions, when together: happiness and anger. There was nothing in between. I got up and got everyone a round of drinks. Two drinks in and things would calm down. Three and we would still be okay. Four and the "troubles" would start again. I decided I would be gone by that time, thinking about what a menu for dinner with Brendan Joyce might look like.

"Hey, Aunt Helen," I said. "While we're on the topic," I added, handing everyone drinks from the tray that I had found in the cupboard next to the refrigerator. "Who was Declan Morrison?" I asked. "Who invited him?"

Aunt Helen sniffed derisively. "He was no one. He was a party crasher."

Mom looked over at her sister, a crease in her brow. Worry. Concern. Something else.

"So you didn't invite him? Caleigh didn't, either?" I asked. "He told me he was her third cousin, once removed, which means that he must have been related to Uncle Jack."

"No!" Aunt Helen said.

"So, he just hopped a plane from Ireland, found Shamrock Manor, and came to the wedding?" My saying it out loud was proof of how preposterous the whole thing was.

"Yes, Bel. That's exactly what happened," Aunt Helen said, and I could tell that she was gearing up for an argument, even though I found that whole scenario hard to believe. Seems she had found a story and was sticking to it. Mom shot me a look, and in that look was the implication that if I asked another question I'd be eating dinner out by the shed. "There are people who do that, you know. Take advantage of situations. Crash parties. I don't know why you find that so hard to believe."

"Because it's ridiculous?" I said.

Cargan caught my eye and drew a finger across his neck. Why everyone was so blasé about a death at a wedding was beyond me, but that's where we were. I decided to let it go and steel myself for the assault to my system the red cabbage would bring.

I excused myself and went into the kitchen to get a glass of water, Cargan at my heels.

"Heard you're consulting on The Dugout's menu," he said, giving me a side eye as he checked his potatoes.

"You too?" I said.

"Me too what?"

"I saw Jed there today and he acted as if I had committed some kind of supreme misstep. I'm just trying to help the old guy. Having good food would up his game."

Cargan tasted his potatoes. "I don't think he wants to up his game," he said.

"Well, he should!" I said, not sure why it was important to me. Why it mattered. "Can't I do something nice for someone?"

Cargan shrugged. "I guess it depends on why you want to," he said, and left the kitchen.

Dinner was a rather low-key affair, with everyone on their best behavior after a rocky start. Mom's roast was the same as always: juicy, succulent, with a crispy skin. Her red cabbage? Meh. I pushed it around on my plate and could have sworn I heard Aunt Helen whisper, "Snob," as she cleared my plate, my dislike for cabbage now a character flaw, apparently.

Caleigh surely didn't lick it off the grass. No sirree.

I ate a slice of store-bought angel food cake and begged off a little after seven, citing some menu preparation that I wanted to undertake in advance of the McCarthy wedding.

"NOTHING FANCY!" Dad bellowed. "AND NO ROASTED PIGS!" Dad's entire being—his gestalt, so to speak—was lived in capital letters, exclamation points. I was used to it by now. I wondered how it flew with the guests at the Manor, the people who booked the joint. Maybe the high ceilings and the vast expanse of dance floor made him feel as if he had to say everything at the highest decibel. Maybe he was just loud. Or maybe he was going deaf. Who knew?

I headed outside and started around the house toward the steps leading to my apartment, passing Dad's studio, one light left on over the big wooden table in the center of the room. From inside I heard the cry of a cat, one who wanted to be outside yet was trapped inside. The door to the studio was locked, but Dad "hid" a key on top of the jamb, thinking no one knew that access to his artistic area was so available, but I reached up and there it was, just like always. I had hidden a lot of stuff in the studio over the years: a six-pack of beer, a pack of cigarettes (really, I was holding them for a friend), that one test that I got a 60 on because I hadn't studied. For all I knew, it was still in there, along with a pair of jeans that I had spent eighty dollars on and the shoes that my mother had pronounced "slutty" and which I promised I had returned but which I had kept and worn with glee when she wasn't around.

Inside, I called for the cat, knowing full well that she didn't know her name but giving it a try nonetheless. "Taylor!" I poked around, looking under boxes and around canvases, but couldn't find her. "Taylor!" I said a little louder, going into the small room in the back where I had found Dad a few days earlier, standing over a box marked "ART." No cat in sight. I picked up a canvas that had fallen and put it on top of the box, noticing that where it had once been sealed shut, it was now open a little bit. From inside I heard the mournful cry of Taylor or some other wayward cat. I would soon find out which it was.

I pulled the lid back from the box of supposed art and

peered inside, waiting a few seconds for my eyes to adjust in the dark of the windowless room. The cat was in there all right, and indeed it was Taylor, but what she was sitting atop wasn't "art."

AK-47s, one stacked atop another, were in the box, the little cat peering up at me from the place she had nestled in beside them.

CHAPTER *Twenty-three*

It took me a long time to go to sleep that night and even longer for me to get up the guts to go to the Manor the next morning and face my parents, one of whom was a liar (Mom) and the other of whom was most likely an arms dealer (Dad). The thought of those two things made my stint at The Monkey's Paw, my almost assassination of the former president, and my fending off a knife-wielding actor seem like child's play.

Dad was a patriot for both his native Ireland and for the good old U.S. of A. But was he such a patriot that he thought that hoarding guns—and maybe sending them back over to his homeland—was a patriotic thing to do? I worried on this and the repercussions of someone finding Dad's stash most of the night. Eugene was supposedly the ne'er-do-well in the extended family, but I wondered if I had made that up in my mind, that the rumors that swirled in my childhood had grown in magnitude over the years, that my brothers had stoked the gossip fires. Dad was the good guy. But between the guns and the murder I couldn't figure out what was going on exactly, and that troubled me.

Not Dad. Never Dad. He was a kind and decent soul, not a renegade. I was sure of that.

I had tossed and turned most of the night but finally dragged myself over to the kitchen at the Manor the next

morning to try out some of the ideas I had come up with
for appetizers. They weren't anything special, just some
tried-and-true treats that might make it past the Irish clientele Mom and Dad seemed to cultivate and appeal to.
Bruschetta on toasted garlic bread; a goat cheese tart; a
chicken *satay* skewer. Nothing that was going to set the
culinary world on fire but a step up from the frozen canapés and pigs in a blanket that were standard fare at the
Manor.

I cooked for a while, avoiding anyone in my family. Dad
was in the foyer doing some additional repair work on the
broken banister and Mom's voice could be heard coming
from the office, her tone low, like she was whispering. I
stepped toward the door of the office that led into the
kitchen; it was ajar. Mom was doing her best to be heard
by the person on the other end but no one else, her back
turned to the kitchen door, the sound of Dad's hammering almost drowning out her side of the conversation.

"Helen, we have talked about this repeatedly. No one
knows. No one will ever know. But for Christ's sake, if you
continue acting like this, people will become suspicious."

I had never heard my mother take the Lord's name in
vain and I wasn't sure what had me more upset—that she
was harboring some secret that Helen seemed to know
about or that it had her so upset that she had actually said
"Christ" in anger. She was quiet for an extended period
while she listened to Aunt Helen, whose voice was traveling through the phone and into the space of the office, her
words loud but unintelligible. "Helen, calm down. I have
work to do and can't spend my days worrying about something like this." She waited as Helen perseverated some
more. "I've got to go. Good-bye," she said, swinging
around and firmly placing the phone on the receiver.

Surprised by the speed at which the call ended and seeing the realization dawn on my mother's face when she

saw something—my checkered pants, my white coat, my wide eyes—in the space where the door was open, I fell into the office, falling into the chair in front of the desk. "Mom, hi," I said.

"Belfast," she said, the wheels turning in her head, figuring out how much I had heard, if she should ask. "Do you need something?"

I realized I was holding a skewer of chicken *satay*. "Want to try this?" I asked, proffering the hors d'oeuvre. "It's going to be new on the menu for the McCarthy wedding this Saturday."

She studied the skewer and finally, after much examination, tasted it. "Well, it's lovely, dear. Just the right amount of spice."

My parents hate spice. Spice, to them, is salt and salt alone. This was high praise indeed. "Do you want to try a few of the others?" I asked.

"No, I trust you. I'm sure they are delicious." She patted her flat midsection, the one I hadn't inherited. "That was Aunt Helen," she said after a few moments of awkward silence.

"I gathered."

"She's upset."

"About what?"

Mom sighed. "It's complicated, honey. I'd rather not go into it."

"Is she okay?" I asked.

"Yes, she's fine," Mom said, and looked down at the ledger in front of her. "Dad and I were talking and we'd like to start advertising that we have a world-renowned chef at the Manor now. Is that okay with you?"

"Well, I don't know how long I'm staying," I said, reminding her of the thing I thought everyone knew. I wasn't long for here even if all of the signs pointed to the contrary. "And I'm not sure I'm 'world renowned.'"

"Just to get us some business in the summer and maybe the fall," she said. "And you are. World renowned, that is."

"Wouldn't most summer and early-fall brides have booked their weddings by now?" I asked, wondering at this crack marketing plan. It was clear to me that Mom thought I was never leaving.

"There's always the possibility that we get some last-minute bookings," she said. "And I'd like everyone to know that you're here and that Shamrock Manor has updated her look"—if she meant the Bobby Sands bust in the lobby, well, that was a stretch—"and that the food is incomparable." She looked up at me, the redlined ledger with proof that the Manor was going down the tubes all the ammunition she needed.

"Sure, Mom," I said. "Advertise away."

"Fabulous," she said. "I'll have Sandree take your photo."

"Old Navy Sandree?" I asked. Feeney's girlfriend didn't strike me as a sophisticated lensman, her skills at selfies undeniable but not supporting her ability to take others' photos.

"Yes. She's got one of those iPhones with the nice camera and I can have her take your photo at Sunday dinner."

"No need, Mom," I said. "I have a head shot from when The Monkey's Paw opened. We can use that."

"Oh," Mom said, looking, in that moment, as if she was wondering what else she didn't know about me, the one-time big-city girl who cooked for presidents and had a professional photo of herself tucked away in an old copy of *Bon Appétit*. "Do you look nice in it?"

"Do you mean do I look thin?" I said, more annoyed than I should have been, but what she didn't know about me couldn't hold a candle to what I didn't know about my own parents. The earring in the sugar. The guns. The preposterous third cousin once removed, now dead. "I have been airbrushed within an inch of my life."

"That's not what I meant," she said, looking down at her ledger, the red numbers indicating failure.

Point taken. The Manor was going under and I was here to help right the ship. "I'm sorry, Mom. Yes, I look nice and it's a great photo and you should definitely use it and me to drum up business for the place. The same guy who takes Oprah's photos took it."

"Oprah?" Now I had her attention.

"Yes. Whatever you need to do. I'm available."

"Thank you, Belfast."

I stood there for another minute, staring at my mother staring at the ledger, listening to my father banging away in the foyer, doing what came normally to him, nothing making it seem as if he was worried that he could outfit a splinter terrorist group with the number of guns in his studio. No, what was their concern right now was a failing business and a broken banister.

Why was I the only one worried about everything else, namely, the guy who had broken the banister in the first place? I went back into the kitchen and looked down at the hors d'oeuvres I had arranged on a silver tray, finally popping a piece of chicken in my mouth and wondering how to get the truth out of two of the most tight-lipped people I knew.

CHAPTER *Twenty-four*

I finished up my work, texted Fernando and offered him a full-time position after clearing it with Mom, and hung my apron by the walk-in. I wrapped up the hors d'oeuvres I had made after Dad turned his nose up at them and refused to eat them, and planned to bring them to my apartment, figuring that the starving Brendan Joyce would enjoy them. Guy seemed to eat anything happily and without complaint.

Before I went back to the apartment, I went into Dad's studio and poked around a bit more. Dad was still in high dudgeon while working on the banister, which would keep him occupied for a while, and Mom was sinking into a further depression while looking at the books and seemed unable to move. I hoped that behind the bizarre paintings of birds—a newfound avocation, it seemed—cans of paint and turpentine, and pieces of scrap metal for his "installations" there wouldn't be any more ammunition or firearms.

Cargan poked his head into the studio at one point, scaring the life out of me. "Whatcha doing?" he asked. Today, he was dressed in soccer training pants, athletic slides like Dad wore, and a Messi jersey, Messi being some kind of *fútbol* Messiah.

I grabbed my heart and thankfully did not fall into the canvas painted with giant eagles, leaving a clue as to my presence in Dad's studio. "Jesus, Cargan. You scared me." I stood upright and adjusted the other canvases. I took a few deep breaths. "Just looking at Dad's work. It's fantastic."

"No, it's not," Cargan said. "It's terrible. And everywhere I go, I see it."

"Is he selling it?" I asked.

"No, he just hangs it places around town like he owns everything. People are too afraid to tell him that they don't want it." He pulled at the neck of his jersey. "You know how Dad is."

"Pigheaded? Loud? Blustery?"

"Stubborn," Cargan said, getting right to the point. "So what are you doing here?"

"Looking at Dad's art," I said.

Cargan looked at me, not convinced.

"Really. Just wanted to see what direction he was heading in. Artistically speaking, that is."

"Looks like you were looking for something."

How could one man be so dense and yet so perceptive? He was like this as a kid, too; just when you thought something had gone over his head, he would say something insightful or profoundly intelligent and leave us all with our mouths hanging open. He had once pronounced one of Dad's pieces "almost Modiglianian in execution," and while Feeney had thought Cargan had said something dirty and had guffawed loudly, I knew enough about art to know that not only had he said the artist's name correctly and with a flawless Italian accent, but he was right: Dad's work did almost look like a Modigliani. If you were kind of blind, but still. Despite the fact that in this instance Cargan was right again, I didn't want to let him on what was happening. "Hey, Cargan," I said, attempting to throw him off the scent, "I never asked you."

"What?"

"Declan Morrison, the guy at the wedding."

"You mean the dead guy?"

"Yes, the dead guy," I said, as if there were another Declan Morrison in our lives. Scratch that; maybe there was.
We Irish tend to gravitate toward the same names over and
over, which was why I had fourteen cousins named Kath-
leen and Ballyminster had their fair share of Declans. "Did
you know him?"

"No, Bel. Never saw him before in my life. Come to
think of it, didn't even see him at the wedding." He looked
up at the ceiling. "No, that's not right. I did see him at the
wedding." He went silent, apparently thinking that that
was enough of an answer.

"And?"

"And what?"

"And what was he doing? Did you talk to him?"

Cargan thought that over for so long that I wondered if
he had forgotten the question. "He was arguing."

I waited.

"With Mark Chesterton. Caleigh's husband."

I let out a little *oomph* of surprise. "Did you tell Kevin
Hanson?"

"He never asked."

"He didn't question you?" I asked. Now the idea of
looking for guns seemed passé, the text of Mark and Declan's argument much more important. "You didn't offer
him this information?"

"He did question me. And I think I mentioned it, but I
can't remember. I think I forgot about it until this moment."
Cargan picked up a paintbrush, still wet, and brandished
it like a sword, feeling the heft of the handle in his hand.
"Kevin said I had an alibi because I was playing music
while the whole thing went down."

True enough. But what about finding out what Cargan
might have known or might have seen? No use in asking

that? I wondered how I could send an anonymous message to Lieutenant D'Amato, letting him know that even though I had buried the past with Kevin and we had reached détente, he was still as dim as a 25-watt bulb. Still cute, but still dim. "You need to tell Kevin, Car. Make sure he knows."

"Tell him that I saw them arguing?" he asked. "I figured it was over the fact that Declan crashed. That's what Mom said anyway."

Mom. Spit polishing the truth once again. "Let's go see Kevin right now." I walked past the giant table in the middle of the room and led my brother outside. "We can walk to the station."

Cargan was hesitant, his jersey stretched between us, me pulling and him holding back. "Oh, I don't know, Bel. It didn't seem like a big thing at the time. Just a little spat."

I took my brother by the shoulders and pressed down, trying to make my point. "Everything related to a murder is a big thing, Car. Everything."

He knew that resistance was futile. We argued about that as we walked down the path from Shamrock Manor into the village and through the front door of the police station, housed in an old Tudor that was original to the area. Kevin was standing at a desk in the front; I recognized its inhabitant as Francie McGee, a classmate of Arney's whom he had escorted to the junior prom, an event that had been held, conveniently, at the Manor.

"Hi, Francie. Hi, Kevin," I said. I motioned toward an office in the back, not sure if it was Kevin's but knowing we needed some privacy. If I recalled correctly, Francie was a bit of a gossip, a trait that got a good workout from her current position as receptionist at the FLPD. Francie looked at me, acting as if she didn't believe her eyes. The last time she had seen me, I was ten years old probably and trying to get a peek at her making out with my brother in the coat-check room at the Manor.

"Bel McGrath?" she asked. "Nice to see you. What brings you here?" she said, and by the lilt in her voice, the excitement lurking beneath the banal questions, I could tell that she had lapped up every salacious detail of my removal from The Monkey's Paw and the murder at the Manor. She was apparently the one *Times* reader in Foster's Landing.

"Just need a word with Detective Hanson," I said, my hand firmly on my brother's forearm, guiding him toward the room at the back of the open office area. Kevin followed behind me and, once inside the room, turned on the light and closed the door.

"What can I do for you, Bel?" he asked, leaning back against a credenza, his hands in his pockets.

I gave Cargan a little poke. "My brother has something to tell you."

"Cargan?" Kevin said.

Cargan turned a deep red before all of the blood drained from his face and he went white. Kevin pulled out a chair and led him to it, pouring him a cup of water from a cooler next to the credenza. He put his hand on my brother's shoulder, showing sensitivity to someone he had known most of his life.

"Bel, why don't you give us some privacy so we can have a chat?" Kevin asked. I reluctantly allowed him to walk me to the door and he gave me a look as I exited that conveyed he had my brother's best interests at heart. I had no choice; I had to trust him. I left the room and wandered over to Francie's desk, figuring I could catch up on the intervening years and what she had been doing beyond answering the phone and any 911 calls at the police department.

I settled into a chair across from Francie's desk, giving

her a wan smile. "Do you like working here?" I asked, not much else to talk about now that my brother was behind closed doors, alone, with one of Foster's Landing's finest.

"I do!" she said, whipping a pen out of a carousel and making a great show of writing something in a notebook. "Something different every day."

"Hmmm," I said, not sure I wanted to know what those somethings were. I prayed that they didn't include any members of my family. I know that Dad had spent more than a night or two at the station bailing Feeney out after one or the other of his punk performances, with his band Bleeding Heart of Jason (yes, he's going to hell), a group who wore their old CYO jerseys. One night at the local VFW hall (which one could rent for a song) had turned into a night we would all like to forget, with Feeney ending up in the one cell in the Tudor's basement.

"You've been gone a long time, Bel," Francie said, not looking at me. "Long time."

"Yes. I moved to New York."

"I guess you had to get out," she said, studying the day planner on her desk.

"Of New York?" I said.

"Yeah, there too."

"You mean the Landing?" I wasn't following her line of questioning.

She made a little noise, affirmative and judgmental all at once.

I sank further in my chair. Because of Amy? Because of the last night we were together? I didn't ask. I didn't have to.

"Because of Amy," Francie said, clucking sadly. "Poor girl. Poor parents. The worst thing that can happen: your child goes missing and is never found."

The second worst? Being the girl's best friend and years later having someone like Francie McGee—and others;

I'm sure she wasn't alone in her thoughts—assign some kind of guilt to you. Some kind of responsibility. I stayed silent.

An hour ticked by and then another one. I texted Brendan Joyce my apologies and told him he would have to take a rain check. The length of time I had been here was a sign that something wasn't going according to the original plan, wherein Cargan would tell Kevin what he knew, we would leave, and Kevin would carry on with his investigation. No, something was definitely wrong.

Into the third hour, Kevin opened the door to the room where he and my brother had been talking and strode across the room, none of the other cops in the area really taking note of him. His mouth was set in a grim line, but he waited until he reached me to tell me what was going on, whispering into my ear so that Francie McGee, she of the fancy pen and pencil carousel, couldn't hear what he was saying.

"Your brother wants a lawyer." Kevin paused. "Preferably not Arney."

Arney specialized in divorce cases and not particularly well, particularly since his clientele was mostly Irish, all Catholic, and thought that divorce was a mortal sin. Business was not exactly booming. I wasn't surprised that Cargan didn't want Arney to represent him. I tried to remain expressionless but wasn't sure how successful I was.

"And a ham sandwich. Hold the mustard."

CHAPTER *Twenty-five*

There was no way to handle this without involving my parents. I could handle the ham sandwich on my own, but I had to let them know that Cargan was at the FLPD and that something was afoot. Needless to say, when I found them at the Manor, both in the office, my father rubbing my mother's feet, they weren't happy.

"What now?" my mother said, pulling her feet out of my father's hands so quickly that she nearly upended herself on her swivel desk chair. "Your brother is where?"

"This doesn't have anything to do with that night at the pool, does it?" Dad asked.

"What? Pool?" I asked. "No." I had to return to that later. "He told me that he had seen Declan Morrison and Mark Chesterton arguing at the wedding, so I took him to see Kevin."

"You did what?" my mother asked, her face turning the color of the pig I had roasted a week before.

Dad was silent. Mom had been protective of Cargan always, casting him in the role of the one who needed protecting, simple almost. I could never figure out why; he had friends in school and had even dated a girl—another one besides Amy—in my class for a couple of months before settling into a life in Foster's Landing that revolved around soccer and the Manor. He was smart in his own way and, if I had to rank them, would put him as the best musician among my brothers, the one who crafted interesting arrangements for the band or who put songs together for a set that allowed people to whoop it up for just as long as they needed before settling into a nice waltz to catch their breath. He had been an all-Ireland fiddle champion three years running, much to the chagrin of the hometown crowd in Ireland, who grudgingly admitted that he was the best there was and that no one in all thirty-two counties could touch him musically. There was a time when he traveled extensively as a musician, his fiddle paying his ticket out of Foster's Landing. He had returned eventually and seemed to be stuck here now after the years before that took him far and wide. Why my mother insisted on treating him as if he were special in some way, in need of constant encouragement and guidance, was something I never understood but, to my mind, had kept him as a sort of man-child in the family, someone whom no one else really took seriously.

"He had to tell, Kevin, Mom. It was the right thing to do."

"Well, Detective Hanson should have been a bit more diligent in his questioning earlier, don't you think?" she asked, her beautiful face hard, unyielding.

I don't know how this had become my fault, but it had. I decided not to argue with her and to just give her the facts. "He wants a lawyer and a ham sandwich. I'll handle the ham sandwich. Can you handle the lawyer?" I asked.

She looked at my father. "Call Arney."

"Not Arney. A different lawyer," I said. "You can ask Arney for a recommendation, but he doesn't want his brother there."

That seemed to incense Mom more than anything. "I am not going to pay good money to someone else when we have a lawyer in the family. Someone who, I might remind you, nearly bankrupted this family by attending law school for far longer than any law student should."

"And how is *that* my fault?" I asked. Yes, I had a list of transgressions that were kept in my mother's brain—the time I knocked Feeney's front teeth out accidentally with a golf club at the top of the list—but Arney attending law school for an extra year should not have been one of them. "Listen, if you want to consult with Arney McGrath, attorney-at-law, I can't stop you, but Cargan asked specifically that he not be involved."

Dad stood, coming back to life. "I'll call Paul Grant."

I had known "Paul" when I was in high school; he was two years behind me and named "Philip" at the time. He was one of the few WASP kids among a bunch of blue-collar Irish and Italian spawn and his sister had graduated with Arney and gone on to Harvard, something that no one before in Foster's Landing had seemed to aspire to or really given much thought to pursuing. Philip was a nerdy kid who had been the belittled and abused water boy for the basketball team and the football team, never having made either team himself, but he seemed to be having the last laugh: he had married Jackie O'Leary of the Society Lane O'Learys, a gorgeous girl who had long legs and was rumored to have had the same breast implant surgeon as Kim Kardashian. He had three whip-smart kids, from what I understood, one of whom Mom said had competed on *Jeopardy!*, during "that infernal kids' week," she had said, a *Jeopardy!* purist at heart. I had seen Paul Grant's signs around town; his office was conveniently located next to the one building that had medical offices. "Slip and fall? Call Paul!" were some of the witty bon mots to adorn his ads. Rumor had it that he had changed his name to Paul because it rhymed with "fall" and that since Paul was an apostle, the Irish in town might be more inclined to hire him. It was a stretch, in my opinion, because Foster's Landing only had one attorney prior to Philip/Paul's hanging out a shingle and that had been Philip Grant, Sr. It wasn't a stretch to think that Philip Jr. would follow his dad into the family business. I just hoped Paul was a better attorney than he was an ad mastermind. I remembered that as a kid he wore far too much Old Spice cologne for anyone, let alone a fifteen-year-old boy, and called everyone, girls included, "son," in some attempt to sound hip.

Mom stood up behind the desk, leaning forward. "And why does Cargan need a lawyer?" she asked. "Let's start at the beginning."

I had asked Kevin that exact question, but he had been vague. He said my brother felt more comfortable with someone in the legal profession in the room, that Kevin's questions were making him "nervous." Any questions made Cargan nervous and he was always stubbornly obtuse. Obviously, this had to do with the types of questions Kevin was asking and Cargan was afraid to screw things up even more than I had to this point. "I'm not sure, Mom. Let's let Paul handle it with Kevin. I'm sure everything is fine. You know how Car gets when there are too many questions thrown at him."

She narrowed her eyes, keeping them trained on me. "This is not how I expected this day to go, Belfast."

Yes, on a scale of 1 to 10, with 10 being that your business was going under and 1 the crate of eggs never being delivered from the local farm, this was about a 22. Sorry I ruined your middle-aged foreplay, otherwise known as a "foot massage."

My father stood stock still by the door, not saying a word. A mad Oona was not a good thing, and while Mom's ill wind only blew through every so often, everyone took cover when it did.

"Me either, Mom, but now that it's going this way, I'll leave the attorney issue to you and I'll make Cargan a ham sandwich." When no one moved, I said, "Agreed?"

Mom shuddered as if to shake off the cobweb of disappointment that had enveloped her, and picked up the phone. She was yelling at my dad to find Paul's number so that they could get him over to the station.

As I assembled a sandwich for my brother, I thought about just what he could possibly need a lawyer for. I hoped it was just standard Cargan overreaction to a simple situation. He watched a lot of television at night in the bedroom that he had once shared with Feeney and still resided in and a lot of his viewing, when it wasn't *fútbol*, of course, was related to detective shows, various iterations of the *Law & Order* franchise, which seemed to be on every channel, every day, at every hour. Maybe he had watched one too many episodes and decided that no one should talk to the police without a lawyer. Maybe that was it.

I could only hope. I cut the crusts off his sandwich, sliced it diagonally, and wrapped it in foil, grabbing a piece of leftover cake from the O'Donnell wedding and adding that to the haul that I was bringing back to the police station.

Dad cornered me in the foyer, just as I was about to leave. "This was a bad idea, Belfast," he said.

I went for broke. "You know what's an even worse idea, Dad?" I said. "Keeping a bunch of guns in your studio."

I could see the wheels turning in his head, practically see smoke coming out of his ears as he thought up a response. "Ah, Belfast," was all he could muster.

"Dad," I said, trying to keep my voice at a whisper. "Why? Is Uncle Eugene still involved in bad stuff? Are you trying to cover for him?" A more sinister thought floated through my head. "You? Are you doing—"

My questioning had given him enough time to come up

with an answer, the lightbulb going off over his head, so to speak, and he cut me off. "An installation!"

I studied his face for some indication that he would change his answer and tell me the truth, but all that was transmitted was his pleasure at coming up with a lie on short notice. When it was clear that that was his story and he was sticking to it, I left.

I trudged back down the hill away from the Manor, needing the bucolic surroundings of the Manor's grounds to help me get into a better head space over this whole thing, my role in it. I wondered just what it was that made my brother "lawyer up," as they say.

CHAPTER Twenty-six

I delivered the sandwich and was told to wait at the front of the station, having tried to get a look at Cargan in the conference room and failed. Lieutenant D'Amato blustered by, gave a couple of orders that sounded fake—just what was a "forty-seven-sixty-nine?"—and went into his office. The cop whom he told to patrol the perimeter of the village pool—a "three-ten-ninety-two" in progress—a place where no one went because of the drought, a place that was gated at night according to Brendan, looked just as confused as I did at the order. Something told me that the Lieutenant was just a wee bit uncomfortable with today's turn of events, the son of Oona McGrath, a woman everyone knew the widowed Lieutenant was sweet on despite the ring on her finger and faithful husband, in police custody. Who could blame the guy? Mom was a flirt, plain and simple. And everyone knew it.

Except for Dad.

Maybe she could flirt Cargan out of an obstruction of justice charge. Or worse. She was that good.

The Lieutenant nodded at me as he passed to go into his office. "Belfast."

"Lieutenant." I looked down at my lap so as not to make eye contact with anyone else in the office. Mom and Dad still hadn't shown up and I could imagine them frantically calling Paul Grant, telling him the story in that back-and-forth style that they used—Dad starting a sentence and Mom finishing it—and probably confusing the hell out of the attorney, our only hope.

Mom was usually the cool customer, leaving the emotional outbursts and carrying on to Dad. I thought back to the day of the wedding, thinking about whether anything seemed out of the ordinary with them, if having a wedding crasher had dampened her spirits at all, knowing, as I did, that everyone seemed rather chummy with Declan Morrison prior to his untimely demise. But all I could think of was Mom in that impeccably cut dress, the high heels, her smile as she went round and round during the spinning portion of the Siege of Ennis, literally kicking up her heels. There hadn't been a trace of discomfort on her face, in her demeanor. It had been the usual Oona McGrath hostess show, the lady of the Manor, the iron maiden, running the place with her usual aplomb and strictness.

"She raised four sons," the women at the wedding had whispered, "and look at her."

Yes, there was a daughter, too, but apparently that didn't count, especially when you spoke of how wonderful an Irishwoman—an Irish *mother*—in her sixties looked after breeding and bringing up four rapscallions, one more trouble than the next.

If they only knew.

The nicest one, the one all of the mothers thought would be perfect for their fair lasses, was sitting a few feet away from me in a conference room, probably near tears at this point, thinking that he was in some kind of major trouble he would never escape.

Paul Grant stormed into the station about a half hour later, his curly hair sticking up wildly, a Hawaiian shirt announcing that he hadn't planned on working that evening. He greeted me like a long-lost friend. "Belfast!" he bellowed. "Great to see you!" He went into some stock small talk that didn't apply to me. "How's the hubs? Kids?"

"No 'hubs' and no kids, Philip," I said. "Just me and my cat," I added, taking ownership of a feral animal that wanted no part of me unless there was salmon in a pouch to be had.

"Cat?" he said, rubbing the beard he had grown to give him some gravitas, or so I suspected. That had been the one thing he had going for him in high school: the ability to grow facial hair in the course of a school day. I could see his mind working and reviewing the file in his brain of all things Belfast McGrath; clearly, he had a home subscription to the *Times,* because the look on his face told me that he knew what had happened. That and the fact that he took a step backward, bumping into Francie's desk, led me to believe that he thought I might cut him at the slightest provocation.

"So, I'm going to see your brother now," he said, backing up slowly and keeping an eye on me as he made his way to the conference room, feeling behind him for sharp objects while making sure I didn't pull any out myself.

Kevin left the room a few seconds later to give the client and his attorney a chance to talk. He came over and took a seat next to me so that while we talked we didn't have to look at each other.

"What's going on in there?" I asked. Before he could answer, I held up a hand. "I know. You can't say."

"I can't."

We sat in silence for a few minutes. "So, how's Mary Ann?"

"She's good," he said, nodding. "She's good." As if saying it twice made it twice as true.

What I really wanted to ask him was how long he planned on dating her, if he ever planned on proposing. I could imagine Lieutenant D'Amato being pleased with the longest courtship on record for his only daughter. "And work?"

"Work's good. It's good."

Francie clocked out for the night, making a great show of punching an actual time card into an actual time card machine. I hadn't seen one of those since my stint working as a line cook at the BHJ convent, a place that housed three dozen nuns, all of whom took a turn at one point or another asking me if I had gotten "the call" or if God had sent me a private message to become a nun. He (or She) hadn't. And if He (or She) had, I probably would have ignored it, my contrary nature having been set in stone at a young age. The universe didn't have that good a sense of humor.

Francie now out of the picture, Kevin relaxed a bit. "I don't know, Bel. Cargan seems mighty troubled by something."

"Does he now?"

"Something about Declan Morrison being his 'mate' and how he wished he could change what happened that day."

His mate? Really, I thought. Cargan had told me they had never met. I shifted uncomfortably in the molded-plastic chair. "That doesn't sound terribly incriminating." Behind the closed doors of the conference room I could hear Paul's usually booming voice, now muffled, and the lower tones of my brother's voice.

"It's not. But he seems to know more than he's saying and he's being very tight-lipped." Kevin pulled a piece of candy from his pocket, a caramel, and handed it to me. "And then there was the asking-for-a-lawyer-thing."

"He watches a lot of *Law and Order*," I said, by way of explanation. And there was the short-lived stint in the police academy a long time ago, a place he left and from where he took off to roam the land with his fiddle, law enforcement not for him.

Kevin gave a little chuckle. "Most of our 'customers' do. Not a lot of what they see on those shows is entirely accurate."

"Don't tell Cargan that," I said. "Those are the only shows he watches." I turned the caramel over in my hand, a memory seeping into my brain, Kevin slipping me candy during Geometry in sophomore year, Amy pegging the move as one designed to get Kevin into my good graces after a year of pining for me, not very discreetly. He had been smart enough to know even back then that the way to my heart was with food, and that much hadn't changed, on either of our accounts. "Really, Kevin, I think you should let him go. Give him some time. I'll talk to him, see what else he knows."

Kevin shook his head. "You know I can't do that, Bel." He looked at me. "Have you given any more thought to the hypnotist?"

I hadn't. And wouldn't.

"See what you know, maybe?" He stood. "We use someone great. A local. Beverly Dos Santos."

"Bev?" I said. "From the Post Office? Beverly is a hypnotist?"

"And psychic healer," Kevin said, as if he, or anyone, knew what that meant.

Before I could express more incredulity, Paul emerged from the conference room. "My client is ready to make a statement," he said, his Hawaiian shirt looking even more preposterous as he made the statement. I hadn't noticed the full-length hula girl that ran up the left side, looking expectantly at Paul's bearded face, as if she were waiting for an answer to some question about hula dancing.

"Yes!" I said, blurting out the one word I hadn't meant to say.

Kevin stopped midway to the conference room. "Yes?"

"Yes. I will be hypnotized," I said, the look on Paul's

face, concern mixed with sadness, all I needed to see to convince me that if I could help in any way and that help involved being hypnotized by the lady who sold my mother stamps, then I was in.

"You will?"

I stood. "I will. Get Beverly over here." I walked over to Paul and grabbed him by the arm, crushing the erupting volcano on his shirt. I whispered in his ear, "Hold him off. I don't know what he plans on saying, but you don't have much of a poker face, so what Cargan plans to say concerns me."

"Okay, Bel." Paul turned to Kevin. "There's been a change in plans. My client would like to consult with me further, so we will need more time."

Kevin looked a little stunned so I gave him a gentle push toward a desk with a phone.

"Call Bev."

CHAPTER Twenty-seven

I learned later that Beverly Dos Santos had been born Spring Lake Autumn Winter in Woodstock during the Summer of Love to Marcia and David Winter, two hippies from Massapequa who still lived close to where the epic concert had taken place. It was all right there on her Web site, complete with a list of things that she purported to be:

Pet Psychic
Crystal Healer
(Regular) Psychic [her parentheses . . . not mine]
Wholistic [*sic*] healer
Hypnotist
Nutritionist
[And finally and inexplicably] Clown

Thankfully, when she showed up at the police station she was not in her clown persona but in full-on hypnotist mode. Or maybe it was (regular) psychic mode. It was hard to tell. She studied my face for a minute.

"You have a lot of pain."

"Not really."

"You do. It's in here," she said, clutching her breast.

My breasts were fine, one of my best features, in my and several others' opinion.

"Your heart," she said, making the shape of a heart with her hands. "It's broken."

"It's really not," I said.

"It is. You just don't know it."

Now, I'm not the most self-aware person in the world perhaps, but my heart was no longer broken. It had been— two times to be exact—but right now it was whole and really kind of mended. And the mending was recent, but still, it was all better. Maybe.

"Someone still loves you."

I looked at Kevin, but he looked away and blushed. She looked at him, too. I'd deal with that later.

"And the cat isn't yours," she said.

My mind flashed on Taylor. "I know she isn't."

"She will never be yours. And she's a 'he.'"

"Got it, Bev. The cat, a boy, isn't mine."

She studied me for a few more minutes, her long blondish-grayish hair hanging halfway down her back. I could just hear my mother if she came into contact with her knowing she felt a woman her age should have a short cut, a bob at the very least. My mother's thoughts as to what "a woman her age," basically anyone over forty, should be doing were well-known. "Shall we get to work?" Beverly asked.

Since the police station only had one conference room, and I use that term loosely, Kevin asked Cargan and Paul to move to a desk where they sat across from each other, Cargan looking forlorn and downtrodden and Paul punching away at his phone, probably sending Khan Academy links to one of the little Grant geniuses. Paul certainly didn't seem interested in my brother or his sadness. I shot Cargan a look and put my hand over my mouth to telegraph,

Not one more word. He gave me a little nod to tell me that he understood.

I didn't have a lot of hope for the session, but I wasn't beyond giving it the old college try. I settled into another of Foster's Landing Police Department's uncomfortable chairs and tried to arrange myself in a way that made me open to Beverly Dos Santos's suggestions of "deep sleep." Thoughts of onions flooded my mind.

The last thing I remember was Kevin's look of concern, Bev's instruction to relax, my saying, "This isn't working," and the clock on the wall ticking away, the time now five thirty. My eyes fluttered open again and the clock—which I was sure someone had messed with while I had my eyes closed—now said six seventeen and Kevin's look had changed from concern to confusion.

Beverly looked at me. "How are you feeling?"

I stretched my arms over my head. "Wow. I feel great," I said, letting my head roll around on my neck for a few minutes. Any fatigue or stress that I had had in my body prior to my session was gone and in its place was a languid, liquid feeling, a sense that everything was good again and that we could resume our normal lives, the ones that didn't include a worried-looking brother in the police station and two irate parents. Outside the room I could hear my father bellowing and the lower tones of my mother's voice, talking to either Paul, Cargan, or both at the same time. It didn't sound like a particularly productive conversation, but then again, when Dad was involved there was a lot of bluster before there was resolution.

Beverly was leaning against the conference room table, looking me over.

"We're done, right?" I said, standing. "Did I remember anything that's helpful in any way?" I wasn't sure which answer I wanted. "Yes" meant more questions for me and "no" meant no resolution for Cargan and his situation, whatever that was.

Kevin had shrunk back into a corner of the room, his arms crossed over his chest. Had I professed a lingering love for him? Said something totally inappropriate and embarrassing? The two other people in the room silent, the only sound the whir of the air conditioner as it kicked into life, I looked at both of them, searching for some indication of what had happened during my session, one that I was surprised had been successful in terms of my going into a trance, or whatever Bev and her fellow hypnotists called it. "What? What's going on?"

Kevin, as I looked at him more, studied his face for an answer, paled. "Tell me everything you remember about that night."

This was getting frustrating. We had been over it a thousand times, or so it seemed. "I told you everything, Kevin. Met the guy at the wedding. Found out later that he had crashed. Heard voices. Next time I saw him," I said, willing my face not to turn red at the lie, "he was coming over the balcony at the Manor. He died. You came next." Short and sweet—that's how you had to keep these things. Otherwise, you'd get tripped up and the next thing you knew you were sharing a prison cell in the local police department's jail with your brother, wondering why you hadn't made two ham sandwiches.

"What else?" Kevin asked, and I knew the jig was up. He tapped the phone in his hand lightly to jog my memory.

"Oh, you mean the text messages?" I asked.

"Yeah, the text messages," he said, not happy.

Bev looked at both of us, thrust into the middle of a drama that she was enjoying thoroughly.

"They were incriminating," I said, rolling my eyes toward Bev. "Can we talk about this later?" I asked.

"Okay," Kevin said, knowing the power of the Post Office gossip chain. "And what else?"

"The earring?" I said.

Kevin looked confused but shook his head. "No, not that."

"Then what?" I asked. "What else is there?"

Whatever it was, he couldn't say it.

Bev was the one who finally broke the silence. "Why did you tell Amy Mitchell twenty-five years ago that she 'would be sorry'?"

CHAPTER *Twenty-eight*

I guess my friendship with Amy and her disappearance was going to haunt me until the day I died. It had been pretty clear that that would probably be the case, but now I had hard proof. And if my subconscious was any indication, I was my own worst enemy in terms of not letting myself off the hook.

Out of respect for my family and our long affiliation with everyone on the police department and in Foster's Landing in general, Cargan was also released, and the two of us began the walk home to the grounds of the Manor, both silent for most of the journey. When all was said and done, he hadn't needed a lawyer, he didn't know very much, and there was nothing more to say. Kevin was not curious enough to follow up on the earring I had mentioned, never asking what I meant.

Kevin knew why I had said what I had said that night; he just didn't want to admit it. And by the look on his face, I knew he was covering his tracks and pretending like he was a good detective following up on a lead when, in fact, he was the reason I had said those things I had said to Amy on her last night. I still wanted to ask him why he had been at the river that night after I had eaten dinner at his house, but I didn't think that doing so in front of Bev was the best idea, so I filed that away.

Kevin and I did discuss the text messages, and if I wasn't who I was and so completely guilt ridden for doing what I did I think I would have been in bigger trouble. Caleigh's responses to Declan's messages were surely included in the ones on his phone but I didn't know how much they revealed. I had deleted Caleigh's messages so quickly that I hadn't had time to read them. But whatever was on that phone, Kevin wasn't saying, out of respect of me, Caleigh, or someone else, it was hard to tell.

Before Cargan and I reached the road that led to the mansion, I turned to my brother. "Why did you ask for a lawyer? What are you not telling me?"

He had already been through this with Mom and Dad; otherwise they wouldn't have left the police station and driven away, leaving me and my brother to do the walk of shame back home, something I had done many times, usually in the middle of the night after a party somewhere in the village or out on Eden Island. He looked at me. "I did what you asked, Bel. I told them what I knew. But Kevin kept hammering away at me like I had more to do with that guy's death and I got nervous." He balled up his hands at his sides, his body stiff.

"There's nothing to be nervous about, Car. You had nothing to do with this. You know that. Kevin knows that. And now that Paul Grant knows it, so will the entire village," I said, trying to make a joke that ended up falling flat by the look on my brother's face.

"This whole thing was a bad idea, Bel. I never should have listened to you," Cargan said, walking away from me and starting for home.

"Why did you say he was your mate?" I called after him.

"It's an expression, Bel. It means nothing," he said before giving me a dismissive hand wave without turning around.

Was that true? An expression? I didn't think so, but I let that go. I caught up with him and stopped him for one last discussion. "Cargan, Dad has guns in his studio," I said, him being the only person I thought I could tell what I had seen.

"Guns?"

"Guns," I said. "AK-47s."

"And how would you know what an AK-47 looks like?"

Good point. "Just guessing."

"Bel, you've been nothing but trouble since you got here. If I didn't know better, I'd think that you thought that Dad was a gunrunner, or worse, and that the entire family is keeping some giant secret from you." His face turned red. "There's nothing going on. A guy at the wedding argued with the groom, probably being cut off at the bar. He died and the police will find out who did it."

"You have more faith than I do, Cargan," I said, attempting a joke. "If it wasn't for you and your tutoring in high school, Kevin Hanson would still be in freshman algebra."

"Dad is making some kind of cockamamie installation. He's not a gunrunner or . . ."

"A murderer?" I asked.

"Oh, Bel," Cargan said. "That's awful. How can you even say that?"

He was right. How could I think it, say it aloud?

"We're not keeping anything from you. Just leave everything alone," he said, the disappointment on his face staying with me as he started down the hill again, leaving me to watch his back as he got smaller and smaller on the road.

I sat down and stretched my legs out in front of me, staring into the copse of trees on the other side of the road. Maybe he was right and I was wrong. It wouldn't be the first time. I wished I had been hypnotized to forget everything unpleasant that had happened, but no, everything

that had happened was now etched in my mind, as fresh
as it had been the day it had happened, particularly when it
came to Amy and our troubles. I remembered telling Amy
that she would be sorry, but it was never as sinister as it
sounded, not as dire as Kevin and Bev seemed to think it
was. She was going to be sorry that she had lost me as a
best friend, that she had committed the ultimate betrayal
that night, as far as my teenage mind could see. She had
kissed Kevin in full view of me and everyone else on the
island that night, a drunken misstep that uncovered the
truth of the situation, which was that we were rivals, not
friends, and that she had seen me always as competition,
not as a soul mate, not as someone on whom she could always count, always rely. As an adult, I could see the truth
and the situation for what it was: teenage indiscretion fu-
eled by cheap beer, a bad decision made worse by the
things that were said afterward, and the fact that after that
night no one saw Amy Mitchell ever again.

Kevin went from pale to deep red remembering that
night, along with the fact that I had had to recount the
whole thing in front of Bev, Post Office lady/psychic/hyp-
notist. Clown. He begged for her discretion, which she
promised, but we couldn't be sure that this juicy tale—the
one involving a village detective, the chef at Shamrock
Manor, and a missing girl—would not be retold thousands
upon thousands of time to every single patron of the Foster's Landing PO.

Who loved me? That's what I wondered, that one piece
of information being dropped by Bev into my proverbial
lap something I puzzled over. I hoped it was Brendan and
not Ben. Not Kevin, even though the look on his face was
odd, embarrassed. Not anyone else but the guy whom I
likely had sat next to at countless assemblies, never really
taking notice of him, my eyes always on Kevin and no
one else.

I sat there for a long time, pondering all of this. Nothing else had come out of the hypnotist's session; everything I had told Kevin was what I said again while in an altered consciousness. Finally, I got up, brushed off the back of my pants, and started up the hill.

Behind me, a car crawled along slowly. I turned and saw Brendan behind the wheel of his old Honda; he gave the horn a little beep in greeting. The passenger-side window rolled down and he leaned across the seat.

"You look like you could use a drink," he said.

At the sight of him, uncomplicated, friendly, and warm, I felt the stress leave my body, my limbs relax. "You're right about that," I said, walking over to the car.

"I was hoping I'd find you here." He reached over and opened the car door. "Hop in. You look like you have a lot to tell me."

On our way to the river, I asked him the one question that had been niggling at the back of my mind since we first met at the empty swimming pool. "Are you for real?" Between Kevin, who had kissed my best friend right in front of me, and Ben, the wanker who let me take the fall for his mistake and had cheated on me, I was unaccustomed to guys as nice as Brendan Joyce. He looked taken aback at the question. "Yes, I'm for real." He turned left out of the street and headed toward the river. "You may not have noticed, but there aren't a lot of opportunities to date here in the Landing, unless I want to go out on a limb and ask Bev from the Post Office out."

My stomach got a little sick at the mention of her name.

"Which I don't, by the way." He turned and looked at me. "By the look on your face, I take it you know Bev, pet psychic?"

"I do," I said, leaving out that we had just become acquainted. I turned and looked out the window, watching the village go by. "She's also a clown."

"Now that's not nice, Bel."

"No. For real. She's a clown, too. It's on her Web site."

"Huh," he said. "Multitalented." He made a left, head-ing toward the water. "She's actually trying to channel my cat, Felix, and help me find him. He ran away about six months ago and I'm lost without the little bugger."

"Hmm," I said, not paying attention to what Brendan was saying, where we were going.

"So, our date," he said, pulling into the train station and driving down to the kayak put-in. "What happened? Why did you have to cancel?"

I explained the whole thing. Cargan, his recollections, the murder. How it was unsolved and no one seemed to have a great urgency to solve it. How Dad had involved Paul Grant.

"You mean Philip?" Brendan asked, pulling into a spot, gravel spraying up around the car.

"Yeah. Remember him?"

"I do," he said. "I guess 'Paul' rhymes with 'fall'?"

"That's my guess. And Paul is a saint."

"Paul Grant?"

"No. Saint Paul."

"Saw his kid on *Jeopardy!* Little bugger is as smart as a whip, but I hate kids' week."

He and Mom had that in common. Here's hoping the kid's father was as smart as a whip, too, in case we ever needed him again.

Brendan and I took a spot at the splinter-covered pic-nic table. Once we sat down and he revealed the items in his reusable grocery bag I asked him why he had shown up. "Why did you come looking for me?"

"I don't know," he said, though I could tell that he did. I waited.

"Well, yeah, I do." He handed me a piece of baguette with a healthy smear of soft cheese. "I wanted to see you.

Felt like things were left off a little abruptly the other day and then you canceled. Just wanted to make sure we were square."

"Square?"

"Solid."

I gave him a little fist bump. "We're square. Solid."

"I guess I've been teaching at the high school for too long. I'm starting to sound like one of the kids."

I laughed. "You definitely do not sound like one of your students. I don't think any one of them would use the word 'square' to sum up a relationship." He handed me a glass of wine and I caught sight of the label as he poured himself one. A good bottle, somewhere in the thirty-buck range. I complimented him on his choice.

"Thanks. I took a class at a local winery one summer."

"To meet chicks?" I said. As far as I knew, that was the only reason men went to cooking class, wine-tasting seminars, yoga.

"To meet chicks," he said, nodding enthusiastically. "It didn't work."

"There was always Bev from the Post Office."

"Indeed."

"But I hear she's taken." She was. According to her Web site, he—Jacob, a blacksmith—was her "one true love," her "reason for being." Okay then. "And a clown."

Brendan snapped his fingers, dismayed. "Damn it." He topped off my wine. "I bet she's flexible. Can probably ride a unicycle."

"Both great traits in a partner."

"It's slim pickin's around here, Bel. You have no idea."

I did have an idea. Since I got back, I had eaten dinner every Sunday with my parents and four brothers. I had no social life to speak of. I knew well of the dearth of possibilities for young, swinging singles in Foster's Landing, having been in my apartment for the last two months with no one to talk to, not one person with whom to hang out.

"Will you be my social life now?" he asked. "Will you hang around with me? I would hate to have to ask Bev to go for a kayak ride or a pint at the Grand Mill."

"Well, that would be cheating, because of her husband. A clandestine love affair," I said.

"Good point." He turned and stared into my eyes. "Will you hang around with me, Belfast McGrath?"

"Brendan Joyce, are you asking me to go steady?" I asked.

He took a slug of wine. "I guess I am."

It had been a long, crazy day. I looked at his open, honest face and didn't hesitate.

"Sure, Brendan Joyce. I would love to go steady with you." And something finally dawned on me. "And I think I know where your cat is."

CHAPTER *Twenty-nine*

Brendan took me home a little before eight and we hunted around for the cat we hoped was Felix. I gave Brendan a description of the cat I had appropriated and he sounded an awful lot like Felix. After searching for almost an hour with no sign of him, we gave up. Brendan said that after he pulled together some paintings for a show that weekend he'd come by and see if he could lure the cat home.

"He likes lo mein."

"That's my cat," Brendan said.

"Ah, well," I said. "I hope I can visit from time to time."

He gave me a quick kiss before I got out of the car. "That can be arranged," he said before driving off.

I stopped by Dad's studio to see if I could smooth things over between us, but he was deep in conversation with Uncle Eugene and Frank the Tank. Uncle Eugene was still in town and not scheduled to leave, I had learned at our last family dinner, for another two weeks. He had spent a week in the Bronx visiting with some old friends and was now back in the Landing and staying in one of the guest rooms at the Manor. The three men were drinking a pint of beer and eating some kind of organ meat, the smell of which filled the studio and made my stomach hurt just by smelling it. I hadn't jumped on the offal train when it became a thing, preferring to stick to clean, delicious food that you didn't need to convince people to eat because it was the latest trend. I was surprised that Frank was partaking, but he was right there with the guys, eating whatever delicacy my father had prepared. Frank nodded silently when I walked in, downing his beer and beating a hasty getaway, mumbling something about Helen and chicken.

Dad watched him go. "Never can understand what that guy is saying," he said, looking at me. "Belfast. Nice to see you."

But it wasn't. I could tell that I was still in trouble for the Cargan mess.

At least Uncle Eugene, who was usually a giant crank pot, looked happy to see me. "Belfast! How are ya, my girl?" He proffered the meat. "Black pudding?"

"Ah, no thanks, Uncle Eugene. I'm full." I gave him a hug. Dad stood to the side of the big table in the middle of the room and avoided my eyes.

"You good, girl?" he asked.

"I'm great, Uncle Eugene." I looked around the room and into the side room, but the big box, the one marked "ART," was gone. "Little excitement here, but that's all over now," I said to him, hoping my father would agree.

"I heard," Eugene said. "Poor lad. Quite a scare sitting in the police department."

"Sure is," I said. "It was all a big misunderstanding."

I heard my father mutter something under his breath. Sounded like "thanks to you."

"It's just that—" I started, hoping to explain what had happened and why.

But Dad cut me off, exploding into one of his patented tirades. " 'It's just that' nothing, Belfast. You put your brother in a very precarious position by making him talk to that wanker Kevin Hanson again. What the heck has gotten into you?" he said, storming about the room. Even

Eugene, who was given to his own flights of bluster, seemed a little surprised and a lot wary. My dad is a big man, and even though he has the heart of a lamb, when he loses his temper it's a sight to behold. It's not like Mom's slow burn; it's a full-on volcano. I'm not sure which was scarier. Right now Dad was winning, but I hadn't seen Mom yet to see if her emotions were at full boil. "You need to remember that family comes first! That we protect our own! That we take care of each other. You had no business marching your brother down to the station."

Nothing like your father losing your temper at you to make you feel twelve years old again. I felt a sob building in my chest and creeping up my throat, so I took a big gulp and pushed it down, hoping that this outburst would be short-lived. When he appeared to be done, I apologized for my role in all of this.

"Apologize to your mother! And your brother!" he said.

"I already apologized to Cargan," I said.

Uncle Eugene put a hand on my dad's arm. "Mal, take it easy."

"I won't take it easy," Dad said, but it was clear that he had run out of steam. "I won't take it easy," he said again, this time with a little less passion. He had one last burst of vitriol left in him. "And stop it with the fancy food! We want what we want. Cook it our way!"

That was a deal breaker, but we wouldn't discuss it now, not with tempers flaring and emotions running high.

Eugene changed the subject to something more disturbing than the menu at the Manor. "We all want to know what happened to that poor chap," Eugene said, "who had it out for him." A look passed between Eugene and my dad that was inscrutable, mysterious.

My dad straightened, calming down, turning into someone else. "Yes. We do. A terrible thing, that was."

"Sure, he was a nice chap," Eugene said.

I felt like I was in the middle of some kind of performance, one where all of a sudden we all cared with the same degree of intensity about what had happened to Declan Morrison.

"Did you know him, Eugene?" I asked.

Again a look between Dad and Eugene. They knew more than they were letting on.

"Well, yes, I did, Belfast. He's a mate from the old country. Grew up around my boys," Eugene said.

"Dad? Did you know that?" I asked.

"Old Eugene here reminded me that we had met the kid when we last went home." Dad went into a ridiculous monologue about he forgets things, how he's forgotten more than I would ever know. "So, yes," he pronounced. "I had met the young man."

"But you forgot. Until right now," I said, wondering if stating that would make him see how ridiculous it all sounded.

He crossed his arms over his chest. "Yes. That's right."

"So you lied to me," I said. "When you said you didn't know him."

"I forgot," he said.

We stood in silence for a full minute. When it was clear that there was nothing left to say on the subject, I looked at Uncle Eugene. "We'll see you at Sunday dinner?" I asked.

"Sure you will," he said.

I turned to leave, but the sight of a woman at the door of the studio stopped me in my tracks. She was small and dark and the look on her face told me that she was not to be trifled with. She looked at first my father and then Uncle Eugene. "Malachy," she said in greeting. She didn't acknowledge Eugene.

Dad looked more defeated than stunned. He bent at the waist, resting his hands on the edge of the table. "Trudie."

"Hi," I said, holding out my hand. "I'm Belfast."

"Yes, I know," she said, accepting my hand. "I'm Trudie McGrath. And I'm here to get my son." When it was clear I didn't know what she was talking about, she elaborated. "Declan. Declan McGrath."

CHAPTER *Thirty*

Not shockingly, Declan hadn't give any of us his real name. True, Dad knew who Declan was and had lied to me. I'm sure Mom did, too. And Uncle Eugene. They all knew and had chosen to keep it to themselves.

Why? was the question.

"We didn't know him, Belfast," Dad said after Trudie left the studio and went out to the car to wait for a ride. "Trudie kept him from us after Dermot left. We never saw him after he was a wee baby." Dermot was Dad's younger brother, someone rarely spoken about, someone I had never met. Declan had been his son, now reunited with his father in heaven, or so said Dad and Eugene, both crossing themselves at the thought.

Eugene nodded in agreement at everything Dad said.

"Why did he show up here, Dad?" I asked.

But there was no answer for that.

Uncle Eugene was the one who offered to take Trudie to the police station to start the process of getting her son's remains shipped back to Ireland, even though it was clear to me that they had a very tense relationship. I could only imagine how Kevin and the rest of the Foster's Landing Police Department would feel once they knew that my parents not only knew the deceased, they were related to him. Well, at least Dad was, by blood. Declan had been raised by his mother, Trudie, in a small village in the west of Ireland that was far from Ballyminster after Dermot left the family, sometime in the early eighties, as far as anyone could remember. Ah, I see, I thought. So, despite the thousands of Declans in Ireland, that's why no one knew our Declan.

God rest his soul, as Mom would say.

Declan was a "bad seed," according to Dad.

A "foul ball," in Mom's opinion, according to Dad.

"And how did you know that?" I asked. "You said you didn't know him, that you were estranged from Trudie."

"We heard things," Dad said, looking at Eugene.

"And the wedding? Why was he there?" I asked.

Neither had any idea as to why he had shown up at the wedding. I don't know what they were making their judgments on about him, what they had "heard," based on the fact that they claimed they had never met the man before Caleigh's wedding.

Dad and I stood in the studio after Uncle Eugene and Trudie left, me staring at him, waiting for an answer that it didn't seem was going to come. "Spill it, Dad," I said. "I want everything. The whole truth."

"Oh, there's nothing to tell, Bel," he said, clearly exasperated with me and the entire situation.

The more I thought about it, the more I came to the conclusion that Declan had looked a lot like my brothers; I should have figured out sooner that he wasn't a "third cousin, once removed" on Caleigh's side as he claimed but a first cousin to me, no relation to Caleigh, thank God. That thought had danced around in my head—that Caleigh had slept with a cousin, albeit a distant one—since the wedding. One tragedy averted. My brothers all had gotten the recessive gene of the thick black hair that ran through Dad's family while I was the only one who favored him and was a redhead. Declan had the same hair color and complexion as my brothers, making him a McGrath through and through. No one was sure exactly what color Mom's hair actually was; she had been blond for as long as we all could remember and we were sure she had some kind of blood oath with her hairstylist not to tell ever what was beneath that shiny patina of golden hair.

"There's a lot to tell, Dad," I said. "Let's start with the guns."

His mouth opened, but nothing came out. "What guns?" he said, but his heart wasn't in it. "The guns."

"Yes, the guns," I said.

The wheels inside his brain turned for a few more seconds before he came up with a big, fat lie. "I already told you. I'm doing a new installation."

"Do I look like I was born yesterday?" I asked. "You had a box of guns and you want me to believe that you were going to use them for an installation?"

"Yes."

"If that's the case, where are they now?" I asked.

"Secret location," he said, as if his using fewer words would make me believe this whale of a lie. "They are guns after all."

Now it was my turn to be mad. Not as mad as the night I wanted to kill Francesco Francatelli, but mad enough. "Dad. Enough. This is getting completely out of hand. We have a dead guy, a box of guns, and now the dead guy's mother who just happens to be your sister-in-law. What else is there? What are you not telling me?"

But he had shut down, nothing else to tell. He went into the back room and attempted to slam the door shut, but it had never been hung correctly and bounced back and hit him in the back of the head. So much for storming off, showing me who was boss.

Secret location, my ass. I went back over to the Manor and to the one place I had hated since I was small: the basement. The basement was where all McGrath detritus went to die, or at least be stored. I hadn't been down there since I returned home but, even so, could probably do a complete inventory based on what I remembered from my youth: a broken Victrola; some of Mom's pageant gowns, moth-eaten and threadbare; bicycles in various stages of disrepair; an inordinate number of tires.

The boys had told me various stories when I was small about what actually went on in the basement, what its main purpose was, the secrets it supposedly held. It was the repository of long-dead relatives, or so they told me. Mom kept the ventriloquist dummy down there that she had used in one of her pageants for the talent portion, and at night it came alive. (There was no talent portion and there was no dummy, I didn't think.) There were wedding guests who had taken a wrong turn and gone down there, never to be seen again. Skeletons. Ghosts. Spirits. Paintings that came to life.

None of it was true, but that didn't stop my heart from pounding just a little bit when I descended the steps, my hands feeling along the unpainted sheetrock that lined the walls along the staircase for the light switch. What was down there was far less thrilling or terrifying. In addition to the Victrola and the pageant gowns, there were also decorations for every season, extra banquet tables and chairs, moth-eaten tablecloths and napkins that Mom had never had the inclination to throw away. The woman had been born years removed from the potato famine but held on to stuff in the event something like that wended its way into our lives again, a depression-era mentality that confounded me.

I picked around the giant space looking for the box of guns and found them, tucked in the corner of the basement, right by the giant furnace that kept the mansion warm in the winter. I wondered about the intelligence of keeping guns next to a machine as big as the furnace, but

I pulled the lid off the box and found that the guns had no ammunition in them and there was none in the vicinity.

What a day. I was starting to rethink my plan of staying here, helping Mom and Dad get the Manor back on its feet. This place was crazier than I thought, much weirder than I remember, my family something of a bunch of odd-balls with a host of secrets that they would go to great lengths to protect. I replaced the lid on the stack of guns, which maybe really were being used for an installation if I believed my father, and turned around, preparing to head back up to the main floor of the Manor and, eventually, end up in my apartment, a giant glass of wine in one hand, the remote in the other. That was the only way to shake off what had been a very strange day.

I started for the stairs but directly in my line of sight, behind a stack of boxes that held the aforementioned moldy linens, their contents marked with black marker on the outside of each box, I saw a night table. And on that night table were a lamp, an alarm clock, and a book, which I could see from where I stood was *Love in the Time of Cholera.*

Cargan had a room upstairs, as did Mom and Dad. Eugene was in a guest room. No one, as far as I knew, lived in the basement, not even the myriad workers who toiled at the Manor, making sure the grounds were kept up and the building itself didn't fall to the ground. I walked over to the bed and put my hand on the blanket, still warm from the body who had gotten up, probably at the sound of my footsteps, when the light had come on at the top of the stairs. The bed had been made with military precision and underneath it was a small suitcase with no identifying tags as to whom it belonged to, from whence it had come. I began to pull it out from under the bed and it got snagged under the bed frame. I lifted the frame with one hand and pulled the suitcase out with the other. The suitcase was locked. I looked around for something to jimmy it open, pulling open the drawer of the nightstand only to find a small piece of paper, a business card for a local extermi-nator.

And a gun.

The lights went out and my heart stopped beating.

CHAPTER *Thirty-one*

Kevin's flip-flops and Bermuda shorts didn't lend themselves to an air of professionalism, but it was late and he was doing other things when Officer Penner, a nice cop who seemed to know at least one of my backstories judging from the judgmental crease in his brow, showed up to start the investigation into my discovery. It didn't take long for them to get here, maybe ten minutes, and when they emerged from the basement, another twenty minutes later, it had been enough time for Mom, Dad, and Cargan to assemble in the office to await the verdict on my discovery and what it might mean. There was another cop outside sweeping the perimeter, looking for any indication that an intruder was on the premises, someone with great taste in literature.

And a gun. Let's not forget that.

I had banged the heck of out of my shin when I started fleeing the basement, running straight into some piece that stuck out of the furnace, the sound not unlike something you might hear on a Saturday-morning cartoon. *Thunk.* I had stumbled up the stairs to the empty foyer and turned on every light I could, the memories of being in the black basement—with possibly a ventriloquist dummy that came alive at night—something that most definitely was going to haunt my dreams. Sitting in the office, I looked down and saw that I had quite a bruise forming.

But everyone else was still in the midst of their own ruminations about what I had seen, who could possibly be living in the basement. Dad's shoulders sagged with the weight of a new set of issues for the Manor, while Mom—clad in a colorful silk kimono and backless, high-heeled slippers—allowed just the barest hint of worry to cross her unlined brow.

"What else can go wrong, Mal?" she asked.

But my father had no answers, slumped in one of the office chairs, his hand over his eyes.

Cargan held the ledger in his lap like a security blanket, saying nothing.

I pointed to my bruised shin. "Wow, this hurts," I said, hoping someone would take the hint and get me a Baggie of ice from the kitchen next door, but Mom and Dad were arguing about the owner of the contents downstairs and just how they were going to explain a box of AK-47s to Kevin Hanson.

Turns out they didn't need to. Kevin came up the stairs from the basement a few minutes later, coughing noisily, having ingested decades-old Manor basement dust during his walk-through. "The AK-47s, Mr. McGrath? Should we start with those?"

"A new installation," Dad said, barely lifting his head.

"Fantastic," Kevin said, and Dad smiled, tone-deaf to sarcasm, especially where it concerned his artwork.

I found it odd that Kevin accepted the explanation so readily.

"The barrels are stuffed with cement," Kevin said, reading my mind.

Knowing that fact would have saved me hours of perseveration. I wished I had taken the time to look when

I first discovered them, the hours spent thinking my father was an IRA gunrunner hours I would never get back. Or maybe the cement was a recent addition.

"So what did you find?" I asked. "Did you see everything? The night table? The alarm clock? The gun? The copy of the Gabriel García Márquez?"

"The 'you look fantastic' guy?" Kevin asked.

"It's 'you look marvelous,' and no, not him," I said. "The author of the book."

"That's Fernando Lamas," Cargan said. "The 'you look marvelous' guy," he added when no one seemed to know what Kevin was talking about.

Dad perked up. "Wasn't he married to Ava Gardner?"

Mom shook her head. "No. Arlene Francis. From *Password*."

Cargan looked dubious. "I thought he was married to Rosemary Clooney. And I think Arlene Francis was on *What's My Line?*"

"That was José Ferrer," Mom said.

"On *What's My Line?*" Dad asked.

Kevin shot me a look—your family is crazy. I couldn't disagree.

I clapped my hands together. "As fascinating as this walk down Hollywood's memory lane is, I'd like to hear what Kevin found in the basement." I looked at Mom and Dad. "You as well?"

Mom pulled her kimono tight around her slim body. "Of course. Continue, Detective Hanson. What did you find?"

It was Kevin's big moment; it was written all over his face. "Nothing."

"Well, how could that be?" Mom asked. "Belfast told you about everything down there."

"No bed, no night table, no alarm clock. No 'you look marvelous' guy or the book he wrote. And definitely no gun," Kevin said, shrugging. "We searched everywhere."

I wanted to ask if they found a living ventriloquist dummy, even though 90 percent of me didn't think one existed, but I kept my mouth shut. Cargan drifted out of the room and went to the kitchen; he returned a few minutes later with a Baggie filled with ice and handed it to me with a sad smile.

I closed my eyes, hoping against hope that what I was about to say was not the truth. "Please, dear God, tell me that that's not where you were putting Trudie up? I know there's bad blood—"

"Trudie?" Mom said. "Trudie is here?"

Dad nodded, not looking at her.

"Yes, Mrs. McGrath, Declan's mother came to retrieve his remains," Kevin said.

Mom looked at Dad and I was sure there was going to be more to this conversation after everyone left.

"Trudie is Declan's mother," I said, waiting to see what Mom would do. "But you already knew that."

Mom surprised me by doing nothing, standing like a statue, willing her mouth not to move. I looked at Kevin.

"I know it all," he said, not the least bit apologetic that he hadn't told me that Declan Morrison was my cousin, not Caleigh's.

"Well, that was a whole heck of a lot of nothing," Dad said, standing. "Can we return to what we were doing, Kevin? Go back to normal here?" Based on Mom's getup and his florid complexion, I had a feeling that we had interrupted a long-planned tryst with my emergence from the basement, the calling of the cops.

"What's normal here exactly?" Kevin asked, the words out of his mouth before he knew it. "I mean, as soon as we look through Bel's apartment we'll get out of your hair." He pulled something from his pocket. "But there is just one more thing I need to discuss with you."

Guy was becoming like Columbo, dropping little tidbits

in the midst of meaningless conversation. He pulled a long piece of wire out of his pocket, on the end of which dangled what looked like a tiny microphone. He screwed up his face, confused. It was the same look he got when puzzling over a piece of band music from back when we were in high school.

"It looks like the Manor is bugged."

"Bugged?" Mom repeated.

"Yes. Bugged. Miked. Being listened to," Kevin said when it was clear that Mom had other thoughts on her mind. Roaches. Mice. Something worse on the vermin scale.

Mom didn't say anything. Dad let out a great gust of air that flooded the room with a garlic-tinged odor and Cargan went deep into himself to a place I wasn't sure we would get him back from.

Officer Penner came back from wherever he had been. "Searched all of the rooms, Detective. Every one is miked."

Mom looked as if she were about to faint. "Every one? Even the bedroom? I mean *bedrooms*? Like where Cargan sleeps?" she asked, making it immediately clear that she and Dad had been involved in something the likes of which none of us wanted to know about. Or it was just a standard night of lovemaking, but because we're Irish and prone to hang-ups about that sort of thing she was still embarrassed.

Officer Penner confirmed her suspicions. "All of the rooms, Mrs. McGrath."

I flashed on the length of wire in the bridal suite, something I had forgotten about until now.

"So let me get this straight," I said. "Someone has bugged the Manor and is living in the basement listening to us."

"That pretty much sums it up," Kevin said.

"And that person was able to dismantle their living situation but not the bugs between the time I ran up here and called you and when you started to investigate."

Kevin was impressed by my deductive skills. "Yes. That's how I would describe it." He asked my parents if he and Penner could look through the studios, my apartment, the rest of the Manor, one more time.

"Of course, Detective," Mom said, laying it on thick. I knew how she felt about Kevin, but in this situation her lack of respect for him lay hidden under the layer of humiliation she felt at standing in front of him in a gauzy kimono and high heels.

Kevin and Penner left and it was just the four of us in the office. I looked at Cargan.

"So, do you want to tell us what's going on?"

CHAPTER Thirty-two

Cargan wasn't talking, but there was no doubt in my mind that the setup in the basement belonged to him. He had appeared too quickly after hearing me shouting from down below and then disappeared for a time, ostensibly looking for an intruder. But like Mom he had a tell, and his was a deep rosiness that started at the collar of his Arsenal jersey and ended at the tips of his ears, something that had made him give away the locations of his ships in Stratego, even though he managed to beat me every time.

There were no bugs in the studios, nor in my apartment, not that having one in my apartment would have been cause for alarm on my part. Unless the person bugging the place had an affinity for listening to me sing the sound track of *The Sound of Music,* which I did to chase away the blues every now and again, they weren't hearing anything they hadn't already heard. A can opening. The refrigerator door slamming shut when I spied lentil crap. The flush of a toilet. It seemed to me that what they might hear coming from Mom and Dad's bedroom was much more scintillating, exciting in a way I didn't want to think about.

I stared Cargan down for a while, but he wasn't budging. It was late. We were all tired. And I, for one, had had enough of this craziness, so I said good night and started back for the apartment. The cops had left. There were reports to be written, details to be noted and saved for additional work on the investigation. Nothing to see here, as they said; show's over.

Outside, I saw a shadow in the distance, standing by the stairs to my home, and recognized that it was Kevin. He waited until I was close, only the moon overhead illuminating us, to ask the question that had been on his mind for many years, I suspected.

"Just how did your family become so weird?"

Rather than become offended, I laughed. He was right; they were weird. And loud and judgmental and neurotic. It was a veritable treasure trove of dysfunction, all wrapped up in what should have been a pretty package: the gorgeous mother, the artistic—well, the jury was still out on that one—father; the fairly successful and independent brothers. And me, wherever I fit in. "I don't know, Kevin."

"Is it my imagination, or are they getting stranger?" With the moon as a backdrop, he looked just as we did as teenagers, his hair hanging over his forehead, not a line on his face to indicate that we had aged.

"Yep. Getting stranger. By the day." I had the benefit of distance on my side, so I could compare the people I had grown up with the ones I knew now. Every idiosyncrasy had become magnified with age. It was probably the same for me, if I were prone to introspection. "Do you want to ask me anything else, Kevin?" I assumed he must have some other order of business; why else would he still be here? I started up the stairs. "I guess it's good that there aren't any bugs in my apartment, right?"

"Yes, that's great news."

"And you knew that Declan Morrison was really Declan McGrath."

He nodded.

"And the texts? You know everything then."

"None of that really changes anything," he said. "There's still a dead guy and we still don't know why. Or who did it."

I assumed he was behind me, but when I turned he was still at the bottom of the stairs. "This drought," he said. "It's been a long time."

I stopped midway up and turned. "Yeah. I wanted to go swimming at the village pool and there's not a drop of water in the place." I laughed again. "All the better to see my mother's face at the bottom."

"Is it your mother's face? Everyone always thought so," Kevin said. "I don't think it really looks like her."

"When have you seen anything my father has done look like it's supposed to?" I started back down the stairs. "That's the hallmark of a Mal McGrath original." I made my way down to the bottom step so that Kevin and I were the same height. "It's my mom, all right, down to the freckle on her chin."

"She's not quite so terrifying as a mermaid."

"That's because you can outrun a mermaid, Kevin," I said, ruffling his hair, an old, familiar gesture that didn't seem completely out of place here. We had fallen into an old conversational pattern, new to the moment but completely part of our history, and something happened right then, a letting go that I wasn't expecting.

He leaned forward and put his hand at the back of my head, pulling me close. The kiss was sweet, like that first time in tenth grade, and, again, familiar. It was the only way I could describe it, words failing me as I drifted back to a time of kayaking in the summer, swim practice, band rehearsals, SATs. Eden Island and beer purloined from our parents' "extra fridge," usually in a basement or garage, stocked to the brim with barley, wheat, and hops. Of me and Kevin, Kevin and me, Amy along for the ride, the happy, self-anointed "third wheel," or so I thought, not knowing that that third wheel wanted to move up in the ranks.

I let it happen, when I thought about it afterward. It's not as if I had wanted it or expected it, but I let it happen when it did, allowing myself to be swept along in a wave of nostalgia that made my heart ache at the thought of it. I didn't know when it started and I wasn't sure when it was going to end, if it was going to end, but the decision was made for us.

"I guess I should have expected this," a voice said, somewhere in the darkness, a voice with a lilting brogue that I recognized as Brendan Joyce's. "I just thought it would take longer to happen."

I pulled away from Kevin so quickly that I nearly fell off the step, the sweet kiss tainted by the discovery of someone I cared about more deeply than I had cared to admit. Or forgotten to remember.

"Brendan," I said, coming off the step and seeing only his outline in the darkness. In his arms was the cat that he said he was coming back to find later that evening. I guessed that time was now. I couldn't think of anything else to say, so I just repeated his name.

"Don't you have a girlfriend, Hanson?" Brendan asked, the cat looking small in his big hands. "What would she think of this?" Although I couldn't see his face, his voice was remarkably calm, given the situation. I wondered if he looked as calm as he sounded.

"This is all my fault," Kevin said, backing away from the steps. "I'm sorry. I've gotta go." He walked toward his car and was out of the driveway, the gravel spraying like it always did, as he peeled out of Shamrock Manor and down the road toward the village.

I was happy that it was so dark and that I couldn't see Brendan's disappointed face. I wasn't sure what to say; luckily, he spoke first.

"It's okay, Bel," he said. Off in the distance I heard a bird let out a loud caw somewhere along the river, probably looking for a safe place to land. I had had that, once, a safe place to land, but with my giving in to Kevin's advance had lost it. I hoped it wasn't for good. "I should have known that you two still had a thing for each other. I just feel bad for Mary Ann. I'm new to this. To you. But she . . . ," he started, trailing off.

"But we don't," I said, the protest not sounding quite as vehement as I would have liked. "We don't. Have a thing for each other, that is."

His sigh was a mix of disappointment and exasperation. "You should sort this out," he said right before the cat jumped out of his arms and ran back to the woods. "Jaysus, Felix!" he said, the cat's departure the final straw, the last indignity.

I watched him walk away, wondering where his car was, why he was on foot. While I thought he would head to the woods, it seemed he wanted off the property of Shamrock Manor as quickly as possible.

What a difference a couple of weeks makes, I had thought earlier. With me feeling the way I did now, it didn't feel that different at all.

CHAPTER *Thirty-three*

I thought that throwing myself into my work would be a good counterpoint to the previous day's unpleasantness, all of it. I went to a local farmer's market and was perusing the tomato selection—still young in the season but not bad—when I felt a tap on my shoulder.

This just keeps getting better and better, I thought as I took in Mary Ann D'Amato's angelic face, her spotless scrubs, these with playful kittens on them. She was holding a zucchini in one hand, her purse in the other. My hand tightened around the tomato I was holding and seeds spilled out into my palm.

"Hey, lady," the kid behind the tomato table said, "that's not a stress ball. It's a tomato."

I put it down. "Got it. I'll take that one," I said, picking out a five from another bushel, "and these. Sorry for the mess," I said, noticing tomato juice on the twenty I handed the kid. I turned back to Mary Ann. "Hi, Mary Ann." My voice sounded stilted and unnatural and I had to listen carefully to myself to make sure I hadn't said, Yes, I kissed Kevin. And I liked it!

Mary Ann's placid expression told me that I had said what I intended. "Bel, I had such a great time that night you came over. Can we do it again?"

I didn't know how to respond.

"And Kevin said you're dating Brendan Joyce, so we could have a double date instead? What do you think?"

My mouth was open, but no words came out.

"I have been working so much and I really need to get some kind of social life," she said. "Kevin has been begging me to cut back on my hours and I should think about that. When he told me you were dating Brendan, I thought that it would be perfect for the four of us to get together."

Her face was so earnest that I really didn't have the heart to tell her that there was no more Bel and Brendan, that we were back to just Bel. So I lied. "That would be great," I said, figuring that this conversation about getting together would be like the ones I had in New York: always promised, never executed. This double-date idea would fall by the wayside like so many other plans that materialized at bars, on subway platforms, and in Whole Foods.

"How about tomorrow?" she asked. "I just finished my thirty-six-hour shift, so I have three days off in a row."

That's what she looked like after a thirty-six-hour shift? That was just not fair. I smoothed down my T-shirt and ran a hand through my unruly red locks. "You know what?" I said. "I'll call you. After I speak to Brendan," I said, not mentioning that I might not ever speak to Brendan again.

"Great." She leaned in and gave me a kiss. "It's so great to see you again, Bel. So great to have you back in town."

"Really?" I said. "We've been keeping Kevin mighty busy over at the Manor." And now in more ways than one, I thought.

She waved a hand dismissively. "It's his job and he loves it." She moved her purse from one hand to the other and put back the zucchini. "Call me when you know if you're free," she said, and gave me one last beatific smile before heading down another aisle of the market.

I put the tomatoes in my eco-friendly bag and picked

up a couple of loaves of fresh bread figuring I would drown my sorrows in some bruschetta, a bottle of red a part of my anticipated feast as well. On the way home, I wondered how I would finesse all of this with Brendan while keeping my distance from Kevin, trying desperately to sort out my feelings for both men as I navigated the road on my way back to Foster's Landing.

I stopped by The Dugout and dropped off a couple of tomatoes.

"So, Oogie," I said, grabbing a knife out of the block on the counter in the kitchen. "This is how you cut a tomato for the BLT we talked about." I demonstrated with the less-than-effective knife how thin the slices should be.

"I think they should be thicker," he said, standing behind me, looking over my shoulder.

Who was I to argue? It was his restaurant. "Just a suggestion," I said, fanning out the slices.

He grabbed a loaf of bread from the refrigerator. "So, how's it going here, Bel? You starting to fit in again? Adopt the Landing state of mind?"

Had he asked me that a few days ago, I would have said it was going great. Now half of my family weren't speaking to me, I had kissed Kevin Hanson and lost Brendan Joyce, and I wasn't sure any of this, the coming home, had been a particularly good idea. I smiled, but my heart felt heavy. "Great, Oogie. I'm loving it here."

He raised an eyebrow.

"Really. It's fine. How are people liking the new menu items?" I asked.

"BLTs are a hit. Everything else . . ."

"Not great?"

"Ah, it's fine."

"No, we'll work on it," I said. "Let me come up with some other bar-friendly options for you." I put the knife back in the block.

"Where do you think she went, Bel?" he asked. "Amy," he added, as if I wouldn't know to whom he was referring.

I couldn't look at him. We had been over this. "I don't know, Oogie."

He waited, as if there would be more.

"I really don't," I said, before pushing through the swinging doors into the bar, where I felt several sets of eyes on me before I burst out onto the street. She was dead. Why couldn't he see that? Girls like Amy don't disappear like that, never to be seen again.

Back at the apartment, I was still a little unhinged but I brought my purchases inside and started chopping tomatoes as soon as everything was unpacked, not being able to shake the feeling that my time at The Dugout, the idea that I could help, was a mistake. Maybe Jed had been right and I did feel guilty. It would be only natural, though I had suppressed the feeling for the years in between when I had originally left and now, when I had come back.

In between the slapping on the wood cutting board and the staccato thoughts running through my head, I heard the sound of footsteps coming up the rickety wooden steps and then the *click-clack* of high heels on the deck outside.

"I'm back!"

Caleigh. Good God. She was the last person I wanted to see right now, tan and rested and sensually fulfilled from her time in Bermuda, the likely recipient of many a massage, back rub, and fruity drink served ocean side. I had made the mistake of looking up the resort at which she was staying; it was all pastel cottages, personal valets, and five-star dining. Jealousy isn't a good look on me, but there you have it: I was jealous, particularly after the last couple of weeks I had had with my family and the Manor and the local police. With a man in uniform and one who just wore a camp director shirt. I gave in to my envy just a bit, taking in her relaxed face, her tanned calves coming out of a pair of Tory Burch Bermuda shorts, her outfit topped off with a pair of Jimmy Choo sandals.

Wow. It hadn't taken her long to fall into the role of rich Westchester wife.

She came into the apartment and, as always, sniffed disapprovingly in the direction of the Ikea sofa with the ketchup stain, my laminate kitchen cabinets, the rug with the hole in it at the foot of my bed. Even before she had come into the money and life that being Mark Chesterton's wife afforded, she had found my apartment "drab" and "depressing." She should have seen my fifth-floor walk-up on Avenue C. She would have loved that, but she didn't go east of Broadway when she went below 14th Street and that had prevented her from seeing a pretty nice apartment that awaited me after hoofing it up the stairs.

"I'm back!" she said again, apparently waiting for a reply from me or some over-the-top reaction.

"Hi, Caleigh," I said. I went so far as to give her a quick hug.

She waved toward the back door. "There's some huge guy wandering around in the woods out there. I hope you know him."

"There is?" I asked. I went to the back door and saw the familiar outfit of camp director shirt and khaki shorts. "Yes, that's Brendan Joyce." I heard him calling Felix's name; the cat must have returned to his one true home with me. At least that's what I told myself.

She curled her lip. "The kid with the braces? The one from school?"

"Yes. Except that he doesn't have braces anymore. He's a grown man who teaches art at the high school."

"What's he doing in the woods?"

"Looking for his cat."

She didn't respond, continuing to look around the apartment. "I brought you something," she said after casting her glance on every surface and finding everything lacking. She pulled a tissue-wrapped gift out of her enormous leather bag and handed it to me. "Ta-da!"

I took the gift and opened it up to find a scented candle with an exact replica of the hotel where Caleigh and Mark had stayed glued to the lid. I opened it up and sniffed it.

"Doesn't it smell just like Bermuda?" Caleigh asked.

"I wouldn't know. I've never been to Bermuda," I said. Honestly, to me it smelled like every single scented candle I had ever smelled—the pumpkin ones, the apple pie ones, the cinnamon and spice ones—all rolled together. For all I knew, she had bought a candle stateside, glued on some kind of art project, and called it my gift. When I saw her disappointed face, I did what I always did: I tried to make her feel better. "It's lovely, Caleigh. Thank you. It will really be a nice addition to the place."

She perked up. "You're welcome! Mark picked it out. He thought you'd like a souvenir from our honeymoon after everything you did to make the wedding a success."

Had she lost her mind? Had the wedding been "a success" and I hadn't realized it? A guy had been murdered. I wouldn't call that a success. "Yeah, about that, Caleigh."

"About what? The wedding? We got some great photos of you, Bel. You look really good!" she said, which led me to believe that she thought I looked chubby and was overcompensating for that thought. I probably did look chubby, because I am chubby. To me Caleigh looked like she hadn't had a decent meal in months, and I knew she had gone on some medically approved starvation diet two months prior to the wedding on which she had shed unnecessarily some twenty pounds. As she stood in front of me, even with the glow from her honeymoon I thought she looked positively skeletal. "Want something to eat?" I asked, my go-to in situations like this.

Her mouth practically watered at the suggestion and I

didn't wait for her answer. Mom had loaded my refrigerator with some lentil crap, a kale salad that wasn't bad looking, and some leftover lasagna from a dinner she and Dad had had at the local Italian joint. I pulled out the lasagna and put it on a plastic plate, shoving it into the microwave for two minutes. She took a seat at the counter. I poured her a big glass of Cabernet, her favorite, and handed her a fork and the plate of lasagna, smoking hot and ready to be eaten.

She shoved a forkful of pasta into her mouth so quickly that she burned her tongue. "Ow!"

"Give it a minute to cool off, Caleigh," I said, pouring a glass of wine for myself.

She nodded, putting her fork down. Outside I could hear the plaintive cries of Brendan, begging the cat to come to him. I had noticed a pouch of salmon in his hand; looked like he had hoped for a strong headwind to bring the smell of the fish to Felix, but it was dead calm out there. "So, what's happened since I was gone?" she asked between mouthfuls of lasagna.

Were we going to go there? I wondered. Were we going to talk about what had happened between her and Declan? The murder itself? Or had life begun for Caleigh after she had said, "I do," with no looking back to the events preceding that declaration? "Well, the police have been investigating—"

She held up a hand. "Don't say it." A trail of marinara wound down her hand and her forearm, stopping at her elbow. I was right: she hadn't eaten anything substantial in a long time. No one makes that much of a mess while eating unless they are starving.

"Don't say what?"

"Don't say anything about anything. About *that*," she said. "I'm happy, Bel. For once."

For once? What happened to all of those years before this when she was head cheerleader, prom princess, accepted into the college of her choice early decision? What about those times? She wasn't happy? Could have fooled me. "You're just happy now?"

She pointed the fork at me. "Don't talk about it. Leave it alone."

"Caleigh, Cargan saw Declan and Mark arguing at the wedding. What was that about?"

"Nothing!" she said. "Leave. It. Alone."

"Did he think that Declan was too close to you? Was he suspicious?" I asked. "Don't worry. He has an alibi. He was dancing with Jonesy."

"I know he has an alibi," she said, sneering at me. "And yes, he thought Declan was too flirtatious." She downed her wine. "I don't want to talk about this anymore."

There was one thing I wanted to know, and even though she was done with the subject I asked her anyway. "Where did you meet him? He wasn't at the rehearsal dinner. And I didn't lay eyes on him prior to the wedding."

She mumbled something between bites of food.

"What?" I said. "It sounded like you said, 'The Dugout.'"

"I did!" she said, wiping her mouth. "I went to The Dugout."

"Oogie didn't mention seeing you there," I said.

"Oogie wasn't there," she said. "Just as well. I didn't want to see anyone I knew."

"The Dugout?" I asked, incredulous. "Hot dogs and horrible beer? And even worse wine?"

"Yes," she said.

"And Oogie is always there. Practically lives there," I said.

"Well, this time he wasn't," she said, defiant. "I just wanted to have one last good time." That made me wonder just what she expected from her marriage. "I didn't realize he was coming to the wedding until after."

"The brogue didn't give it away?" I asked.

"He wasn't even invited."

"Yes, but a guy you had never seen, with a brogue, in the Landing?" I asked. Seemed obvious to me.

"Lots of people in the Landing have brogues."

She had a point.

"I suspected that he might know one of us," she said, "but I wanted the whole thing to be anonymous. Dangerous."

"Oh, it was dangerous, all right, Caleigh. So dangerous that he ended up dead."

"Which is not my fault," she said. "Just leave it alone, Bel."

There were times, over the years, when I had wanted to lose my temper with Caleigh, but something had stopped me. Maybe it was guilt. Something about her being family, my almost sister. But I didn't have that kind of restraint anymore, not after everything that had happened in my life and even the day that I had had, everyone now angry with me over what I thought was a sensible decision regarding my brother and his recollections, recollections that still didn't amount to much or warrant his getting a lawyer and putting me in hot water with my parents. "Caleigh," I said, speaking slowly. "A man died at your wedding. A man you slept with—"

"Shhhh!" she said, clasping a saucy hand over my mouth. "Don't say another word."

I took her hand from my mouth. Outside I heard Brendan clomping up the stairs to the apartment. "Do you realize that now that you're back you have to talk to the police again?" I asked through clenched teeth. "That if this murder goes unsolved any longer, the suspect list will widen again and everyone will be questioned again? I'm surprised Kevin didn't meet you at the airport and bring you in. They are going to want your phone."

By the look on her face I realized that she didn't know about those last texts, because I had deleted them before she had seen them.

"My phone? Why?"

It was like ripping off a Band-Aid, me blurting this out. "He was texting you. During the wedding. When you passed out, I deleted all of the texts not realizing that a) he would die and b) those texts would still be on his phone."

She dropped her fork on the plate, her appetite gone. "Nice going, Bel."

"I'm sorry."

"So why would they want my phone?" she asked. "If everything is gone?"

"I guess to see if you had anything else related to him on it."

Her face went blank and I wasn't sure why. "I tried to get rid of everything, Caleigh. I was trying to help."

"Thank you?" she said. "I'm probably a suspect now."

You probably should have always been one, I wanted to say, but I didn't.

Brendan knocked lightly on the back door and I called to him to let himself in. He walked in cradling Taylor/Felix, the smile that was on his face usually replaced by a thin-lipped frown.

"He keeps coming back here," Brendan said, petting the cat's head. "I don't know why."

Because he loves me? I wanted to say. But Brendan and I weren't at the point where we could joke with each other, the tension between us completely understandable but uncomfortable nonetheless. Caleigh didn't seem to notice.

He took in the two of us, Caleigh staring at her lasagna and me glaring at my cousin. "Am I interrupting something?"

Caleigh stood, wiped her hands on the paper towel I

handed her, and smoothed down her Bermuda shorts. "Hello. Caleigh Chesterton."

"I know you, Caleigh," Brendan said, and something dark passed across his usually cheerful face. I couldn't tell if it was directed at Caleigh or me. "We went to high school together."

"Yes. We did," she said, her clipped staccato indicating that her memories of him weren't pleasant and I suspected had to do with some dismissal of him by her and not the other way around. "Bel, thanks for the lasagna. I'm going to leave now." She passed Brendan on her way to the door. "Nice cat."

When we heard her car speed off, the gravel road alerting us to her departure, Brendan looked at me. "She's as delightful as she was in high school, I see."

"No love lost?" I asked.

He was too much of a gentleman to say. His last comment was indeed his last on the subject of Caleigh Chesterton, née McHugh. He held on tight to the cat. "He's gained some weight," he said, lifting the cat up and down and feeling his heft.

"He's been eating well."

Brendan nodded toward the back door, the last place Caleigh had been. "Caleigh didn't look happy when she left."

"She wasn't."

"I hope it wasn't my appearance here."

"No," I said, not saying what it was. I walked him to the back door and ruffled the cat's fur. "It is okay if I visit with him occasionally?"

"I don't know, Bel," he said.

"Maybe I can bring him salmon from a pouch?" I said.

Brendan smiled, but it was sad. I was getting a lot of sad smiles these days from various people, which was really starting to bum me out.

"I guess that's a no?" I said.

"Your life seems a little complicated right now," he said.

That was one way to put it.

I waited until he was gone before I really let what had happened sink in, how I had ruined probably the best thing that had happened to me in a long time. I had no appetite anymore, which was how I knew that things were really serious.

I guess that's what happens when you move on as quickly as I had from a former life without one backward glance.

I texted Mary Ann D'Amato and told her that unfortunately, we wouldn't be able to make it to dinner after all. No use operating under false pretenses anymore.

CHAPTER *Thirty-four*

"Bring your boyfriend to dinner," they said.

"We'd love to see him again!" they included.

"It will be fun!" was the consensus.

I didn't have the heart to tell them that I no longer had a boyfriend, that that relationship had been the shortest in the history of relationships. It was fine, though, because what my family left out when they begged me to bring him was that they wouldn't be on their best behavior, their best behavior something that they had misplaced somewhere along the way, along with class, couth, and the ability to sit down, *en famille,* at the large table and have a discussion that didn't include Mom clucking about someone's lack of grooming, Dad blustering about the lack of accolades for his new installation, or Feeney poking Cargan about a recent musical arrangement to the point of an almost fistfight. I made up an excuse about Brendan planning for the week at camp, which was a Herculean task given that most of the days at the camp previous to this summer had the kids swimming for most of the day.

The McCarthy wedding from the day before had gone off without a hitch, my new hors d'oeuvres making quite a splash and everyone complimenting Dad on the food as they left. The boys had played flawlessly and no one had fought in between sets. No injuries during the Siege. More important, everyone had lived. All in all, it had been a good day.

I wondered if everyone had just lost their collective spark all at once. I knew it couldn't last.

Caleigh showed up for dinner without Mark, who I guessed had had enough of my family to last him a lifetime.

Mom raised an eyebrow in disapproval. "Busy?" Mom asked, a smile plastered on her face not disguising her disdain for a husband who didn't accompany his wife to Sunday dinner at her family's.

"He's talking to the contractor about our new quartz countertops," Caleigh said, checking her teeth in her knife. You could take the girl out of Foster's Landing, but you couldn't take Foster's Landing out of the girl.

"On a Sunday?" Mom asked. "More peas, Derry?" she added, showing everyone who she liked best at that moment.

Derry took the bowl and helped himself to a heaping spoonful of peas; I had bought them at the farmer's market along with the tomatoes. Cargan and I had shelled them in the kitchen, side by side, in silence. I assumed we were still in a fight over my taking him to the police station, a situation that was taking an inordinately long time to blow over.

Before everyone arrived, I asked Mom if she had invited Aunt Trudie to dinner, a question that was met with stony silence. I guessed that that was a "no"?

"Yes. Mark is very busy," Caleigh said, licking her lips. She had Mom's tell, too. Must have been a family trait. "The contractor is very busy during the week, too, so he bids and consults on the weekend."

Liar, liar, pants on fire. It was written all over her red face.

Feeney got to the point. He pointed his knife in Caleigh's direction. "I don't think he fancies us much." Feeney's girlfriend, Sandree, had begged off this week, a fact about which I was disappointed; she had promised me some Old Navy Super Cash and I was looking forward to acquiring a new collection of yoga pants. That, and she had written some new songs and we were going to miss their debut.

"Probably thinks we're a bunch of hooligans," Derry added. Another county heard from, so to speak. "And rightly so."

Arney chuckled around a mouthful of peas.

"That's not what he thinks," Caleigh said. "He likes you all just fine. Very much, in fact."

Frank the Tank chimed in from the end of the table, "He's a fine fellow."

We all turned in unison and looked at Frank, shocked to hear his voice for the first time in days.

"Well, he is," Frank said. "And he deserves our girl here."

We didn't mention that Caleigh wasn't technically "his girl." She blushed deeply at the emotion coming from a previously emotionless man and nodded her head to him in silent gratitude.

We all went back to eating, Feeney finally breaking the silence. "I got questioned again by Hanson." He sighed. "Jesus. You get one vandalism conviction in high school and you're forever a suspect."

"A perp," Derry said.

Arney chimed in, "There was also the drunk and disorderly. Oh, and the public indecency."

"Dismissed," Feeney reminded him. "Lack of evidence."

"Actually, it wasn't lack of evidence. Everyone saw you

with your pants around your ankles at The Dugout. Oogie dropped the charges," Arney said, a stickler for the truth and accurate details.

Feeney waved his hand. "There was a line for the men's room," he said, looking around for the person who guffawed at the revelation. It was Frank. He couldn't help it. Feeney high-fived him over the pot roast on the platter in the middle of the table.

"And there was that time at the concert," Arney said.

Dad slammed his hand on the table. "Enough! Youthful indiscretions. All of them."

Cargan excused himself from the table, the thought of going back to the police station seeming to bring on some intestinal distress. The door to the bathroom at the end of the hall slammed shut behind him.

"Poor lad," Frank said, shaking his head.

Him or the dead guy? I wanted to shout, but no one seemed terribly concerned about the murder. Still. I decided to go for broke. "So, Caleigh," I said.

At my tone, she shot me a look. Cease and desist. Shut your piehole. But I wouldn't.

"The police say that Declan was a wedding crasher, even though we now know he was a relative. Our relative, but a relative nonetheless. Are you still sticking to that story?"

Arney sat up straighter, stiffening. And considering he was a stiff to begin with, the straightest of the bunch, the most reliable and dare I say "normal," that was saying a lot.

Caleigh, directly across from me, met my eye. "Yes, Bel. A crasher. No one knew him."

"That's not true. He said he had met you in Ireland a few times. He was my cousin but he said he met you. And even though everyone else denied it, Aunt Trudie's arrival certainly confirms that it was true."

I turned to Dad, who had suddenly fallen silent at the head of the table, his previous exhortations on Feeney's indiscretions, the state of Ireland, post–Celtic Tiger, and a host of other topics getting the attention of Frank and Brendan; we had all heard it before. "Really? You seemed to know him pretty well, Dad. He was your nephew. When was the last time you saw him? You said it was when he was a 'wee baby' but that can't be, can it?"

Mom spoke for him. "Let it go, Belfast. This is not the time."

I looked at Aunt Helen. "Not a clue? No idea?"

Helen looked down at her plate, a lone dollop of mashed potatoes sitting in the middle of the free stoneware that we had collected as kids and that Mom still used. "I didn't know him, Belfast."

I looked at every member of my family: Mom, Dad, Arney, Derry, Feeney, Cargan, Caleigh, and Aunt Helen. "Not one of you?"

I realized this wasn't the best time to interrogate the family at large, but we wouldn't be together for another week and that was another week that the murder of some poor bloke—something no one else seemed to care about—at Shamrock Manor went unsolved.

Maybe this wasn't about him, I thought as the family stared back at me like I had lost my mind. Maybe my impending hysteria was about something else. Maybe this was about Amy. Unsolved mysteries. People who appear and then disappear without a trace. Maybe this was about my own guilt, my own sadness.

I didn't realize until that moment that I had stood and was gripping the edge of the table. I sat down and looked down at my lap.

"You knew him, Caleigh." It was Cargan, having returned from the bathroom, the collar of his soccer jersey damp from when he had washed his face earlier. When she didn't answer, he continued. "I saw you together. Stop saying you didn't know him." He said what I had been thinking for weeks.

Aunt Helen threw her napkin onto her plate. "Well, I never!" she said.

Feeney looked at Aunt Helen. "We always suspected that."

Helen looked at him, furious.

"That you never," Feeney said, earning himself a cuff to the head from Dad.

"I didn't know him, Cargan." Caleigh tried to laugh it off. "You've had a few, haven't you? Bless your heart." She looked around the table for support but seeing everyone's downcast eyes, sad expressions, knew that she was alone.

As beautiful as she was, at that moment she was really ugly.

"I'm not drunk, Caleigh, and I'm not stupid, like you've always thought. Like you used to say."

Caleigh looked around for support, but she got none. "Well, you weren't the sharpest tool in the silverware drawer," she said.

Mixed metaphors notwithstanding, I saw red when she said that, an image of us as little kids floating into my head, Cargan, about ten, in bright red swim trunks at the village pool, me, the younger sister trying to teach him to do the backstroke. Caleigh, in a snappy one-piece with cutouts on the side, saying, "What's the matter with you? Are you a baby? Are you stupid?" And me, getting grounded for a week because I had held her head under the water, not long enough to drown her or cause brain damage (well, I hope not), but just long enough to teach her a lesson.

"I saw you together after the rehearsal dinner. Outside

of The Dugout." He closed his mouth suddenly, not sure he wanted to continue. But continue he did. "You knew him. I saw you kiss him." He sat down at the table. "And now, I think I would like a beer."

CHAPTER Thirty-five

Caleigh had left in a huff after dinner and Cargan's revelation, denying everything that Cargan saw. I believed Cargan over her—everyone did—and she knew it. I never did get to ask her if she had been back to the FLPD to talk to Kevin, as he had promised she would be. She protested heartily to us and for a long time, but it was written all over her flushed face: she knew Declan and more than a little bit. And now others at the table knew what I had known all along. I'm not sure Aunt Helen or any of the other elders made that connection, but Feeney surely did and when he looked at me he rolled his eyes, never having been a fan of our dear cousin.

In the kitchen, I asked Cargan if he had told Kevin about the kiss. "On the advice of counsel, I plead the Fifth."

"Car, we're not on *Law and Order*. I'm your sister. You can tell me."

But he had just repeated himself and turned his back on me, giving his full attention to the sink and to the roasting pan that was crusted with dried gravy.

Before I walked out, he whispered, "They have a cell phone. With lots of messages."

I knew that, but now I was the one keeping secrets. I kept my mouth shut and made a hasty exit. "How do you know that?" I asked.

He was caught. "I overheard something at the police station."

"Did you also happen to overhear anything about why anyone would have bugged the Manor?" I asked.

"No."

"What do you think?" I asked. "Who do you think did that? Maybe Declan?"

"I don't know, Bel. Let the police figure it out. It's complicated, I'm sure."

I eyed him before I left, seeing if he would give something else up, but he was tight-lipped, putting away the leftovers.

Aunt Helen was crying copious tears at the table as I departed, Frank in the same position he had been in at the wedding, his arm around her, consoling her. "It will be okay, Helen. He's gone now," he said in his deep baritone. I wasn't sure who he was referring to—Declan or Cargan— but Aunt Helen wasn't having any of his consolation. She threw his arm off with a strength that surprised no one— she was one of Mom's Pilates acolytes after all—and stormed from the house, slamming the door in my face before I could leave myself.

I turned to the stunned members of my family. "Well, that went well," I said, but that proclamation didn't break the tension like I thought it might. I left right after that, thinking that those first early days when I slept all day, the covers pulled over my head, after my dismissal from The Monkey's Paw and my broken engagement seemed like the glory days compared to the past couple of weeks here. I left and went to the only home I knew now: the apartment.

I was lounging on my stained couch when Kevin showed up a few minutes after nine. I wasn't expecting him and told him, indelicately, that he was the last person I wanted to see.

"Sorry about that," he said. He noticed the healthy pour of red wine in the goblet on the counter. "Got another one of those?"

I only had one wineglass, so I took a water glass from the cabinet and filled it halfway. "This will have to do," I said. "I'm short on anything that matches around here. All hand-me-downs." I thought about Mary Ann's perfectly appointed house on the other side of town and how good it had smelled that night I had had dinner there. I didn't know where he lived exactly and wondered how it could compare to his girlfriend's place. "How's Mary Ann?" I asked. I couldn't meet his eye. It was too uncomfortable after the kiss.

"She's good," he said. He shifted around in his suit, still on the clock, the red wine notwithstanding. "Hey, Bel. Is Caleigh back from her honeymoon?" he asked. "She was supposed to call me as soon as she got back to the States. I've been trying to reach her, but she doesn't answer her cell or her home number. And I've been in touch with Bronxville PD and there's no sign of her at the house."

I wondered about that. Maybe she was the person living in our basement? Was she in hiding? She had been back at least two days that I knew of, but coupled with Cargan's admission of seeing her with Declan it was no wonder that she hadn't called Kevin. "She is," I said, not sure how much I should reveal. She's a pain in the ass, but she's my pain in the ass and I didn't wish her ill despite her duplicitous nature. When I thought about it, she'd probably sell me down the river for a new Hermès bag, a thought that was beneath me but probably the truth.

"How long?"

I told the truth. "Not sure, really. Two days? Maybe three?" I gulped down some wine. "Why? Is there something going on?"

"Might be," he said. "We just need to question every-one again and see if any memories have been jogged over the past two weeks."

"Isn't the case growing colder by the day?" I asked, hearkening back to something I had heard while watching *Castle* with Cargan when I had first arrived home. "Isn't it going to be harder to solve?"

"Yes. It's getting harder by the day, but we have some new information—" he said, stopping himself from going any further.

"New information?" I asked.

"Never mind, Bel. It's nothing."

"Do I need to be questioned again?" I asked.

"I think we have everything we need from you," he said, effectively letting me know that I was off the suspect list, if I had ever been on it. It would have been virtually impos-sible for me to kill Declan Morrison, run down the stairs, and then witness his death. Even Kevin could figure that out. He hemmed and hawed for a few minutes and it was clear he had something to tell me.

"Spit it out, Hanson. You were never good at keeping secrets," I said.

"We have a search warrant," he said, drinking his wine down in one gulp. "Two actually."

"But you already searched the Manor."

"Not for the Manor."

"And you already looked around my apartment and the studios." I thought about what it could be. "The bugs? Do you have something on that?" The wheels turned in my head. Cargan lived in the Manor and I thought a thorough search had been done of the premises, including his room and Mom's office, as well as the bedroom where Caleigh had gotten ready. "Where else is there to look?" I asked.

He blurted it out. "We need to go back to the studios. The Pilates studio. Your father's place."

"Now what would you hope to find there?" I asked. "There's lot of torture equipment in Mom's studio and there's just . . . bad art in Dad's," I said, regretting my honesty.

Kevin smiled. "It's not so bad. His 9/11 tribute was nice."

No, it wasn't. Just ask anyone in the village. "What are you hoping to find?" I asked. "And didn't you search the other night? The night you found the bugs?"

"Like I said: new information."

I gripped the glass in my hand thinking of Dad talking to Declan at the wedding, looking chummy, running across Mom the week after his death in the wedding suite, crying. My eyes went to the sugar bowl on the counter, the one with the earring in it. They both had acted very strangely and that was saying a lot, because they were a bit strange on a normal day, a day that didn't include a relative's wedding and a murder. "And if you tell me, you'll have to kill me?"

Like every joke I had told this week, this one fell flat, too.

"Just tell me, Kevin. Do I need to worry? Do my parents?"

"Not if they don't have anything to hide," he said. Outside the sun finally set completely, and the apartment was almost completely dark, so dark that I could barely see him. I switched on the overhead light in the kitchen, making him wince. He finished his wine.

"When?"

"Tomorrow morning," he said. "We were going to come in tonight, but McDougall called in with a bout of scurvy."

"Is he a pirate?"

"Nah. Just a hypochondriac."

"He'd better get that looked at. Or have an orange."

"He thought he had mange last year. It was poison ivy."

Kevin headed for the door. "Well, okay. Bye," he said, looking at me like he regretted everything, everything he had said, everything he had done.

He was warning me. I didn't know why and I didn't care; obviously, he had no idea I was as nosy as I was and that the minute I knew he was out of sight, I would be out of my apartment and into the studios. I waited for the sound of gravel spraying, kicking up onto the lawn of the Manor, before I put my clogs back on and ran down the stairs to Dad's studio, hoping against hope that I wouldn't find anything that would incriminate him in this sordid case. We already knew that the guns weren't anything to worry about, their barrels stuffed with cement and ready for an installation. Mom I wasn't so sure about. She lived her life close to the vest, and if there were someone in my life to whom I needed to entrust a secret, something that I would want them to take to their grave, it would be Mom. All my life, and I don't know why, I felt as if she was holding back, as if she was keeping something from me and maybe even Dad. I wasn't sure I ever wanted to know what that was, if anything, but the stakes were higher than they had ever been.

The former Rose of Tralee, the mother of four boys (and me, of course, even though I never felt like it counted among her friends, the Irishwomen who thought that raising boys was akin to herding cats and worthy of a Nobel Peace Prize), the grande dame of Shamrock Manor.

My mother, the enigma.

CHAPTER *Thirty-six*

Dad's studio was clean.

Well, as clean as any place that housed used bits of scrap metal, oil-covered paintbrushes, and giant canvases splattered with the musings of what I suspected was kind of a tormented mind. There weren't any more guns and there was no trace of firepower anywhere, no ammo, no clips, no shiny pieces of metal that seemed to be part of a larger, more deadly contraption. I crept across the small expanse of lawn to Mom's studio, housed in another out-building, fronted with large windows that on a sunny day let in warm sunlight that bathed the place in a soft glow, the bodies glistening in the heat and under my mother's watchful eye.

I had a key. Back when I had first arrived home, I had answered the phones for exactly three days but had tired quickly of looking at sinewy women dressed in expensive athletic wear. I had taken over for an "exhausted" Aunt Helen, who had needed some time off from the job and gratefully accepted me as her replacement for a spell. Once I left the position, Helen's exhaustion dissipated and she returned, using the small office as her unofficial wedding planner central location, booking flowers, and ordering cake and making sure that everything Caleigh wanted Caleigh got. Within reason, of course. Caleigh still had her wedding at her aunt and uncle's wedding hall, a place she associated with proms past and the Irish step-dancing recitals of our youth.

I didn't dare put on a light; what with the large windows in the front everyone would be able to see me, get a gander at what I was doing. I had grabbed a small flashlight from one of the drawers in the apartment and held it in my teeth as I wrestled with the door, which always stuck and required a jiggle or two to open. In the dark, the studio was even creepier than it was during the day, all of those contraptions standing at attention, just waiting for my mother to bark orders in her low, "inside" voice to the grateful women who benefited from her physical ministrations. I broke out in a light sweat at the thought of the contortions that the women twisted their bodies into, all in the name of "health." If that was health, leave me out. I'd continue with my foie gras, good wine, and delicious chocolate and die happy, probably at a much younger age than the women who came to the classes. I was okay with that, a life well lived and all.

I wended my way around the equipment and went back into the office. Mom had two desks—one for her and one for Helen—but a quick spin through Mom's told me that she kept nothing here, one drawer containing only a few business cards, another holding a stash of pencils, and the last four used ChapSticks. Helen's desk was a different story, the contents revealing just how different the sisters were from each other. Papers spilled from the drawers and it was hard to open them, even tougher to close them when I tried. Old client contracts, new client contracts, stuff that should have been filed but had never been, the history of Oona's Pilates Studio right there in all of its messy glory. I riffled through the papers in each drawer, the flashlight still between my teeth, my mother's voice in my head saying, Belfast! If it's not food, don't put it in your mouth. I had taken those words to heart, for the most part, but in the dark, and with so much to examine and read, I had only one option. The mouth it was.

I slammed the three desk drawers shut and turned my attention to the drawer that slid right under the top of the desk, the one where one would keep extra paper or pens and papers, paper clips. Not Aunt Helen. I pushed aside a half-eaten peanut-butter sandwich and dug around, feeling around in the drawer for anything unusual, something not a client contract. My fingers grazed a manila envelope, stiff and unyielding and, when opened, revealing a bunch of photographs.

Ireland, 1986. Or so said the inscription on the back, Dad's mullet on display in the first photo, taken at JFK Airport, and Aunt Helen's shoulder pads in the second supporting the date. I remembered that trip. It was years before the chicken pox vaccine was required for all kids and getting the virus was a rite of passage; everyone eventually got it, and if you had four brothers the chances were that you would be next in line once the last brother's scabs had healed. The day we were to leave to visit the family in Ireland, I had broken out in it, my body covered with sores. Mom stayed home, canceling her ticket for the family trip, giving me flat soda when I had a fever, dabbing my body with calamine lotion when the itching got too much. I remember crying like I had never cried before when Dad and the boys drove away, Cargan the only one showing any sympathy for me, knowing, as he did, that I wanted to go on this trip more than anything. His face, staring out of the Vanagon, his fingers waggling a little good-bye to his sister, was an image etched in my brain.

I looked at the photos, the memories flooding back. My brothers were in one photo and Caleigh was in another. And as I looked at the last one, a photo of a handsome boy, good-looking in a dark-haired, dark-eyed way, a few freckles dotting his nose, it occurred to me how much he looked like Arney, a younger Feeney. I turned the photo over.

"Declan," it read. "Age 10."

In another photo, my father was crouched down in front of Declan, handing him something that looked like an envelope, the boy accepting it and smiling.

Mom was so quiet that I never heard her enter; that or I was so engrossed in looking at the photos that I wasn't aware of anyone else in the room until I heard her voice. "Bel? What are you doing?"

I dropped the photos on the floor, the one of Declan Morrison/McGrath as a young boy going facedown, his image hidden from view. "You did know him. You all knew him."

"Sit down, Bel," Mom said, less angry than I thought she would be at finding me in the office of the studio.

"I will not sit down," I said, my voice sounding like an extended hiss. "You all lied." I shook off the hand she had put on my arm, the pressure not subtle at all. "Did you lie to the police? I thought you said that none of you knew him really, even though he was Uncle Dermot's kid?"

By the look on her face, it was clear they had.

"The boys don't remember him," she said. "At least, I don't think they do."

"Cargan?"

"Definitely not," she said. "He was too young when they met."

"How do you know?" I asked.

She was silent. She knew just like she knew that not telling me had been a huge mistake.

"Mom," I said as calmly as I could, "Kevin has a search warrant for this office and Dad's studio. He warned me, essentially, because I can't think of any other reason a good detective, which of course we are not sure Kevin really is, would let someone know about a search. You have to come clean. This is serious."

"I know it's serious," Mom said. In the gloom of the office I got a glimpse of the woman she had been forty or so years prior, one with dewy skin and innocence in her expression, one who would soon meet my father and start a life with him, not knowing how mercurial he might become, how his "art" would become a singular focus, to the detriment of the business they built together. Even though the room was dark, I could see that she had tears in her eyes.

CHAPTER Thirty-seven

I went to bed, confused, a little sad, and a lot angry. If there's one thing I hate, it's being kept in the dark.

And onions. Thanks to hypnosis, I hate onions.

"Caleigh knew him," I had said, the enormity of everything pressing down on me. My parents lying to the police, Caleigh disavowing any knowledge of a man she had met in Ireland a long time ago.

"She only met him that one time. And she was little," Mom had said. "How old was she, Mal? Eight? Nine?"

And there began a heated discussion of how old Caleigh had been in 1986.

Finally, I ended the debate. "Who cares?"

Mom was beyond doing the math at that point. "I'm not sure she put the pieces together at the wedding."

I wondered if Caleigh and Declan's pillow talk had included his admission that they had played Ring Around the Rosie in Ballyminster back in 1986. I suspected not. But the idea that she had met him when they were children haunted me as I tossed and turned and tried to fall asleep. Was she really that dense? That dumb?

I decided, right before I fell into a dream-filled, tortured sleep, that yes, she was.

No one had even a guess as to why he had shown up to

crash Caleigh's wedding. He was a family member, so was he really crashing? Or just representing his side of the family?

When I woke up in the morning, just like he said he would Kevin brought most of the police department with him—sirens turned off, thankfully—and searched Mom's Pilates studio and Dad's art space. Mom had canceled the morning session the night before, so thankfully we didn't have an army of taut middle-aged women stomping around the grounds, waiting to be tortured by Mom in her spandex leotard.

Mom and Dad seemed preternaturally calm about the whole thing, even going so far as asking me to whip up a buffet breakfast for the cops while they trampled through the various rooms at the Manor and its outbuildings.

"A little fry-up," Dad said, ushering me into the kitchen when I emerged from the apartment.

"Should I whip up a pitcher of Bloody Marys, while I'm at it?" I asked.

He thought on the question for longer than it deserved. "I don't think so. They are all on duty after all."

It took all morning, with various boxes being carted out by the uniformed cops, who each took a break to have a meal in the dining hall of the Manor. "Great sausage, Bel!" one said, and I recognized him as Jimmy Hanry, my former dodgeball nemesis.

"Glad you're enjoying it," I said, going back into the kitchen to cook some more food. These guys were eating as if aliens were about to descend on the Manor and spirit us all away.

Cargan showed up a few minutes after ten, sweaty and nervous. "Are Mom and Dad suspects?" he asked.

"Don't know," I said, handing him a hotel pan and instructing him to dish the eggs I just made into it. "It was the weirdest thing, Car. Kevin came by last night and told me that this was going to happen." I thought of the photographs that I had found in Aunt Helen's desk drawer, now between my mattress and box spring. "Does that sound like normal police behavior to you?"

He thought about that for a few seconds. "Well, on one episode of *Law and Order: SVU,* Olivia warned a guy she was sleeping with that her partner liked him for a rape in Brooklyn."

Wow, he really did watch a lot of crime shows. "Liked" him? That was something only the cops on television said. "I think that's different," I said. "Kevin isn't having a relationship with anyone here." That wasn't entirely the truth, but it wasn't a lie, either. I willed myself not to blush at the thought of us sharing a kiss at the bottom of the stairs a few nights earlier. I was not successful.

Cargan started scooping eggs into the hotel pan. "Yeah, but he did."

"That was a long time ago, Car."

"I see the way he looks at you," my brother said, unable to meet my eye.

"He's with Mary Ann."

"Yeah, but they're not married."

"But they are in a committed relationship," I said, whipping up a bowl of pancake batter, which in and of itself, after all this time, was strange. Out in the dining hall, the natives were getting restless. I wondered if I kept feeding them if that would distract them from the task at hand.

"But they aren't married," Cargan said, his love of the literal trumping everything else. Like reason. And common sense. "And I wonder why that is?"

"I'm not interested," I said. I thought about Brendan Joyce and what a perfect guy he was. Had been. Still was. But he wasn't mine anymore. After Kevin, and then Ben, I think I was learning to trust again, and that was a comfort. When I had first arrived home, emotionally battered and bruised, I wasn't sure that time, or anyone, could heal those wounds. "Back to the investigation. Did you know that Declan Morrison was our cousin?" I asked.

Cargan focused on the eggs. "Mom told me this morning."

"You didn't remember him from that trip to Ireland in '86? The one I couldn't go on because I had the chicken pox?"

"I didn't remember, Bel. Heck, I can barely remember what I had for dinner last night."

"I can tell you: leftovers from the McCarthy wedding last weekend."

He looked up and smiled.

"Any time I package stuff up and then find it gone, I know it's you."

"I had a midnight snack," he admitted. "And your food is so much better than Goran's."

"Thanks, Car."

We went back to preparing and serving breakfast to the cops and finally, around eleven, they left. Mom retired to the office, where I could hear her tapping furiously on her MacBook. I poked my head in. "Everything okay, Mom?"

"Grand," she said, not looking up.

Today's investigation had nothing to do with me, so I could think of no reason for her to be mad at me. I decided that until this kind of attention was off the Manor she was going to be in a perpetually bad mood and I would bear the brunt of it because I was always here.

"Oh, and Belfast?" she said as I pulled out of the doorway.

"Yes, Mom?"

"We were just trying to protect you. . . ." She paused.

"From what?"

"The unpleasantness."

"I saw a guy die, Mom. I was already part of the un-pleasantness."

In the kitchen, I started washing up the pans I had used, thinking about what my mother had said. Growing up, the five of us had been shielded from unpleasantness almost never. The horrid details of Uncle Eugene's missing leg, how a British bomb had blown it off along with the head of a local bartender. My maternal grandmother's remem-brance of the time one of her childhood friends in her small village had actually starved to death. (That one came in particularly handy when Derry, a picky eater, refused to eat his vegetables or, really, anything else on his plate.) The baby who had died, along with its mother, in child-birth, my paternal grandmother—a child herself—the de facto midwife on call. My father's recounting of his arrival at Ellis Island—something we later came to find out was a lie; Ellis Island had closed its doors in 1954, six years before Dad even thought of coming abroad. Aunt Helen's telling of the horrible fight that took place between Uncle Dermot and my father one night, both of them ending up with bloody noses. That's how we grew up, and those were the stories we listened to. Now that we were adults, it seemed much too late to try to right the narrative ship and only tell stories that cast everyone in a good light.

I had been away a long time. I had to keep that in mind. People changed. I had changed. But when did they become completely different people?

That's the question I found myself thinking about a lot.

CHAPTER *Thirty-eight*

Before the police left, I found Kevin. "Did you find Caleigh yet?"

"I did," he said. "She came in on her own. Finally."

"And she gave you her phone?" I asked. I was tired of everyone else's lies, so I decided to come clean.

Kevin nodded.

"Anything else on there?" I asked.

He didn't answer, all of sudden deciding, it seemed, that he would be a real cop and do things by the book.

I stood on the lawn for a while, figuring out what to do next. After all of the cops were gone, I made my decision. It was a long shot, finding Declan's mother, but I decided to give it a try.

There aren't that many places to stay in Foster's Landing, so it didn't take me long to find Trudie McGrath. For obvious reasons she had elected not to stay at the Manor, and I didn't get the sense she'd be welcome there anyway, the way everyone reacted to the sound of her name making her seem like persona non grata. The next morning, after doing some prep work in the kitchen, I ran down the list of four bed-and-breakfasts in town, and found her on my third try. The receptionist at the B and B was someone I used to know from swim team and she put me right through to Trudie's room. After a little negotiation on time and place, she agreed to meet me at the Grand Mill for an early lunch.

I couldn't remember ever meeting Trudie formally, though I had heard about her. Apparently, she was the second most beautiful gal in the small village that she, my father, and my mother had grown up in, but unlike my mother, she hadn't aged quite as well in the intervening years since they were rivals for the local pageant crowns. The little woman who walked into the Grand Mill looked a full ten years older than my mother and clearly wasn't into Pilates, either, being doughy and soft. I hugged her and fell into an ample bosom. I told her how sorry I was for her loss.

She sat down, adjusting her napkin on her lap. "Thank you, Belfast. You're the image of your dad's ma," she said.

I had heard that before, so it didn't surprise me. "She was the redhead, from what I understand."

"Yes, and your mother herself had a bit of red in her hair before she started keeping it blond," Trudie said, looking down at the table.

"I'm so, so sorry about Declan," I said, repeating myself but at a loss for words.

"You saw it happen," she said.

"I did."

She looked at me expectantly and I knew what she was asking.

"No. He didn't suffer. He died right away," I said, but I couldn't be sure. It had been a horrific, violent death but fast? Who knew? I thought so, but I also knew that in this case I would be forgiven for lying. "Is that what you were told?"

She nodded and I was off the hook. One less sin to atone for.

The waitress came over and Trudie ordered a cup of tea but nothing else. "You're not hungry?" I asked.

"Sure, I haven't eaten in days," she said, her eyes filling with tears. "He was my only boy, you know."

"Can I ask you a few questions?" I said. It seemed as if she might be the only person who would tell me the truth. I waited for her tea and my soda to come and I asked her the question that no one seemed to be able to answer. "Why did he come to the wedding, Trudie? After all these years?"

"I don't know, Bel," she said, but that was a lie and we both knew it. She made a show of preparing her tea, tasting it finally to see if it was to her liking. It wasn't. I could tell by the look on her face. American tea. Not as good as the tea back home.

"Trudie, please. The more we know the easier it will be to find out what happened."

"Oh, we know what happened, Bel. Everyone knows what happened."

"We do?"

"Yes. My son was murdered at a family wedding. That's what we know."

This was getting me nowhere. "Do you have any idea who might have wanted to kill Declan?" I asked. "Any idea at all?"

She sipped her subpar tea, grimacing. "Any number of those people. Your father. Your mother. That infernal Eugene."

I gripped my glass, the condensation seeping between my fingers. "My mother or father?" Uncle Eugene was such a wild card that it didn't surprise me that he was included in this rogues' gallery of potential murderers.

She shook her head. "I've said too much. That was inappropriate. I'm sorry."

I leaned in. "Trudie, please. Tell me what's going on. What happened to Declan? We need to know."

"I will put it this way, Bel: He knew the secrets. Where the bodies are buried."

Before I could ask, Real bodies? the waitress came back to take our order. "We need a few more minutes," I said to her disappointed face. She wanted to serve us, turn over the table, and collect another lunch check; we were messing up that plan. I turned back to Trudie, waiting for an answer, but she was ready to leave, her purse in her hands, her lips in a grim line.

"Good-bye, Belfast." She started for the door. "I have a plane to catch."

I threw a twenty on the table, all I had, and raced after her, following her onto the sidewalk. She was hurrying somewhere, probably the B and B, even though it was clear from the way she was looking around that she didn't really know in which direction her temporary accommodations were. I caught up to her and grabbed her arm. "Trudie, wait." I was a little winded; the old gal could walk faster than I thought someone her age could or should. Must have been all of that traipsing around the little village where she still lived. "What is it that you can't tell me?"

She turned and fixed me with a look, part sad, part angry. "Ask your father," was all she said as she set off.

"You're going the wrong way!" I called after her, my voice drowned out by the sound of a car whizzing past.

I got back in the Volvo and drove in the completely opposite direction.

Uncle Eugene was having lunch with my father when I arrived, the two of them ensconced at a wrought-iron table at the back of the Manor, a beautiful river view a backdrop to their meal. Dad sat up a little straighter when he saw me; whether the fact that he was up to his elbows in leftover canapés from the McCarthy wedding or that he had something to hide, it wasn't clear. He pushed his plate away and threw his napkin on top of it while Uncle Eugene heartily consumed a pig in a blanket, a potato with caviar, and some duck liver mousse that I had covered with plastic and put in the refrigerator two days earlier.

"You look mad as a wet hen, Belfast," Eugene said, his eyebrow raised. "What have you gotten into now?"

"I should ask you the same thing," I said, standing next to the table, facing the river, the sun hot on my already red face. "Why does Trudie McGrath think that the two of you know more than you're saying? That you know maybe why Declan was killed and who did it?"

Dad hid his face in his hands. "Oh, Bel. Don't go jumping to conclusions. Trudie is crazy."

"And so are you!" I said, pointing at my father. "And probably you!" I hooked a thumb in Eugene's direction. "And everyone else on this godforsaken estate. You're all nuts." I pulled out a chair and fell into it. "Does that make one of you a murderer, too?"

"Now what is this ridiculousness?" Eugene asked, not missing a beat with his food. He had a pint of dark beer, a Guinness with a thick, foamy head, a backup bottle next to the glass. "Bel, let the police do their jobs and keep to the kitchen."

Insults on top of dishonesties. It was almost too much to bear. Uncle Eugene had been a shadowy figure from my youth, someone the family saw on a regular basis until he moved back to Ireland, his "troubles"—something to do with guns—widely known but whispered about. A stint in some Northern Ireland jail, despite Caleigh's contention that he was never convicted. A wife he had left. A son or two or three, the number always changing, left along with Eugene's bad reputation in their sleepy village. But he was welcomed back always when he came here and greeted us when we went there, his "troubles" pushed under the carpet.

He wasn't even that nice of a guy, I thought, not even a relative. Why had we kept up a relationship with him, let him be part of the family? With his rumored backstory, many details missing, at least to me, why he was embraced by my family was another mystery to be solved, right after the one about the dead guy at the wedding, the one no one seemed to care about in the least.

"Keep to the kitchen?" I asked.

Dad saw the storm brewing from my furrowed brow, the set of my jaw, and stood. "Now, Bel."

I looked at Eugene, shaking Dad's hand off of my arm. "And who are you really?" I asked. "You're not a relative of ours. You have no family that I can discern, either now or when you lived here all those years ago, yet you came back for Caleigh's wedding. Who are you besides some guy that hangs around our side of the family and got into some trouble with guns in Ireland?" I looked at my father. "Is that where you got all of those guns? Are you really going to make an installation with them? Or is that just a convenient cover?"

Dad blanched. I was completely out of control, not unlike how I was that night at The Monkey's Paw when everything fell apart.

"He's our friend, Belfast," my father said. "Jack's cousin. We grew up together."

"You're more loyal to him than you are to us," I said. "Why is that?"

Behind me I heard Mom's voice, soft but stern. "Bel. Stop." When I turned, she was looking back and forth from my father to Eugene. "This is enough. We're done with the lies." My father wouldn't meet her gaze, but Eugene stared at her. "You can tell her, Eugene, or I can, but either way, someone is going to tell the truth finally."

My dad and Eugene seemed at a loss for words, so Mom continued. "Yes, he's Trudie's son and was raised by Uncle Dermot for a time, but he came to the wedding to confront his real father."

I thought back to the wedding and all of the times I saw Declan and my father together. Right before the wedding, deep in conversation at the bar. During the wedding itself. How the thought crossed my mind more than once that Declan looked so much like Feeney and Derry, who, despite their dark hair, favored my dad in looks.

I looked at Dad. "Please don't tell me he was our brother."

CHAPTER Thirty-nine

Uncle Dermot, Dad's brother, was never up to the task of being a husband and a father. At least not to Trudie and Declan, the two people he left in a small village in the north of Ireland to fend for themselves, Trudie with not much going for her beyond her great looks and fine figure, as Dad called it, and Declan trouble from the start. Dermot set out for parts unknown, a gay man in 1970s Ireland, and landed in London, where he lived out his days before dying of AIDS in the mid-eighties pretty much alone, his own parents having disowned him, my father being the only McGrath sibling to have kept in touch. Their last meeting, at a beautiful town house in Notting Hill, Uncle Dermot having made a name for himself as a shoe designer before passing, was when he revealed that he wasn't Declan's biological father.

But Eugene Garvey was. He just hadn't known until now.

Trudie and Dermot had been best friends in that village, born on the same day and sharing more than just a birthday, including a love of Yeats, cooking, and drawing. Dermot drew shoes and Trudie sketched birds, and together these two best friends forged a friendship that would help hide the fact that Trudie was a pregnant nineteen-year-old with parents who would send her to live far away if they knew.

Dermot and Trudie knew what happened to girls who got into trouble and it wasn't pleasant. There were convents and orphanages and halfway houses, none of them places Trudie wanted to end up. Dermot, on the other hand, was attracting looks and gossip already as the only boy in town never to have kissed a girl, never mind dated her. Some said he was holding out for Trudie. His own mother thought he would become a priest, was saving himself for the Lord. He made the former the truth tellers when he proposed to Trudie one afternoon, her tears mixing with the torrential rain that fell outside the thatched cottage where she lived, Dermot cooking up the plan that would help both of them remain respectable members of their community while plotting their getaway from the repressive place.

Trudie told my father that the truth had come out just weeks before the wedding, Caleigh stupidly and unknowingly sending an invite to Trudie McGrath, seeing the address in her mother's address book, thinking that any McGrath was welcome at her celebration. Whatever had happened, that invitation had sparked an outpouring of revelations from Trudie to her only son. He came, determined to get the truth from someone, anyone.

Little did he know that among this crowd being a keeper of secrets was almost a birthright.

"It was I who told Dermot to leave," Dad said, the tears streaming down his ruddy cheeks. "I told him that he could help Trudie and Declan financially but that he only had one life to live. And he had to live a true life."

"Is that why you fought?" I asked. The three of them looked at me, confused. "Aunt Helen said you had a terrible fight and Uncle Dermot ended up with a bloody nose."

Dad chuckled. "No. That was over football. There was a little drink involved." He choked back a sob. "I loved him, Bel. Dermot. He was a kind soul."

Dermot had helped for as long as he could until medical bills forced him into bankruptcy. Dad picked up the slack, but for Trudie, raising a teen on her own, it was never enough and Declan fell into pursuits that he shouldn't. Drugs. Alcohol. And worst of all, just a chip off the old block—*allegedly,* as the family said with regard to Uncle Eugene—guns.

"He came here looking for his father, looking for money, trying to blackmail me into helping him get guns out of the States and into the wrong hands in Ireland," Dad said. Eugene had remained silent this whole time, his face a mask of sadness. "That's why there were guns in the studio. He bought them, got them somewhere on the black market here. After he died, I filled them with cement so that no one could ever use them again."

"And you?" I asked, looking at Uncle Eugene. "You had a child you never supported?"

"Bel," my mother said, a warning in her tone.

"Would you want me for a father, Bel?" Eugene asked. "Don't answer that. That's what we call a rhetorical question."

I stared at him blankly.

"I don't want the answer to that one." He took a slug of his Guinness. "And anyway, no one knew the truth. Until now."

"You had no idea you had another son?" I asked.

"Just found out myself. And now it's too late," he said, and in his saying that I saw that there was pain there, the not knowing, the quick, murderous turn of events. "And before you can go there, I have an alibi for when he died," he said, answering my next question before I even knew to ask it. "I was trying to calm down that big lummox your aunt Helen calls a boyfriend."

I was pretty much done with this conversation, but that raised my hackles a bit. "Frank the Tank? He never says a word. What was his problem?"

"Something about Declan not being nice to Caleigh," Eugene said, throwing up his hands. "I never could tell what he was talking about." He looked at my father. "Not much of the orator, that one."

"Yes, he's a bit of a mumbler, not so much on the conversation. Mumbles Mouth McGee," Dad said, taking the napkin off his plate and resuming eating, now that the cat was out of the bag and we were all on the same page. "Nice guy. Don't get him started on 9/11. Thinks there was a conspiracy. That the government was involved."

I tried to ask what "not being nice to Caleigh" meant, but the two of them were off on another tangent, fortunately not about José Ferrer or Arlene Francis, but meandering nonetheless.

"There was!" Eugene said, nodding. "And what about the Asian plane that went missing? You think we'll ever see that again?"

I drifted away, Mom on my heels, while the men on the back porch discussed falling towers and missing planes and, of course, the IRA. Sinn Fein. The Troubles. Talk about not being so much on the conversation, as Dad put it. Those two were like a broken record.

I went into the kitchen, the place where all of this had started. Mom leaned against the counter and watched me as I started making a lasagna that I would put in the freezer for the coming Sunday's dinner; it was Cargan's favorite and something he had requested when I had first arrived home. As I put water on to boil, I looked at Mom. "So, do the police know all of this?"

"Of course they do, Bel. We keep some secrets from the family, but we're not liars." She seemed to think that there was some distinction, something that set her apart from other people with lesser morals. The secrets were doozies, but when you have secrets, keep a lot of them, it seemed that they all fell on the same neutral part of the moral spectrum after a while.

"I wish you had told me," I said. "This whole situation has been making me crazy."

My mother surprised me by giving me a hug, maybe the tenth or fifteenth I had gotten from her in my entire life. Her body felt as it did when I was small, taut and lean, with just enough cushion to make the hug feel good and comforting, and I let myself be loved by her without trying to pull away too soon or be stiff within her embrace. When we did finally separate, she straightened her spine and acted as if the hug had never happened, so I continued fixing the lasagna, laying out what I needed.

"And Mom, don't worry about me anymore," I said, thinking of the lentil crap in my fridge that I needed to throw out.

"I'm not worried about you, Belfast," Mom said.

"You know what I mean," I said, smelling the mozzarella to make sure it was fresh enough to use. "Going into the apartment. Cleaning. Leaving food."

"I haven't done that in days," she said. She put her finger to her lips. "Maybe ten days ago? I left some lentils even though I know you don't like them."

"Really?" I said. Every day, there was evidence of her being in the apartment, a footprint here, a depression in the sofa there. A pillow moved. A glass in a different spot. "Ten days?"

"At least ten days," she said, and there was no sign of her tell, the lip-licking tic to let me know that she was lying.

I put the cheese down and watched as she walked away, going through the door and into the office, and heard the sound the chair made when she sat in it. I thought about the story they had told me, my uncle Dermot, gay and trapped in Northern Ireland, Trudie pregnant and trapped in her own way. The "troubles" both national and of the Uncle Eugene variety. Of the yearbook on my bed, open to the page with me and Amy. Of hot dogs and how they smell, how when you make them the odor lingers on your clothes. Of peanut shells and how I found one behind the toilet in my bathroom.

Of Oogie Mitchell and the haunted look on his face that first night I had found myself in The Dugout, out of sorts and out of place, someone with nothing to hide and nothing to lose.

CHAPTER *Forty*

I thought about going to The Dugout, but I didn't have to. I hadn't seen Oogie in a few days, hadn't been in to check on the menu. The times we spent together left me feeling a little hollow and sort of sad, so I had put some distance between me and my old hangout, and Amy's father. I left the kitchen the next day to get a knife I knew I had, somewhere in the apartment, probably in one of the boxes I had yet to open after moving in.

Oogie Mitchell was standing in my bedroom, his hands on his hips, looking for something. He didn't look startled when I entered, nor was he at all sorry that he was caught in my bedroom by me, somewhere he shouldn't have been ever. "Bel, I keep feeling like I've lost something."

I didn't know how to feel. I wasn't scared, but I wasn't completely at ease, either. The look on his face told me that he had been drinking. That and the stench emanating from his thin body. "What did you lose, Oogie?" I asked, keeping my distance, standing in the doorway of the room.

He looked at me but didn't respond. "I feel like what I lost might be in here. Or there might be a clue. Or that you know."

I thought about the peanut shell behind the toilet and realized that all this time, when I thought it was Mom lurking around, it was Oogie. He had been in the apartment several times and left telltale signs of his presence. "I don't know, Oogie. I've told you that all along. I wish I knew where Amy was, but I don't."

"She's not dead, you know," he said, angry. "They all say she's dead, but she's not."

"Who says she's dead?" I asked, backing into the hallway, trying to keep him talking long enough so that I could move toward the back door.

"Everyone!" he said. "And that damn candlelight ceremony. That's what everyone thinks. That's she's dead. That's why they come."

"Why?"

"To mourn. To tell me how sorry they are that she's gone and never coming back." Without warning, he pulled out a gun from behind his back and shot at the ceiling. That's how I knew it was loaded. Plasterboard rained down on his head, a huge chunk missing him by a few feet, landing on the pillows on my bed. "Is it up there?"

I put my hands over my ringing ears but could still hear him. "Is what up there?"

"What you know!" he said, as if expecting me to give him answers I didn't have. "Everything! The clues!"

"There are no clues, Oogie," I said, taking another step backward, trapped in the bedroom. It was tight and I had nowhere to go. "There are no clues," I repeated in an attempt to get him to understand that I knew less than he did, that I had no idea where Amy had gone or why.

"You know more than you're saying," Oogie said. "You always have. You went away and took the truth with you."

I held my hands up. "I know nothing, Oogie. I never have. I wish I knew something that could help you or anyone else who is looking for it find out the truth."

"You went away. You took the truth with you."

"I went to college, Oogie. And then I went on with my life." The minute the words were out of my mouth, I realized how hurtful they sounded. Amy wouldn't go on with her life because someone had taken it. I was sure of that.

He let the gun drop to his side. "Tell me everything. Tell it all."

"There's nothing to tell, Oogie. That last night, we had a fight. I'll always regret it, but that was it, the last I saw of her."

He considered that, chewed it over. "What did you fight about?"

To say it aloud, it sounded silly, trivial. And it was. But when you're seventeen and the world revolves around a few people in a tiny town the magnitude is greater. "A boy."

"Hanson?"

"Yes, Hanson," I said, my cheeks flaming. What a hold he had had on me. Then it made sense. Now it was just embarrassing. I was taken over by sadness. Amy. My best friend. The closest person to a sister I had ever had, something I would never tell Caleigh, who thought we were closer than we were.

A shot rang out and I waited for the pain, but there was none. I had a feeling that someone else was in the room, maybe behind me, but I couldn't be sure, waiting for blood to start running from my body in a steady river, ruining the rug that Dad had laid before I arrived home, the remnant with the hole in it. I lurched forward at the sound of the shot, if not the feeling, and thought about The Monkey's Paw and Ben, the drought and Mom's face at the bottom of the swimming pool, the mysterious bed and book in the basement.

It wasn't like my life flashing before my eyes, more of an accounting of the last few weeks, an inventory really, and when I was done, in an instant, all went black, like someone had turned out the lights.

CHAPTER *Forty-one*

In my family, people never say, I love you, or anything approximating a nice sentiment. We don't hug or kiss. We can't have a truly playful time where everyone is laughing at once; someone is always mad even in the midst of hilarity, up in arms over some slight. We are a very sensitive bunch. But we do things to help one another and would have each other's backs if the chips were ever down, even though afterward we would each tease the other about being weak or needing help.

There was unmerciful teasing and sometimes fisticuffs, but I knew I could count on my brothers to be there for me, to pick up the pieces or bandage the wound, both seen and unseen, and make me whole again.

We would take a bullet for a brother, or sister, if need be, putting our own safety second. It was kind of like being in a special secret service of crazy sisters and brothers.

It's not perfect, but it works for us. I just never expected that anyone would have to take an actual bullet for me.

When the dust settled and then cleared, I realized that I was on the floor of my bedroom, the acrid smell of something foreign all around me; I later learned it was gunpowder, buried in my nostrils. My face was pressed into the Berber pile, a great weight on my head and my body. In front of me, the light in his eyes dimmed, was Cargan, looking at me as if to say, A hand, please? even though we were both prone and side by side, in the same predicament. One arm was thrown behind him, the other stretched out in front, a gun in his hand, his fingers wrapped loosely around its handle.

"Car?" I said, trying to reach out to touch him, my arm immobile. It took me a few seconds to realize that there was a piece of the ceiling on top of me, heavy and unwieldy, making every movement difficult, if not impossible. I touched my brother's face and felt a waxy coldness and that was all I needed to feel as brute strength overtook the weight of the plasterboard that covered my body. I flung off first one piece and then another, the piece that had hit me in the head rolling off to the side, and stood, taking in the carnage in the room, my breath coming out in short gulps.

Oogie Mitchell lay across my bed, his face in my down comforter, one arm dangling off the side, the gun having dropped to the floor when he could no longer hold on. Great chunks of the ceiling were strewn about the room, letting me know that more damage had taken place after I had been knocked out. I knelt beside my brother, not caring if Oogie was dead or alive, and took Cargan's face in my hands.

"Car? Cargan!" I said again, and not getting an answer, just that blank stare, I ran into the kitchen and grabbed my phone, calling Kevin's cell and saying something, I don't remember what, when he picked up.

I don't know how my parents or anyone else on the property missed what was going on, but they only came running when they heard the sirens. I sat beside my brother, thinking he was still alive, hoping I was right, and holding his hand, cold and lifeless in my own. Kevin was the first person through the door, followed by a uniformed officer who had never seen such carnage, the look on his face indicating that he may have chosen the wrong line of work after all. Soon there were other cops and then people I recognized from various parts of my life and who were involved in the volunteer ambulance corps. I was shuttled about and moved to the living room, where I immediately stained my white slipcovered Ikea sofa with the blood from a wound I hadn't remembered getting, didn't know I had. I put my hand to my head and came away with a palm full of thick, red blood, my hair knotted and soaked with it.

It was all a blur, Mom next to me as Jane-Marie Bell, a girl from freshman algebra, combed through my hair until she got to the wound that was responsible for all of the blood, remarking at how I hadn't changed a bit, how pretty I still was, asking if I liked being a chef, all in such a way that even I, in my addled state, knew that she was making small talk to keep me preoccupied.

A body on a stretcher came out of the bedroom, and then another one. I looked at Mom, but she was as she always is: Composed. Perfect. Poised.

She watched the activity by the door. "Guns. They will be our downfall." She put a hand on my arm when Jane-Marie walked away to confer with her boss. "After we get through this, I'll tell you everything."

"There's more?" I said. How much more? And what could it be? I wasn't sure how much more I could handle.

"Just a little," she said, and licked her lips.

CHAPTER Forty-two

I had to wear a head scarf to cover the part of my head where they had shaved my hair away and that morning, two weeks after everything, added a pair of giant hoop earrings to add a look of whimsy to the getup. I'd be a gypsy until my hair grew back. I had moved back into the Manor proper, temporarily, or so I told myself, while my apartment was turned from a crime scene back into a suitable place for living. We had gotten through the last two weddings with a little help from my brothers, who in addition to rehearsing for their performances, served as prep cooks in the kitchen in the days prior to the events, helping me silently when I gave them assorted tasks: chops these carrots. Trim this beef. Roll this dough.

Today, before I started prepping for the upcoming weekend's wedding, I made a nice fry-up, as Dad would call it: Bacon, two eggs over easy, fried potatoes. Fresh orange juice. A grapefruit cut up with a little sugar dusted on the top. Two pieces of toast slathered with Irish butter. A strong cup of coffee laced with real cream.

I carried the tray up the stairs and knocked on the door to the bridal suite, the largest room in the Manor with an en suite bathroom, most suitable for someone recovering from a catastrophic injury. "Knock, knock," I said before toeing open the door and peering in.

As he had been for the last week since he had been home, Cargan was sitting in the Queen Anne chair by the window, looking out over the barren Foster's Landing River. "Hiya, Bel."

"Hiya, Car," I said. The doctor said that it was a miracle my brother was still alive, and credited his survival to what the doctor called my quick thinking and fast action. If he meant calling Kevin and screaming into the phone and that qualified as "quick thinking," well, then okay. When I first opened my eyes that afternoon in the apartment, I thought for sure Cargan was dead, having taken a bullet for me, not knowing that his own quick thinking, and agility from years of playing soccer, had allowed him to move just enough so that the bullet tore through his side and exited out his back without touching a major organ or his spine.

That and his training.

The police had gotten there so fast because Cargan was one of their own. Deep undercover, but one of them, nonetheless, that deep cover blown when I had discovered the setup in the basement and Kevin the bugs all throughout the Manor. Kevin already knew about Cargan from that day at the station, the two of them enacting an incredibly convincing play for me that included Cargan asking for a lawyer and keeping up the façade that he was not as smart as the rest of us. Thing was, he was smarter. Way smarter. He had been pulled from the Police Academy—we had been told he flunked out—and put into a special antiterrorism unit years before. His last gig had been so dangerous that he had been given a leave of absence and returned home to the Manor—the place he considered home base anyway—to figure out what he would do next. He didn't need to wait long: he suspected Eugene was still in the gun business, a few clues dropped his way to indicate that he was correct, and the wedding, his living in the

Manor, afforded Cargan the opportunity to figure out if that was the case.

Turns out that those years Cargan had spent traveling and touring "playing music" had been the years he had trained with a special unit of the NYPD that investigated terrorism in all of its nefarious incarnations. He was especially helpful in unmasking the leader of a rogue IRA group assembling in Brooklyn—a guy who was the head usher at a rather large church in Brooklyn while plotting to take out the royal family during a trip to the States—and averting tragedy for the British monarchy. Cargan had uncovered yet another group who wanted to assassinate the Pope when he had visited Yankee Stadium. People continually underestimated my brother and that made him perfect for the work. He was as close to a superhero as one could get while still maintaining the façade that he was the simple one, the one we needed to protect. What else he had done was a mystery and I wanted it to stay that way because the thought of my sweet brother, "the wee, poor soul" as I had heard Aunt Helen describe him once, struck a fear in me that would beat right alongside my heart.

Simple? Hardly. Wee, poor soul? You couldn't be more wrong, Aunt Helen.

Eugene was in the weeds, and Cargan was seriously rethinking his plan to put in a good thirty years on the force, the hole in his side making him think long and hard about the life he lived, the loneliness he faced on a daily basis.

He pushed the food around on his plate before looking up at me, the bags beneath his eyes making him look a whole heck of a lot older than he was. "Thanks for breakfast," he said as he did every day since he had come home.

"You're welcome. Thank you, too," I said, but I wasn't referring to his enjoyment of the bacon, the eggs. It was for him being there when I needed him, just like I had been there all those time when he had needed me, but under far less critical circumstances. "How you feeling, Brother?"

"Like I've been hit by a truck, Sister," he said.

"Every day is better, right?" I said, hoping the answer was a resounding "yes."

He looked over at me and smiled. "Yes," he lied. "Every day is better. Right." He looked at his plate.

"Soccer soon?"

"Soccer soon."

"I'll come to a game," I said, just as I had said all those times previously but still had never done.

"Good. You'll love the guys. They play the game like they're possessed." He pushed the food around some more and looked out the window. "Some of them are single, Bel."

I held up a hand. "Stop right there. I think I'm off men for a while."

He smiled and pointed at the river. "The drought. I wonder when it will end."

"Crazy."

"It was a good time to add the eyelashes."

"Huh?"

"I helped Dad add eyelashes to Mom's eyes."

"What do you mean?" I wondered if he was this obtuse with his colleagues. It was a wonder not all of them had died from cryptic communication.

"The village pool," he said. "I snuck in with Dad and helped him add eyelashes to Mom's eyes. On the mermaid."

"Oh!" I said. "Well done. Brilliant, really. I saw them recently and they are spectacular, Cargan. The whole thing is really lifelike."

He pushed the plate away, our small talk done. The joking over. "I want to meet someone, Bel. I want to have kids. I'm tired of being in basements and in vans. Of being with guys all the time, the kind of guys who can never tell the truth to the people they love. I'm tired of trying to figure out if Dad's best friend is a gunrunner or just some rube with a fake leg."

I sat on the bed, my hand instinctively going to the spot on my head that had been sewn shut, able to be closed, my brains staying where they belonged, thanks to my brother's quick thinking. "I hear you, Brother. Now, eat your fry-up," I said, at a loss to say anything else.

He told me that Mom knew; Cargan could never keep anything from her. That was the "more" that Mom had alluded to that day in my apartment. Like a good Irish son, he had kept Mom in the loop, despite his promise to keep his identity and his job a secret from everyone else. I made him promise that the Pilates studio, and the women who went in there daily, wasn't a front for some secret MI-5 faction. He assured me that it wasn't, but knowing what I did now, that the brother I thought I knew wasn't that brother at all, made me rethink everything.

Those were a lot of fit women. If they put their heads together, God knows they could fight some kind of war, win some battle against something besides carbs. But most of them were too busy starving themselves to fit into jeans that were meant for women twenty years their juniors to be of any help to a paramilitary organization with peace and order on its mind.

"So what do you think?" I asked.

"About the fry-up? Great," he said, turning his attention back to his food and devouring his bacon. He never could resist bacon.

"No. Uncle Eugene. Terrorist or rube with fake leg?"

He smiled and I saw a hint of my old brother, the one without all of the baggage and sadness, peek out from within. "I'd tell you . . ."

". . . but then you'd have to kill me?" I was using that joke a lot lately.

"Something like that."

We sat in silence until his plate was clean. "And Oogie? Did you know?"

He stared out over the dry river, not meeting my eye. "I had an idea that he was about to go off the rails. I was keeping watch." He looked down at his empty plate. "On him. On you."

Oogie had waved the gun around, but it was not in his nature to shoot. He had fired another warning shot into the ceiling, but instead of the bullet going straight up, it had hit the ceiling fan and ricocheted, hitting my brother in the side. Another thick chunk of plaster had hit Oogie in the head, and like me, he had been the recipient of a boatload of stitches. It was unclear what would happen to Oogie now, what charges, if any, would be pressed. Although everyone in the village was heartbroken by the turn of events, most agreed, from what I heard, that Oogie had been spiraling downward the past couple of years and my reappearance in town was the final straw, another reminder of that aching hole in his heart. I tried not to think about that as I lay awake in my bed at night, thinking that my original decision to become a hermit might have been the best one.

"We all knew something was coming," Cargan said. "Oogie hasn't been the same for a while."

I wished my brother had been my sous at The Monkey's Paw. Maybe none of what had happened would have happened the way it had. "You've always had my back, Car."

"And . . . ," he started, and we were back at the swimming pool, my mother's face staring up at us with her long eyelashes, though not quite as long back then, imploring me to do the right thing, Caleigh making fun of him, me holding her head under the water. His little, skinny legs in his red bathing suit. Her cruelty. There were other times, times Cargan and I didn't mention. The time I had punched Larry McGovern in the mouth after he had called Cargan an idiot came to mind. I think I still owed the Lord Jesus three Our Fathers for that one, having lost count that afternoon in church after confession. It had mostly gone one way, me fighting the good fight, Cargan being the victim. Things had suddenly changed. Maybe that's why he had done what he had, fighting that good fight, in secret, in private. He swallowed hard. "You've had my back, too, Bel." He nodded almost imperceptibly. "Thank you."

"Eat your fry-up," I said, the sob in my throat making my voice sound stuffy and trapped. There was no fry-up left to eat, though, just the two of us, knowing what he had done and why.

We did love each other, I wanted to say. We just don't say it. I love you, Car; you're the best brother a girl could have, ever. It was also there, but stuck in my throat.

The fry-up would have to be enough. I ruffled his short buzz cut and took care not to knock over the fiddle by the window and left him, staring out at the arid riverbed, knowing that he would always have my back.

And that was enough.

CHAPTER *Forty-three*

There were two people waiting for me in the kitchen when I returned. One I desperately wanted to see; the other I wished a painful death. Neither I had seen in a while. I started with Franceso Francatelli and figured I would deal with Brendan Joyce next. I pulled a big knife out of the knife block and held it in one hand, a ripe tomato in the other. I threw the tomato in the air and cut it into two perfectly symmetrical halves, catching one in midair in my knife hand, the other behind my back.

"Franceso, I had hoped you had contracted dysentery in my absence and died of dehydration," I said.

Not my finest hour or opening line. I had thought of all of the things I wanted to say to Francesco if we ever had the opportunity to meet again, but that wasn't it. Nor, in my fantasies, was I wearing a head scarf underneath which a chunk of my head was missing.

He laughed, an actor used to responding on cue. "Bel! You always were such a jokester," he said.

"Not joking, Francesco." I looked at Brendan Joyce, wondering why he was there. He looked away, sheepish. Part of him, I could tell, was in awe of being in the presence of an award-winning actor. "What do you want?"

"Bel," Francesco said, throwing his hands out. "Friends? Again?"

"No. Not friends," I said. "What do you want?"

Always the actor, his face went into some approximation of sadness, but underneath that was the empty void that was his personality, his lack of soul. "Bel. I want you," he said.

I looked over at Brendan Joyce, united in our incredulity. "Are you getting a load of this?" I asked.

Brendan nodded dutifully.

"You want me to come back?" I asked. "To The Monkey's Paw?"

"That's what I want," he said. Francesco Francatelli, a guy who had no business opening a restaurant, never mind playing a sweet, genius paraplegic with a heart of gold. The guy didn't have an idea of how to run a restaurant. And he didn't have a heart. "Ben isn't working out."

I laughed out loud. "Brendan, we didn't even need Beverly Dos Santos to tell us that that was going to happen." Francesco came around the corner and I brandished the knife. "Stay back," I said.

"Didn't you go to anger-management classes?" he asked, looking like he wanted to give me a hug. I didn't like hugs and I certainly didn't want one from him. The tall, good-looking guy in the corner? Now that was a different story.

"I did. One intense class where I learned that if I feel threatened, I need to remove myself from the situation." I looked at Francesco in his expensive loafers and with his hair plugs and stepped back. "As a result, I am going to remove myself from this situation by asking you, Francesco, to leave."

He put his hands in his pockets. "Here's the thing, Bel," he said, chuckling. "You see, receipts are down. Reservations are almost non-existent. And the only way

Max Rayfield will do a show is with you," he said, referencing the cable bigwig who had wanted to film me for a
reality show and who had been in the restaurant that fate-
ful night. "The Monkey's Paw needs you." He put his
hands out again. "I need you."

"You threw me under the bus, Francesco. I did not leave
that fish bone in there and you know that."

"I know that!" he said.

"You know that?" I asked. "When did you know that?"

"That night!" he said. "You're too good. You never
would have prepared something yourself and let it leave
the kitchen unless it had been perfect." He looked aggrieved. "Why, Bel? Why did you let the fish go out like
that?"

I hated having to say this in front of anyone, let alone
the two men in the room. "Because I trusted him."

Francesco let out a throaty laugh. "Guy is a wanker,
Bel. That was your first mistake."

"So, why all the drama? Why the public firing?" I
asked, forgetting that Brendan Joyce was in the room and
that we had unresolved business.

"Max was there," Francesco said. "I figured it would be
good business. Good for the show." He smiled again, his
teeth fake and all the same size and shape. "Drama. I figured she'd love that."

I approached Francesco, the knife still in my hand.
"You ruined my life," I said before realizing that he really
hadn't. He had saved my life, when I took time to think
about it. I was done with Ben. I was done with New York.
I stepped back and put the knife down. "Please leave."

He waved a hand around, surveying the room. He could
tell I was serious and that changed his demeanor for the
worse. The soulless stare was back and he was done with
me and Shamrock Manor. "This is where you work now,
Bel? In a kitchen in a wedding hall? For Irish people? You

are so much better than that. The Irish don't even appreciate good food."

"And how would you know that, Francesco?" I asked.
"How would you know that every Saturday I serve a
gourmet meal to approximately one hundred to one hundred and fifty people who eat my food and drink the
wine and dance and have a wonderful time because they
are good people, not pretentious people? How would you
know that?" I turned my back on him. "That's right.
Because you're a pompous ass who made one or two good
movies and thought he knew how to open a restaurant." I
pulled another knife out of the block, just to see him squirm.
"And you're wrong. The Irish love good food. And laughter. And life." I looked at Brendan. "Right?"

Right on cue, Brendan nodded vigorously.

"But you didn't see my people in The Monkey's Paw
because it was missing the laughter and the life. The good
food was always there."

He went to a line that Ben had used on me. They must
have rehearsed together. "You'll never work in New York
again."

"I sure hope you're right," I said.

I looked around, at the kitchen, at the giant cans of carrots, at the walk-in, which I knew held more fresh ham
than any one wedding party could consume. I looked at
Brendan Joyce in his khaki shorts and camp polo shirt. I
looked at my brother Cargan, standing in the doorway to
the kitchen, wondering what all of the commotion was,
making sure I didn't need a hand. I spied my gorgeous
mother in the office, pretending that she didn't hear every
single word that had been said and that she wasn't on pins
and needles waiting for the conclusion to this drama. I
saw my father in the foyer of the Manor, installing his
latest installation, *Twenty-One Guns,* not knowing that it
was named after a Green Day song and meant something

completely different from what he meant. I looked at Francesco.

"I'm not better than that," I said. "I don't need to be in New York. I'm right where I belong."

CHAPTER Forty-four

The Finnegan wedding went off without a hitch.

And after a rocky start, Brendan Joyce and I were getting back on track as well, with me promising that I would never kiss a not-married-but-committed man ever again. I still hadn't invited him to Sunday dinner because . . . well, my family. Enough said, right? Kevin had given me wide berth and I had dodged Mary Ann's suggestion to come over or double date, citing my not-as-bad-as-I-made-it-sound head wound as a convenient excuse to lay low. Every time the subject came up, and it came up a lot because I seemed to run into Mary Ann D'Amato everywhere, I would point to my head and say, "Stitches."

She must have thought I had gone to Dr. Frankenstein with the length of time it was taking for my wound to heal.

It was after the Finnegan wedding, a Saturday night, that I lay in my temporary accommodations in the Manor, listening to Mom and Dad in the next room wonder about Uncle Eugene's whereabouts, Dad's voice coming through loud and clear, Mom's more hushed. No one had seen Eugene since that day on the back porch, which made us wonder if maybe Cargan was on to something about our dear, unrelated "uncle."

As I lay there, I remembered our conversation. Into my head popped one line, something Eugene had said while we were talking, before I had lost my temper.

"I was trying to calm down that big lummox your aunt Helen calls a boyfriend."

I hadn't seen the lummox since the last Sunday dinner, a few weeks ago, and wondered if he would come to dinner tomorrow. I had never seen Frank the Tank lose his temper; in my opinion, he barely had a pulse, which made him the perfect boyfriend for the flighty, flaky, and kind-of-annoying Aunt Helen. Mom had promised no cabbage for our upcoming family meal, as it really didn't go with the lasagna I had made, so I was hopeful for the meal in general.

Caleigh was coming, as was Mark, or so she said.

This would be an interesting one.

The next day, I went over to the family kitchen a bit early and put the lasagna in the oven. Cargan limped in a few minutes later and peered in at the Italian casserole, making an appreciative noise at the look of it.

"I'm so happy we're not having cabbage," he said.

"Me too," I said. "But lasagna on a hot summer day is a bit of culinary anomaly, too. A good gazpacho would have been nice."

Cargan laughed. "Let me guess: Mom said no."

I put my finger to my nose. "Bingo."

The family assembled at the appointed time and all were in awe of the appearance of Mark Chesterton, fresh from the links, still in his golf clothes, down to his cleats.

"Sorry about that. I forgot a change of clothes and didn't get home in time to freshen up," he said, pointing to his tasseled shoes. He sat on a bench inside the front door and took them off, placing them neatly underneath. "It was a long eighteen today. Stuck behind a group of elderly women," he said. "No disrespect, Mother," he said to Aunt Helen, giving her a winning smile.

"None taken," she said, but obviously there was some taken. She was insulted by the fact that she was included in a group described as "elderly," but being as both she and Caleigh were still in the honeymoon period when it came to their individual relationships with Mark, Helen let it go.

Frank the Tank was in the dining room in his usual seat, nursing a glass of beer. Aunt Helen took her seat next to him and fussed with her napkin for a while, which apparently wasn't folded to her liking. I couldn't figure out what the two of them saw in each other, beyond companionship. They went together like a doily and a carburetor, one all fussy and precious, the other stolid and silent. I took a seat I wouldn't normally so I could sit across from Frank and get a sense of whether or not he was acting any differently than usual, but being as he was as close to a corpse as one person could get and still be alive, I figured I wouldn't have much luck on that account.

Mom brandished the lasagna like it was the Holy Grail. She was like that with most things I cooked, but particularly Italian food, which to her was incredibly exotic. "Lasagna!" she proclaimed as she set it on a trivet, protecting the table Dad had built from the hot cookware, even though there was enough polyurethane on that thing to keep a boat afloat in an angry sea. Mom had frozen the lasagna and then thawed it out on the counter. I prayed that in the summer heat the cheese hadn't turned bad, leaving all of us with a bad case of food poisoning when the night was over.

We all ate in silence for a long time, no one sure what to say; there were so many hot topics and so many things we shouldn't talk about that it was better to keep quiet. Silence kills me. I've been working in kitchens for almost two decades, and if there is one thing about a professional kitchen it's that it isn't quiet. Ever. Unless it's empty. So to be sitting among a group of people all capable of making a lot of noise and seeing that they had all fallen silent, I looked for an excuse to talk. I looked across at Caleigh, sitting demurely beside her husband, someone in the dark but a pretty good guy, I suspected.

"So, a lot has happened," I said, for want of something to say, anything to break the silence.

Caleigh nodded. "It sure has." She glanced over at Mark and smiled.

Uh-oh. This smelled of a Caleigh revelation.

She didn't wait, blurting out, "We're pregnant!"

The reactions were all over the board.

Dad: "That's great?"

Feeney: "So soon?"

Mom: "Lovely, dear."

Aunt Helen: "It's all about me!" (Well, that's not what she said, but that's what I heard.)

And I, using every ounce of will that I had, bit my lip and didn't ask, "Whose is it?" but smiled politely.

"You see, they have these new tests that can tell you almost to the moment of conception," Caleigh said, wide-eyed at the thought of this new technology and giving everyone the impression that she was as pure as the driven snow on her wedding night. Johnnie McIntyre, her first boyfriend and the boy who took her virginity, would have been surprised to hear that.

Mom leaned toward Caleigh and patted her arm. "That is lovely, dear, but we really don't talk about such things at the dinner table."

Mark picked up the slack. "We couldn't be happier."

"When are you due?" I asked.

"End of March, beginning of April," Mark said.

Ah, the old honeymoon baby. Or the two-nights-before-the-wedding baby.

Caleigh looked at me. "Bel, aren't you going to say anything?"

Did I have to? I guess I did to keep up this charade. "That's wonderful, Caleigh. Mark. A new baby. How grand."

Even Caleigh wasn't dumb enough not to hear the sarcasm in my voice. I had tried to keep it at bay, but I couldn't. Mark gave me a quizzical look.

"No. Really. I'm delighted," I said. "A baby!" I jumped up and brought the two of them together in an awkward hug, looking across at Cargan to see if my performance was convincing. By the look on his face, I would say it was not. He was the actor; he had proven that in spades.

"How do you feel?" Mom asked.

"A little morning sickness," Caleigh said. "But other than that, all good."

"I only had morning sickness with one pregnancy," Mom said, and I knew what was coming before she looked at me. "Maybe you're having a girl, too."

"As long as the baby is healthy," Mark said like a dutiful father-to-be.

We went back to eating, the excitement over the lasagna superseding the excitement over the pregnancy. Hunger always wins out in my family and today was no exception. So I was surprised when Mark brought up the murder at the wedding.

"Well, it's the elephant in the room, so we might as well talk about it," he said. I thought Mark and his people were more tight-lipped than mine when it came to things we didn't want to talk about, so Mark's opening of the topic that no one wanted to discuss took the entire table aback. Aunt Helen, in particular, looked like she was about to faint. "I spoke to Detective Hanson this morning, and while things have been rather quiet in the investigation, they are tracking down a lead." He put his fork down and wiped his mouth on one of Mom's linen napkins. "A good lead. A solid lead."

Aunt Helen blanched. "What kind of lead?" she asked, her hand at her neck.

"A lead on the killer," Mark said, his choice of words dramatic and inelegant.

"They know who it is?" Helen asked, and I was starting to think that maybe she knew more than she let on. Frank the Tank sat in stony silence, one of his giant arms snaking around her shaking shoulders.

"That was the impression I got," Mark said. He looked over at Derry. "Pass the sauce, please?" He doused his lasagna with a ladleful of my marinara. Despite the conversation, I was happy to see him enjoying his meal. Once a chef, always a chef.

"And who do they say it is?" Helen asked, her voice quavering just a tiny bit.

I looked over at her, as did Cargan. Derry, Arney, and Feeney were oblivious, a side conversation starting about the free fall that the Yankees' season was in, their limited chances of making the post-season unless things turned around before the All-Star break.

"They didn't tell me," he said, his mouth around a giant lasagna noodle. "But thankfully, we'll be able to put this behind us soon and concentrate on what was so wonderful about our wedding." He turned and looked at Caleigh, her face as white as her mother's, her eyes cast down on her plate. Her appetite appeared to be gone. "Like how beautiful this gorgeous woman looked. The food. Your wonderful hospitality. How we are now one family."

This guy was growing on me. Where I had once seen

someone wooden and emotionless I now saw a real gentleman. I'd have to remind myself in the future to be less
judgmental and more accepting when coming upon
someone new. He loved my cousin and only wanted the
best for them as a couple. He seemed genuinely concerned
about the murder at the wedding. That made him a kindred spirit to me, the only other person, it seemed, who
wanted to get to the bottom of this.

"Who wants dessert?" Mom asked, dinner not over yet.

"It was only because he hurt our girl," Frank said, his
voice still almost unrecognizable to everyone because we
had hardly ever heard it.

Across from me, I saw Cargan flinch slightly, seeming to know what was coming next. Everyone else was
still in the dark, Derry concerned with a dollop of sauce
that had landed on Mom's beautiful white tablecloth,
Arney speaking to his wife about how they were going
to ditch the kids and go on a date night after dinner was
over. I heard it all even though I was still turned toward
Frank and Helen, wondering what he was going to say
next.

"What do you mean, Frank?" Cargan asked, no one but
me focused on the conversation that was taking place between my sort-of-secret-cop brother and the guy at the end
of the table.

"He hurt Caleigh. Took advantage of our sweet girl."
Frank's grip tightened around Helen's shoulders. "He
wasn't nice to Helen here, either."

Caleigh heard her name and perked up. "What? Who?
What happened?"

Frank stood and placed his napkin over his uneaten lasagna, as if pronouncing it dead on arrival. "The lasagna
was delicious, Bel," he said. "But I have to go."

I should have figured this out way earlier. The hushed

arguing I heard right before Declan came crashing through the banister. The strength it would take someone to haul someone into the foyer below. Frank's connection to the family. His love for Caleigh, his devotion to Helen.

I just didn't have a motive for why Francis Xavier Connelly, otherwise known as Frank the Tank, had killed Declan "Morrison" McGrath. Until now.

Frank started for the kitchen and from there would probably go through the foyer and out to the front of the Manor. Cargan looked at me helplessly. Although we both knew that he would be well within his rights and duties as a police officer to arrest Frank—both of us coming to the same conclusion at the same time—still no one besides me and my parents knew that my fiddle-playing, Manor-managing, soccer-loving brother was really a cop. My brothers thought he had interrupted Oogie's confrontation with me, not aware that Cargan had tracked the old man's movements for weeks. Cargan excused himself from the table and gave me a warning glance that said, Don't move.

I had to move, though, because with all of the lying and the secrets I felt that if we could get this out in the open, this one truth, we could move on from here. I followed Frank through the kitchen and into the foyer.

"Why, Frank? You're not a killer," I said.

He turned and looked at me, the big lummox, as Uncle Eugene had referred to him, tears streaming down his face. "I love them both, Bel. I didn't want anything bad to happen to them."

"Who?" I asked. "Helen and Caleigh?"

He ran his hand over the bust of Bobby Sands, his hand lingering on the top of the sculpture's head. "Yes. My girls."

I waited for more, hoping it would come, and it did, in a steady, albeit short, monologue.

"I saw him coming out of the wedding suite and I saw Caleigh was in there, too, crying." He rubbed the sculpture some more. "I'm not stupid. It was clear what had happened."

"What happened, Frank?" I asked.

He didn't respond directly. "Who crashes a wedding and takes advantage of the bride?"

That part made sense, even if the rest of it didn't. Another puzzle with missing pieces. I couldn't imagine Caleigh confessing to Frank what she had confessed to me, but she had been one drunk bride.

Loose lips sink ships and apparently lead to murder as well, if this half-baked story was any indication.

"Who speaks to a lady like that?" he asked to no one.

"Caleigh?" I asked.

"Helen," he said.

I didn't want to tell Frank that Caleigh had accepted Declan's advances—or he hers—and that no one had taken advantage of anyone. Frank's heart looked broken already; no need to go any further. I wasn't in any danger—that was clear—so I asked him if we could sit on the stairs and just talk for a while. Kevin came in as Frank got to the end of the story, Cargan by his side.

"Does Helen know?" I asked.

He shrugged but the look on his face told a different story. She knew. And she hadn't said a word to anyone.

Mark entered the foyer and we all fell silent. "Ah, Frank," Mark said, his voice tight. "Tell me this isn't true."

"Which part?" Frank said, but before he could go any further, reveal the truth of what happened that day, Kevin took over, reading Frank his Miranda rights.

Before they left, the big man in handcuffs, Frank turned to me. "I never meant to hurt anyone, Bel. I hope you know that. I didn't mean to—"

I put my hand over his mouth as he started to form the word "kill." "Shhh, Frank. Get a lawyer."

I believed him. None of us ever meant to hurt anyone, but judging from what was left in our wake—both physical and emotional—it was hard to argue the point.

CHAPTER *Forty-five*

After hearing every story, every tale of blackmail that accompanied Declan McGrath's appearance at the wedding, it was hard to argue for his continued existence on this planet. Thinking that landed me in Father Pat's confessional the next Saturday, the kitchen in the capable hands of Fernando and Eileen, the server with the adorable lisp, who seemed capable and confident of their abilities to keep things running until I was purged of all sin, having said my three Hail Marys and four Our Fathers and an Act of Contrition.

There was the whole thing about Dad and blackmailing him to smuggle guns. And Declan had some stuff on his biological father, Uncle Eugene, that he had planned to take to the Feds if anyone revealed his plan to run guns. (His untimely death ensured that he took that information to the grave, and no one came to find out exactly what it was.) Uncle Eugene never knew about Declan, Dad told me, and finding out this son had died at the wedding broke the little man into what seemed like a million pieces. How he would know that, with Eugene in the wind, was beyond me. I really hoped—prayed actually—that Dad was as feckless as he seemed and that he wasn't involved in any of this on any level.

Worst of all, the biggest secret that Declan revealed had been kept all of these years and I never saw it coming.

Caleigh was adopted.

Why Aunt Helen went to such great lengths to protect that secret, one that was not worth keeping, was the last mystery to solve. Caleigh had come from a place similar to the one that Trudie never wanted to go when she found out she was pregnant with Declan and would have lived out her childhood days in an Irish orphanage if not for the circumstances that brought her to Helen and Jack, a couple unable to have their own biological children.

Cargan knew more about what had happened and shared it with me, our bond stronger than ever, his faith that I wouldn't reveal anything to anyone secure. When Frank found Declan on that second floor of the Manor, worried that Helen had been gone from the wedding a long time, he found him threatening my aunt with the truth about everything, including Caleigh, something he had learned from his own mother. Frank alleged that Declan had threatened violence to him and my aunt and that, coupled with Frank's assumption that Caleigh had been violated in some way, was when things went south, both literally and figuratively, Declan being winged from the second floor to the first.

Mom tried to explain it away, "There never was a good time to tell Caleigh that she was adopted and then it became too late."

I didn't see the logic in that, but I held my tongue. I decided that I was now living among a group of really repressed people, people who needed more therapy and medication than one doctor could administer or prescribe. It was if they hadn't evolved past the Roaring Twenties, their ideas about what was right and normal and just seeming to come from early in the last century.

We didn't know what would happen to Frank, some

kind of defense in the works with Paul Grant. I hoped for the best. Frank was a nice guy. A little impulsive, if the events were any indication, but a nice guy overall.

I returned from confession that Saturday and went to work in the kitchen, hearing the strains of "Locomotion" coming from inside the wedding hall shortly thereafter, the McNulty wedding in full swing. Word of the changes at Shamrock Manor had gotten out, and Cargan had been busy booking new weddings for the fall and into the new year. Dad's creativity was sparked once again, and his *Twenty-One Guns* installation found its way to a permanent spot on the back lawn, where on days we had weddings Mom partially covered it with a sheet and some ribbon so as not to turn off our guests. It looked sort of like a crazy, mixed-up Maypole, but so far no one had complained. To me, it was Dad's anti-gun statement writ large. The new menus were a hit, and I was now involved in the booking process, catering specifically to individual brides and grooms, finding out what they liked, what they expected, what would work for their guests.

Dare I say I was happy?

I started to visit Brendan's cat at his apartment; he had finally gone home for good it seemed. And Brendan and I started to settle into a relationship that was free of drama, absent of angst. After his appearance on the same day as Francesco Francatelli, we had made our peace and finally put to rest the kiss that meant nothing.

And then it was over, the two of us going back to a nice, uncomplicated relationship.

Pauline came into the kitchen. "Head table! Salmon all day!"

"Salmon all day!" I repeated, throwing some butter into two different pans and cooking eight salmons to order for the wedding party, putting a dollop of potato puree under each and handing them to Fernando, who had transitioned seamlessly from sous to expeditor in the course of the day.

Mom came into the kitchen, looking gorgeous in a pale-blue silk sheath dress. "The McNultys think the food is divine, Belfast," she said.

"Thanks, Mom." I ladled some melted butter onto a piece of filet in a pan, a serving for the groom, who wanted surf and turf and who seemed to be protein-loading in anticipation of his wedding night.

"And Belfast?" she said before starting for the door.

"Yes, Mom?"

"Please stand up straight."

CHAPTER *Forty-six*

Still residing in my childhood room in the Manor, I lay awake that night, wondering why everyone accepted Uncle Eugene's disappearance with such nonchalant resignation. He was a bad guy; I think we had established that in a few different ways. Delinquent father. Possible gunrunner. Kind of an ass in general. So why did everyone go about their lives not wondering where he was, where he had fled? Clearly, they didn't want to know.

Below me, in the main dining room, I heard the lilt of an Irish tune being picked out on a fiddle. I got up, leaving the room and walking the length of the hallway, peering over the repaired banister to see who might be having a midnight sojourn in the empty hall, the wedding having come to a spectacular close, with Feeney doing a more-than-passable Elvis impression in a medley that included "In the Ghetto," which fortunately everyone forgot after he launched into "Burning Love," the last song the boys played before everyone left. Although it would have insulted him to the core to hear it, I thought that maybe Feeney's true calling might lead him to Vegas and a pair of stick-on sideburns rather than tormenting the rest of my brothers in the band here at the Manor, but I kept my opinion to myself in the name of family harmony.

The tables were bare, all dishes and linens having been

swept away by the busboys at the end of the day, but a few candles burned on what had been the head table. Cargan, his back turned to me, sat with his feet up against the sill of one of the large windows that faced the river, idling on his fiddle, the notes of "The Dawning of the Day" familiar to me as it was one of the first songs he had learned and one that I had heard him play no fewer than a thousand times.

I started singing to his playing, ". . . Came a fearsome roar from a distant shore / On the dawning of the day. . . ."

He turned. "Ah, you can still sing like a bird, Bel." He patted the seat next to him. "Come sit."

"What are you doing?" I asked.

"Waiting," he said, picking at the strings on his violin. "It won't be long now."

"Waiting?" I asked. Outside, shadows danced on the lawn, the *Twenty-One Guns* installation standing guard over the shapes that the clouds made on the grass. The river, illuminated by the full moon, was alive and moving, the light reflecting off its little waves. "For what?" I asked.

Behind me, a familiar voice filled the almost empty hall. "Not what. Who."

Cargan stood and turned, gently placing his violin on the table. "Eugene Garvey. I thought you might return."

Uncle Eugene clomped across the floor until he stood on the other side of the table, regarding both of us with hostility. "Now why would you think that, Cargan?" he asked.

From his pocket my brother pulled out a passport. "You weren't getting far without this."

"Where did you get that, Cargan?" I asked.

"His room," Cargan said. "It was convenient that he overstayed his welcome."

Knowing he couldn't reach over quickly enough to grab it, Eugene stood there, the look on his face vacillating between hopelessness and anger. "We underestimated you, Cargan. I remember your mother telling me that they gave you kids IQ tests in school and that yours was higher than everyone else's, but no one believed it. Thought there was a mistake. I can see now that we were the ones mistaken." He peered in the darkness at my brother. "How'd you pull off the moron act for so long?"

Cargan didn't respond to that question. "It has nothing to do with intelligence, Eugene. It's just common sense. You didn't come back here for the wedding. It was never about that."

I looked from my brother to Eugene and back again. I hoped someone knew what was going on because I was completely in the dark, both literally and figuratively, as one candle had blown out, the moon our major source of light now.

"My father is a good man, Eugene. But that's what you were banking on, wasn't it?"

I looked at Cargan, tried to discern his face in the moonlight. "Car, what is this?"

"I saved his life, lass," Eugene said. "Back in those days, you didn't tell the IRA that you weren't interested in being part of their plan, of helping them move what they wanted to move in those big boxes that he packed his 'art' in. I got them off his back. And what does he do? Moves here." He swept an arm out. "To this. To America. To the glorious Shamrock Manor." He smiled at me, venom behind him. "I saved his life. And payback, as you Yanks say, is a bitch. All I wanted was for him to accept a shipment on my behalf. That's it."

"But he wouldn't," I said, knowing that Dad, as crazy as he was, had a very steady moral compass. I had doubted that once and that had been a mistake. "And not only did he not do it; he accepted you into his home, no hard feelings." I wanted to know. "So why were you running,

Eugene? Why didn't you just stay, since you and Dad clearly had moved on?"

He pointed at Cargan. "The village idiot here. He knew the whole story. You," he said, giving Cargan a look that was pure hatred, "bugged my room. Just what was the game in that?"

"Just curious, Eugene. You came back after a long, long time. I always had my suspicions about you, but I got what I . . . I mean what the police needed."

Eugene shook his head. "I remember you taking apart radios. Putting them back together. Once I found the bug, I looked no further than you." He moved closer to Cargan. "Now give me my passport, boy."

"This passport?" Cargan said. "The one that was issued to Martin O'Mallory? If that doesn't sound like a made-up name, I don't know what does."

I stood, not sure what to do. If Eugene was guilty of all of the things we suspected, we were in big trouble. But this was a man we had grown up with, whose home we had visited. Just how far would he go to get out of here? Was he capable of hurting two people he had known since they were little kids? Knowing now what I did about Cargan, I felt marginally safer. But in his baggy shorts and T-shirt I wasn't sure exactly where he could hide a gun. And thinking about that, the limited possibilities, I decided I didn't want to know.

Eugene played his last card, pulling a revolver from inside his jacket pocket. "Turn it over."

"I knew you'd be back, Eugene," Cargan said. "Martin O'Mallory. Or whoever you plan on being. It was just a matter of time."

I had a theory and that was that Eugene wouldn't kill us; he couldn't. I could see in his eyes that he wasn't bloodthirsty, that he couldn't shoot us in cold blood and live with himself. It was all there on his face, evident by his shaking hands. He looked confused and broken and not sure what to do, he obviously went with a not-very-well-thought-out Plan B.

Dad has a lot of theories. One of them is that old people don't fall and then break their hips; rather, their hips break and then they fall. It was hard to tell what happened in the case of Eugene when he made one quick move, the move that was going to catapult him over the table and into Cargan, but his hip did break, he did fall, and I'll never be sure what happened first. All I know is that when Cargan called 911 we had the pleasure of greeting both an ambulance crew and a group of cops.

Denny Dougherty, an old pal from kindergarten, was now Sergeant Dougherty; he asked me upon arrival, after the usual questions about what had happened, if now, just this once, I could make him a bacon-and-egg sandwich. McDougall couldn't stop talking about the fry-up I had made during one of the previous investigations and, apparently, my breakfast spread was the talk of the station house.

I looked at Eugene, on a stretcher and manacled. When I turned around, I saw other members of my family, all in various poses that summed up their personalities to a T.

Dad stood at the bottom of the grand staircase, tears on his face, his friend, the friend who had once saved his life, betraying him. Again.

Mom two steps above him, staring at Eugene as if she could kill him with her own bare hands, the story Eugene had told us just having been told to her for the first time.

And Cargan in the office, idling playing with the Rubik's Cube, which someone had messed up and made a cluster of unmatched squares, putting it back together in record time, placing it atop the ledger, now filled with more black than red.

I stood in the foyer for a time, long after everyone else

had left, processing what had happened and what was to
be, coming to my conclusion:

> *This place is an insane asylum, but it's my insane
> asylum. These people are all crazy, but they are my
> crazy.*

I went into the kitchen and, despite the late hour,
made Dougherty a bacon-and-egg sandwich and when
that was done, started prepping for the next wedding.

EPILOGUE

The last unofficial day of summer was gorgeous. Bright, sunny, and cool enough for a stroll along the banks of the Foster's Landing River with a handsome guy who seemed to think that I was the bee's knees, as my father would say. I was happy to be out of the kitchen at the Manor. Brendan and I went back behind the mansion and down to the edge of what remained of the water. I spied a blue heron perched on one of the now-exposed rocks along the drought-ridden river, more dry dirt than water as far as the eye could see.

Brendan opened a bottle of my favorite Bordeaux and poured us each a glass in the plastic cups he had brought along. "If I'm not mistaken, I would say that this is our eight-week anniversary?" he said, not sure.

"Seven, but who's counting?" I said. "There was that little break in there." My relationship with him was easier than any other relationship I have ever been in. He was calm and kind and easy on the eyes. He took me for what I was and didn't expect me to be someone else. So far, he hadn't kissed my best girlfriend, but then again, I didn't have any girlfriends here in the Landing, surrounded by men to whom I was both related and unrelated. He hadn't run when things had gotten tough and secrets had been revealed; he claimed to have a few of his own, but I doubted it. The guy was as uncomplicated as a golden retriever. Feed him and he was happy. Rub his tummy and he was even happier.

He touched his plastic cup to mine. "Here's to the next seven," he said.

"Are you for real?" I asked before I had time to think. In the distance I heard sirens.

"I think so."

"Good," I said, and leaned in to kiss him.

The sirens got closer and the serenity of the afternoon was pierced by their high-pitched wail. In minutes the police cars reached the edge of the river, about an eighth of a mile west of us, all lined up. Finally, the police boat, a local vehicle with the FLPD logo painted on the side, started along the riverbed, right down the middle where there was still enough water to make its journey possible. I counted five cops, Kevin included, on the boat, heading toward Eden Island, if I had to guess.

I grabbed Brendan's hand. "Come on. Let's see what it is."

He hesitated. "Do you think we should?"

"We'll stay back. We won't interfere." We got up and walked along the north shore of the river, keeping the boat in our sights. "Stay close to the shore," I said. "We have had enough go on. I don't think we want an obstruction of justice charge leveled against us."

"Or anything else for that matter," he said. He blanced. "I don't want to do this," he said, but in spite of that protestation, he followed me.

Every now and again, along the shore, there was a puddle or a deeper pool of water, one that was in the shade and hadn't evaporated in the drought. That's where the birds dipped their heads in to take a drink but where there was no life evident. I wondered where all the fish had gone in the absence of a real river in which to swim.

Brendan lagged behind. "Come on," I said, taking his hand, but he was reluctant to go farther. "Bel, I'd rather not," he said. "I have a bad feeling about this."

I left him finally at the shore, standing beside a puddle while I followed the sound of the sirens. Dust-like motes danced in the sunlight that splintered between the trees. After a few hundred feet, I found out that I was correct about the location of the activity. The police boat was parked in front of Eden Island and all of Foster's Landing's police department, or so it seemed, had gathered there. There were three young boys standing at the edge of the island, all being questioned at once by a uniformed cop.

I knew this river like the back of the hand. After all, I had grown up on it, since the Manor had the river as its glorious backdrop. I circled around to the backside of the small island where we had partied as teenagers and walked through the trees, the police too preoccupied with what was going on to notice me. I crept around, wondering where Brendan was, if he had gone back to our spot at the bottom of the hill in back of the Manor, why he wouldn't follow me. He either had had a bad run-in with the law that he didn't want to reveal or wasn't as curious by nature as I was. Either way, I figured we would find each other after this little adventure and I would get the truth from him.

I hung back, as I was closer to the action than I originally thought. One of the cops, whom I recognized as Jed Mitchell, Amy's older brother, turned from the scene of the action and walked directly toward me, not seeing me or anything else as he knelt and put his head down.

I remember later thinking what a beautiful day it had

been to that point, how gorgeous and sunny. How happy I had been, my life finally coming together, my family finally revealing all of the secrets that they had kept close to their own hearts, not wanting to bring me any more pain or trouble than I had already endured since returning home.

I could see a bunch of items on the ground. I left the shore and waded into the shallow water, trying to get as close to the island as I could without revealing myself. Now up to my knees, I circled around the back of the island and crept ashore, staying low, the trees my cover. On the ground was an old, wet backpack, the remnants of a soggy blue-and-gold pennant—the colors of Foster's Landing High School and all of its sports teams—hanging off its strap. It looked just like Amy's backpack, the one she had carried everywhere, from school to home to the island when we partied. The sneakers, soaked and covered with mud, looked like hers as well. There were all sorts of things, things that someone had taken out of the backpack: A key chain. A host of plastic newspaper bags that Amy had used on her dog-walking jobs. A Foster's Landing High School sweatshirt, which, when spread on the ground, revealed just enough so that we knew the name of the owner. An M. An I. And a TCH.

It was all there, like an Amy Mitchell time capsule, having been beneath the water for who knew how long. Whether she or someone else had put it there was something that I wondered if I'd ever know.

I looked around, hoping to see Brendan, looking for a pair of strong arms into which to fall, but he wasn't there. I was all alone in amidst the copse of trees, staring at what would seem like a bunch of meaningless objects to most but that meant so much to me.

In the distance, Kevin turned and, almost like he could sense my presence, locked eyes with me across the short, sandy beach, and in that look the last decades melted away and we were two kids joined together by this tragedy, one looking for the answers, the other trying to forget.

I just wasn't sure which one I was.

Or who I would be as this story continued to unfold.

Read on for an excerpt from

Bel OF THE BRAWL

**the next Belfast McGrath mystery from
Maggie McConnon and St. Martin's Paperbacks!**

CHAPTER *One*

When we were kids, we used to say that if heaven did indeed exist on earth, it had taken the form of Eden Island.

Set in the middle of the Foster's Landing River, a little tributary that flowed into the mighty Hudson, it was lush and green and covered with spongy ground cover that protected the ecosystem below its surface. My friends and I knew the island well, had walked every inch of its pristine landscape, taking great care to remove the dead cigarette butts and empty cans from overnight expeditions that the local police department turned a blind eye to, mostly because they themselves—homegrown all—had spent a night or two there looking up at the stars, a little buzzed, marveling at both the good luck and the horrible misfortune they had to be growing up in a river town like Fosters Landing with everything and nothing to offer.

It had rained a lot that year, the year I graduated from high school, so much so that Eden Island was the only island still above ground, but the water was creeping over the island's banks, closing over the edges of the little land mass, making its way toward the trees that sat in the center like a copse of sentries protecting their territory.

That early summer morning, years earlier and following a night fuzzily remembered at best, when I was a teen

who forgot to wear sunscreen (much to my mother's chagrin), was always covered in bug bites and wore a bathing
suit under my clothes most of the time, I woke up and
turned onto my side, surprised to find myself outside and
exposed to the elements. I could hear a little rumble of
thunder in the distance and feel a light rain falling between the hanging leaves, the ones so low I could almost
touch them. The moss beneath my cheek was cold and
damp and provided a soft cushion for my throbbing
head. My sweatshirt—Foster's Landing High School Swim
Team—was soaked through. I sat up, feeling the back of
my head for a wound that I was sure was there but found
nothing; this pain was just a result of having slept outside
and having had maybe a go or two at the keg that some
older kid had brought. My usual go-to, a plate of greasy
diner eggs and sausage, wouldn't allay the queasiness that
the briny smell of the small river brought to my nose, nor
the shakiness in my legs.

   I looked around, alone in familiar surroundings but
with a feeling of dread spreading icy tendrils through my
limbs. "Hello!" I called out, wondering about the whereabouts of the rest of the usual quartet that accompanied
me everywhere—Amy, Kevin, Cargan. The island wasn't
big, maybe six hundred feet across, an eighth of a mile
long, and a quick check of the perimeter on all sides told
me that I was alone.

   In those days, I wore Keds that were always threadbare, having been white and clean for about a week before my pinkie toe started to peek out from first the right
one, then the left. They were beside me, soggy and soiled.
I searched the pockets of my cut-offs and found a soggy
dollar bill and the key to my house but nothing else. I
looked out across the northern edge of the island and
stuck a tentative toe into the water: high tide. The water
barely came up to my knees when I waded in, and deter-

mined to get home before the real rain came, the thunder rolling and rumbling closer to the spot where I stood, I strode across the expanse toward the other shore.

From the trees behind me, I heard a rebuke. "Where you going, Bel?" they seemed to ask as they swayed and rocked in the wind, getting increasingly more violent as the thunder reverberated, this time a little closer. I waded in deeper, my sneakers skidding and slipping on the rocks below. "Where you going, Bel?" the trees seem to ask again, their cadence not unlike Kevin's when he asked me the same question the night before, the one that was buried in the deep recesses of my brain. Where I was, why he had asked, and where I had been going were all questions I couldn't answer. A thought went through my clogged brain, the synapses firing slowly but in this case, deliberately.

I have to say I'm sorry, I thought, for the first, but not last, time.

The water was cold, colder than it should have been for June. It was all that rain making it chilly, bracing. Up to my thighs now, the water rushed from Sperry's Pond to the north, where rapids had stranded more than one overly brave kayaker out for a relaxing paddle on a gorgeous summer day, the kind of summer days that normally I lived for. I waded closer to the shore, turning back once to make sure I really had been alone on the island. My addled mind was playing tricks on me, and a place I loved was quickly turning into somewhere sinister and foreboding, a place that I needed to escape.

Finally, because it was easier, I began to swim, short strokes while bent at the waist, the current getting stronger, the wind picking up. The shore, which always seemed so close when I was on the island with my friends who seemed to have deserted me, seemed far away now that I was alone. Unreachable. I pushed through the water, my legs—short but swimmer's legs nonetheless—doing the work, my arms splashing at the water but really not helping my progress across the expanse. I pulled off my sweatshirt, noticing a purple handprint around my right bicep and Kevin's words as he caught me as I came out of my kayak—"That'll leave a mark!"—ringing in my ears.

Where was everyone? More importantly, where was Amy? I had left my best friend on the shore the night before, telling her she would be sorry and that I would never speak to her again but a night on the beach, alone and wet, had convinced me that I had overreacted, that it hadn't been as bad as I thought. Maybe she hadn't looked at me the way I thought she had after kissing Kevin—my boyfriend—right in front of me. But the truth was that she had. I held onto the hope that Amy never would have ended the night without finding me first. We were a team. A duo. We were never apart.

Until now.

When I finally reached the shore, out of breath and soaked to the skin, a clap of thunder exploded directly overhead and the spot where I had lain just moments earlier was struck by a bolt of lightning so thick and sustained that I knew I would have been killed had I not awoken when I had. Something had roused me; I had no internal clock. Anyone who had seen the number of tardy markings on my report would know that I was never on time, ever. I looked back across at Eden Island, squeezing the water out of my sweatshirt and putting it back over my head.

"Where *am* I going?" I wondered.

I decided I didn't know.

I lay on the shore, looking at the murky sky overhead. It would be raining steadily soon but it didn't matter; I was already wet. Behind me, footsteps approached but I was too tired to be wary. The person crouched by my head and held out a hand.

"Ready to go home, Bel?" my brother asked, the sight of him bringing tears to my eyes.

"I had a horrible night, Cargan."

He had, too; he had been up all night. It was written on his face.

"I know," he said. "Let's go. Mom and Dad are worried sick. We've been looking for you for hours."

"I was right there," I said. "I was right where you left me."

He shook his head, his dark hair wet and flopping onto his forehead. "No. You weren't." He leaned over and hugged me, and the sound of a great sob—his or mine, I wasn't sure—disappeared in the latest clap of thunder. Over his shoulder, I spotted my other brothers—Arney, Derry and Feeney—clamoring down the hill behind the Casey's house toward the river, their voices loud and raucous, excited. I had been found.

In the distance, there were sirens and voices, coming together in a panic-filled cacophony. I looked at my brothers for the answer to the unspoken question, the worry on his face still there in spite of the fact that I had been found.

Only Cargan spoke. "We found you."

There was something more, something ominous. It was written on his face.

One tear slid down his face. "But Amy Mitchell never came home."

CHAPTER *Two*

"Beets?" Gerard Mason, the groom-to-be, asked, sniffing the air as if just the mention of the root vegetable could produce an odor.

"No beets?" I asked, looking down at the hand-written menu that I had labored over for the past several days. Beet salad was part of my entrée, adding a bit of color to an otherwise colorless meal—in my opinion anyway—of filet mignon and scalloped potatoes. It was a meal I could make in my sleep, even for one hundred and fifty guests. Behind me, I could almost feel my mother's eyes boring into the back of my head, her words ringing in my ears: *We left the old country so that we wouldn't have to eat beets, Belfast. No beets!*

The bride looked at me expectantly. "And goat cheese? Will it have goat cheese?"

"It can," I said. "And candied walnuts, if you'd like."

The bride, Pegeen Casey, looked at her fiancé. "It sounds delicious, Gerry. I think we should do it."

I heard a door slam in another part of Shamrock Manor, whether by chance or on purpose, I wasn't sure. Mom really had a thing against beets. And outdoor weddings. And off-the-shoulder dresses on brides. Something about the way the cake was cut. And a host of other things that I couldn't remember but which came to me every once in a while, in a rush, making my head spin.

Gerry looked at his bride-to-be. "Whatever you want, baby."

Good answer, Gerry, I thought. "Do you have any other special requests?" I asked, scanning my list. We had covered the cocktail hour and the main meal, which left the bar and the cake. "Any special requests for the bar? A specialty cocktail?" I asked, holding my breath. Seamus, our long-time bartender, was pretty one-note—he could pull a pint like no one's business, but everything else was up for grabs. He didn't know the difference between Chardonnay and Sauvignon Blanc and thought Merlot was something you got from a tick bite.

Pegeen Casey shook her head. "It's a pretty standard crowd, Belfast. Your bartender can handle pouring pints and a few hundred glasses of Chardonnay, can't he?" she asked, smiling. I loved a bride with a sense of humor; it made everything easier. Pegeen was as far from a "bridezilla" as one could get, and I appreciated that.

"He can handle those two things," I said. "And the cake? Will we be making that for you?"

"I've ordered a cake from La Belle Gateau in Monroeville," she said. "Are you familiar with them?"

"Yes," I said. "Many of our couples use them for their cakes."

"Please tell me that they're good," Pegeen said.

"The best," I lied. Their icing was too dense and their fondant flowers often required some emergency surgery after the cake was delivered to the Manor. But Pegeen Casey didn't need to know that. Her wedding was in a week and I didn't want to add to her stress about the big day. I made some adjustments to the order sheet, signed it and handed her the original. "We're all set," I said. "If you think of anything in the meantime, please let me know and we'll do our best to make sure that everything is just the way you want it."

She smiled. "Thank you so much, Belfast. I was a little reluctant . . ."

Gerry interrupted her. "Yeah, who wants to have their wedding where a murder took place?"

She put her hand on her fiance's arm. "You understand, don't you?" she asked. "It's nothing personal. Nothing against Shamrock Manor."

"I do," I said. "But that was months ago, and it was really all just a tragic misunderstanding. I promise that you'll be perfectly safe here and that your wedding day will go off without a hitch."

Gerry reached into his jacket pocket. "Well, if anything ever happens again, here's my card."

I looked at the card: Gerard Mason, Private Investigator.

"I can't imagine that the Foster's Landing Police Department has the manpower to handle those types of investigations," he said.

I looked at him blankly, the idea that a private investigator had fallen into my lap, just when I needed one, muddling my thoughts.

"A murder," he said.

"Right. Yes," I said.

The local PD doesn't have the manpower or the investigative skills. They bungled along for weeks on the case of the victim at my cousin's wedding. "Well, thank you," I said. "But we won't be in need of a private investigator any time soon." I knocked on the molding surrounding the entrance to the dining room.

I led them into the foyer, where a bust of Bobby Sands, Irish martyr and rebel for the cause, stood in the center. His poor head misshapen and hardly resembling a head at all, he had become a "talking piece" as my father, the artist in question, described it. I hadn't met too many brides or grooms who wanted to talk about Bobby Sands or his distorted visage. "See you in a week," I said, holding the big front door open for them and watching them drive away.

Private investigator. That was a new one. Maybe I had been lying just a bit when I'd said that I wouldn't be in need of a private investigator any time soon.

Maybe this was exactly the time I was in need of one.

Too bad Gerard Mason ended up not being able to help me, his own wedding day being the last day he lived to see.